BITTERROOT AND CAINE'S TRAIL

TWO FULL LENGTH WESTERN NOVELS

CAMERON JUDD

WOLFPACK PUBLISHING
— EST 2013 —

Bitterroot and Caine's Trail: Two Full Length Western Novels
Paperback Edition
Copyright © 2022 (As Revised) Cameron Judd

Wolfpack Publishing
5130 S. Fort Apache Rd. 215-380
Las Vegas, NV 89148

wolfpackpublishing.com

Paperback ISBN 978-1-63977-509-5
eBook ISBN 978-1-63977-310-7

BITTERROOT AND CAINE'S TRAIL

BITTERROOT

BITTERROOT

This book is dedicated to Hix Stubblefield

CHAPTER 1

T hat he was a man of the mountains was obvious to all who saw him. Rough-hewn, unshaven, lean, he rode a big gray that plodded down the center of the wide dirt street. The rider had the easy slump of one used to the saddle. The stub of a cigar jutted from the corner of his mouth, and the shadow of the brim of his campaign hat hid his dark eyes. He looked straight ahead.

And yet, he gave a subtle tip of his hat to the ladies who passed him. The men he sized up silently, out of habit, noting their glances and reading their expressions.

He looked very much like any other trail-weary drifter, and such were common on the streets of Henley, Montana Territory, nestled as it was at the foot of the Bitterroot Range. His trousers, made of wool, fit loosely. Leather thongs strapped his calf-high moccasins to his legs. He wore a long-tailed gray coat, apparently of Confederate origin, and beneath it a faded yellow linsey-woolsey shirt. In a holster on his hip rode a .36 Navy Colt, and the boots on his saddle held two rifles. One was a .44-caliber scope-mounted Henry, the other a .52-caliber government surplus Spencer repeater.

At the low-roofed, bloodred Henley's Pride Saloon, the

rider stopped. He tied his gray to the hitching post, flipped the cigar butt to the dust, and walked to the open door. He stood there several moments, surveying the interior, then went back to his horse and unbooted his rifles. Turning again, he entered the saloon.

The Henley's Pride had no piano, no women, not a single spittoon. The interior walls were painted the same brilliant red as the exterior, but in the dim light, they looked black. The place reeked of rotting tobacco spittle and stale cigar smoke.

The stranger picked a corner table and headed for it. He leaned his rifles against the wall and dropped into the chair. He tilted it back against the wall and propped one foot on the tabletop.

The barkeep, a nervous young man with HULON embroidered on his armband, skittered around the end of the bar to the table. His wide, childish eyes glimmered beneath thick spectacle lenses.

"Sir, the guns. There's to be no long arms inside. Owner's rule, you understand—not mine."

The stranger tipped back his hat and studied the barkeep.

"Whiskey, son, Kentucky whiskey, if you've got it. Make sure it's a full bottle."

The barkeep swallowed. "Yes, sir—now, if you'll just let me lay the rifles behind the bar—"

"And one of those cigars in that jar yonder. I could use a good cigar."

The barkeep again swallowed, and his eyes grew wider yet. He trotted obediently back to the bar, more nervous than before and thankful his employer was not here to see his rules violated so casually.

He returned with a bottle and cigar and popped the cork with much trembling. He hurried back toward the bar.

"Friend."

He turned, and the stranger flipped him a coin. It clinked to the floor, and it took him two tries to pick it up. He blurted thanks and slid behind the bar, ashamed of his timidity in the presence of this man.

Sunlight streamed through the doorway; dust and tobacco smoke floated in the rays. The red-stained checkerboard window beside the door, in combination with light reflecting from interior walls, cast a ruby glow across the front of the saloon and a man seated there.

The stranger did not look directly at that man but studied him in the corner of his vision. The face was vaguely familiar.

The man was slaughtered-hog fat and sported an auburn mustache nearly as broad as his face. He wore a derby, and on his right hip, a Colt. He stared openly back at the newcomer in the corner.

At length, the big man rose and approached him, boots clumping loudly on the pine board floor. He brought his bottle and glass with him and gave it a little wave as he stood smiling in what apparently was supposed to be a cordial manner. The stranger wasn't fooled by the smile; he could read the eyes.

"Good day, sir. May I join you?"

The stranger said nothing but swung his foot off the table and straightened his chair. With his cigar, he waved at the empty chair across from him.

The other man sat down with a grunt, making the chair creak. He poured himself a drink, raised his glass in salute, and downed the hot liquor in a swallow.

"Powerful stuff, powerful," he said. The smile returned, this time accompanied by a subtle tilt of the head. "You're new to town, I believe."

The stranger drew on his cigar and said nothing.

"New—but I've seen you before."

Still, the stranger did not respond. He looked past the fleshy face and out the open door.

"Just where I don't know—could have been almost anywhere. A man in my profession moves around a lot."

He waited for the obvious question. It was not provided. Finally, he gave the answer unsolicited.

"Brannigan's my name. Clinton Brannigan. I'm a peace officer of sorts. Mostly, I'm a bounty hunter. You've heard of me?"

Still no answer.

Now the smile drained from the jowled face. Clinton Brannigan leaned forward and spoke intensely: "And you, friend, are Simon Caine, and you're mine."

Simon Caine looked into the porcine eyes. "Don't try it. It'll cost more than you want to pay."

Brannigan laughed. "But my battle's won, Caine! You see, aimed at your gut under this table is the daintiest little Bitterlich you've ever seen, and if you twitch even a hair, I'll use it. You bring as good a dollar dead as alive."

Caine took a drag on his cigar and blew smoke into the bounty hunter's eyes. Brannigan winced and sputtered but did not move.

"It ain't worth the price, Brannigan. Fair warning."

For a half second, the bounty hunter hesitated. His broad lips twitched; uncertainty played through his eyes. Then his gaze hardened again; a cold smile flashed.

"Get up slow. Slide the pistol out with your left hand, and hand it over easy, by the barrel."

"Give it up, Brannigan. Walk out with your life."

"Move, Caine!"

Simon Caine's hand whipped to the butt of the Navy Colt as his right foot shot upward beneath the table to pin the bounty hunters left hand to the underside. The derringer clattered to the floor, and Brannigan bellowed in pain, but at the same time, he went for his Colt with his right hand.

Caine was faster. His pistol boomed and filled the air with blue smoke. Brannigan's end of the table splintered. His bulky form kicked backward and tipped over his chair. He landed face up on the sawdust-and-spittle-covered floor.

Piggish eyes stared in disbelief at the red ceiling, hands groped the air, then his expression went blank, and he was dead. There was no sound but the wheezing whimpers of the terrified barkeep.

Caine stood. He looked at the body on the floor and shook his head. He clamped his teeth around the cigar and holstered the Navy Colt, then picked up his rifles and strode to the door.

A man loomed before him, silhouetted against the sunlit street beyond. Caine pushed him aside and walked to his gray. He booted the rifles and unhitched the horse, then swung into the saddle.

The man in the doorway looked into the saloon. He saw the body of Brannigan in the rear, the barkeep pale and frozen like a marble statue behind the bar.

Then he shouted: "He's killed him!"

Caine turned his mount and galloped down the street. He cursed the late Clinton Brannigan. The bounty hunter's intrusion could have come at no worse time nor rendered impossible a more important rendezvous than it had.

The only good thing about it was there was now one less bounty hunter seeking the price an unforgiving federal government had placed on his head.

He bent low and spurred his horse. From behind came sounds of mounting confusion: men shouting, dogs yapping, women screaming. A man came to the door of the gunsmith's shop and fired a rifle.

Caine spurred the gray again. One more corner, and he would be out of town, in the foothills, bound for the mountains that for more than a decade had been his home.

The gray trumpeted and reared as it almost collided with

a buggy that came around the corner. On the seat was a young man with a badge on his vest, and next to him a beautiful young woman with a small child in her lap.

Caine was caught between the buggy and the wall of a building. Behind him, he heard the man from the gunsmithy coming at a run. There was one way out.

He drew his Colt and aimed at the lawman's face. The lady screamed and drew the child to herself.

There was a commotion behind, growing ever closer.

It still was not too late. During the war and many times after, he had escaped tighter spots than this.

But not this time. It would not be the rifleman behind who stopped him, nor this startled lawman. It would be himself—and this lady.

He lowered his pistol and flipped it in the air. Catching it by the barrel, he thrust it butt first to the lawman, who only just now drew his own sidearm. All the while, Caine looked into the face of the pale young mother who clutched her crying child.

The lawman took Caine's pistol. The man behind slid Caine's rifles from their boots and the knife from his belt. Caine raised his hands and smiled around his cigar.

"Mister looks like you've got yourself a prisoner."

CHAPTER 2

In early afternoon, a chill swept down from the mountains, and clouds thickened on the horizon. Low rumbles of thunder shook the atmosphere. The gathering storm rattled shutters and sent dust demons spiraling down the street.

Town marshal Jim Ballentree put down the flyer he had been staring at and aimed his gaze at the pot of coffee boiling on the stove.

"Hulon wasn't lying, Charlie. It all matches, right down to the scar at the hairline. I can't believe it. Simon Caine!"

Charlie Bradley, Henley's full-time gunsmith and part-time deputy looked like a man struck ill. A trickle of tobacco juice escaped the corner of his mouth and ran like a tiny brown river into a forest of whiskers.

"No mistake?"

"No mistake."

"You know what this means?"

Ballentree was in no spirit to answer. He walked to the heavy oak door separating the office from the cellblock in the rear. Three cells: two empty, one occupied by a man who to Ballentree had been only a legend.

The door closed behind him with a dull thud. For a time, the lawman lingered before Caine's cell, watching the tall outlaw who stood with his back toward him. Caine was looking through the shattered pane of the cell's lone window, which was crossed with rusty iron bars. The cell was dark, illuminated only by a feeble glimmer from a coal-oil flame in a wall lamp. The wind, gusting through the broken pane, caused the flame to flicker and flare, setting disjointed shadows into constant motion on the cell wall. Outside, thunder rumbled more often and more deeply.

"I know who you are, Caine," Ballentree said. "The bounty hunter spoke your name before you shot him." The outlaw did not turn nor indicate he even had heard. In a different tone, Ballentree said, "Do you know whose town this is?"

Caine turned and looked straight into Ballentree's face. For a second, something in Caine's eyes brought to mind the fierce sadness of a caged grizzly or a treed puma.

"I know." Caine's voice reverberated against the walls of the cell.

"Then why ride into the town of a man who hates you like William Montrose does?"

"I had a reason."

"But the risk..."

"I'm used to risk."

Ballentree fished a cheroot from his vest and struck a sulfur match. The smoke drifted across the cell and joined its scent with the dank odor of mildewed stone walls. After a moment's hesitation, the marshal offered the smoke to Caine and was slightly surprised when it was accepted. Caine sat on his bunk, leaning against the wall and keeping his eye on the window.

"We're going to have trouble when Montrose finds out you're here. He probably knows already. The barkeep works for Montrose, like everybody else in this town."

"You too, Marshal?"

"No." Ballentree brought out another cheroot and lit it. The tip flared red in the shadowed cellblock. "I got little use for the man, and he's got less for me. I think he was surprised when I was named for this job. Didn't make his wishes clear enough to the town council, I suppose. But that's all to the side. What I'm trying to tell you is that it will take days for the territorial folks to get up here and take you off my hands. And in the meantime, Will Montrose isn't going to sit up there in his big house when he's got his brother's killer right under his nose. And he sure isn't going to be satisfied to let the court, have you. Do you understand me, Caine?"

"I understand. Will Montrose will send his boys down here to string me up. Probably scalp me, too, like I done his brother."

The skin on the back of Ballentree's neck tightened. "I always wondered if that old tale was true."

"Not all of them are. That one is."

"Did Robert Montrose really murder your family?"

Caine flinched like a man does when an old wound stabs at him. "He should have killed me too. Instead, he just tried to scalp me, but he was too drunk. When I tracked him down, I showed him how to do it right."

Ballentree noted the dispassion of the voice, the expressionless face. Lightning chiseled the line of Caine's profile against the wall. It was weathered, angular, somehow handsome. But dead cold.

"Will Montrose has always bragged about killing you someday, Caine. I'll do what I can to protect you. It's my duty." He paused. "Besides, you could have killed me out there today."

"I ain't worth dying for, Marshal. You got a fine family. Don't go getting killed and leaving them alone for the likes of me. A family's the most precious thing a man can have."

For a second, the coldness melted. Something different touched the weathered creases around his eyes.

"Why didn't you kill me today, Caine?"

The lamp's flame danced in a sudden gust from the window. Lightning flashed again, and Ballentree saw once more that look of intense sadness.

"Like I said, Marshal, you got a fine family."

Simon Caine walked back to his window, and Jim Ballentree left him alone.

Charlie Bradley was scared. His face was pale, and his eyes glazed. Ballentree had never seen him look that way before. He realized he was scared too.

"Look out the window, Jim," Charlie said.

Across the street, six men stood looking toward the jail. They leaned against the mercantile storefront, smoking and idle, one with his hat pulled low on his forehead.

Ballentree knew them and why they were there. These were Montrose's men, and with their mere presence, they were sending a quiet message. A warning.

At length, the one with the lowered hat raised it and looked across at Ballentree. Then, with a slow and lazy gait, he stepped from the boardwalk to the street and walked away. The others followed.

"It's starting already," Ballentree said.

———

Charlie Bradley shook his head. "No. It's too much for one man. I can't leave you here by yourself."

"You're my deputy, Charlie. That means you got to do what I say. And I'm saying for you to go to my place and watch out for Susan and Joe. I've got a feeling ... I don't know just what. Montrose might threaten my family to get Caine. Besides, against Montrose's men, two aren't much better than one."

"They'll kill you, Jim."

"Maybe. But I'm the marshal, and it's my job to stay—not yours."

The storm had nearly gone. The pattering of rain on the shingles above declined; thunder rolled like a giant turning in his sleep somewhere over in Dakota. Down the street, a dog barked.

Charlie Bradley finally relented. "All right. I'll go. But your wife will skin me for leaving you alone."

The deputy thrust out his hand, a move that seemed awkward as he did it. Ballentree took it; each noted the trembling of the other.

"Take care, Jim."

The door opened and closed, and Jim Ballentree was alone. He loaded a Winchester, then a sawed-off shotgun.

His eyes fell on Caine's two rifles leaning in the corner and his saddlebags beside them. Hesitantly, Ballentree picked up the latter and sat down on the corner of his desk. He examined the contents, not sure what he was looking for. He found extra ammunition, strips of jerky, some sort of medicinal salve, a bit of cloth with needle and thread, and at last, a photograph.

It was of a woman, quite young, posed stiffly in a fanback chair. She wore a high-collared dress with lace about the sleeves. Her hair was pinned up. She reminded Ballentree of his own Susan.

He dug farther into the saddlebags and touched something he could not identify. He pulled it out.

It was a scalp lock, stretched over a small willow hoop, the hair reddish-brown, the skin scraped as clean as quality leather on the underside.

Robert Montrose. Ballentree's stomach lurched. He stuffed the scalp back into the saddlebag with the rest of the items, then washed his hands.

At the other end of the street, lamps were lit in the town

livery as silent men gathered. Entering through the double doorway, they regarded without comment the nimbly working hands of the livery keeper. Bent and concentrating on his work, he cast a shadow in the lamplight, which was huge and misshapen and in constant shuddering motion.

He stood, grinning without teeth, and tossed his bit of craftsmanship over a beam. He stepped back, admiring his work. The lamps played light on it from their various angles.

"A right pretty noose, if I do say so," he said.

In the doorway, a tall man with graying hair and fine clothing nodded approval from atop a big dun gelding. He clicked his tongue and spurred the horse through the darkness toward the massive log house atop the hill overlooking town.

CHAPTER 3

Ballentree answered the knock on the jailhouse door with caution, expecting trouble. What he found was a young preacher clutching a thick Bible.

His sandy hair was close-cropped, and he was sunburned. He was quite wet from the recent rain.

The marshal eyed the newcomer, then glanced down the street to the weirdly lighted livery. Phantom shapes of men moved in the doorway. He felt a shudder not entirely caused by the night wind.

"What can I do for you, parson?"

"My name is John Crosston. I'm a minister—Methodist —and I've come to see your prisoner."

Ballentree noted the preacher's accent. British, he thought. An unusual inflection to hear in a small town at the foot of the Bitterroots.

"Why this particular prisoner?"

The preacher nodded toward the livery. "Because he is a sinner likely to stand before his creator quite soon."

Yes, thought Ballentree. With me right beside him.

"I see. Come in."

John Crosston stepped inside, apologizing for the dripping water from his clothes. He looked around the room.

"Got an interest in jail offices?" Ballentree asked.

Crosston smiled. "An interest in anything American, I suppose. I've been in this country less than five months."

"I never thought to see a preacher in Henley. This place is about as remote as the far side of Hades. I didn't figure the Lord would range out this far."

"But he does, though he hasn't gotten the notice he is due. That's why I'm here. I've been sent to establish a congregation. I'm told religious influence is lacking."

Ballentree thumbed toward the livery. "Well, you can bet what that bunch has planned ain't a Sunday school picnic. Preacher, if you're to see my prisoner, I'll have to search you. For all I know, you may be one of them. And you got to be ready to get out when I tell you because when they work up the courage to come this way, there's nobody gonna stand between them and Caine. You understand?"

"Of course, the presence of a man of God might influence them to—"

"A preacher don't mean jack to them. They got one lord and master, and he lives in that log house on the hill and smokes two-dollar cigars. So when I say move, you move, and don't hang around for benedictions."

"Agreed, Marshal. Now may I see Simon Caine?"

Ballentree searched the preacher, who, with arms and Bible aloft, looked like he was making an altar call at a Missouri camp meeting.

The search produced only pocket change and a small penknife. Ballentree confiscated the latter, then opened the door to the cellblock.

"Visitor for you, Caine. Meet the Reverend John Crosston, come to save your soul."

Caine was still at the window. His expression had been stern, but he smiled when he saw the preacher.

"You know you're done for when the preachers start coming around," he said. "Save your breath for my funeral, padre. Not even you could convince the Lord to take this dirty old soul."

"Salvation is closer than you think," Crosston said. "Marshal, may I speak to him privately?"

"Well—"

"I'm no risk. He does have the right to discuss final matters in privacy."

Reluctantly, Ballentree nodded. "All right. But remember what I told you."

When Ballentree was gone, Caine turned to his window again. Torchlight played across the little strip of street he could see. There were loud and drunken voices. Not long now, he thought.

"What's it like to die, padre? I've always wondered. I've helped a lot of men find the answer to that question. Now it's my turn."

"Don't talk about death, Caine. I'm coming to give you life."

"Then you're a miracle worker. Listen—you hear them? Sounds like they're grouping up."

The preacher spoke in an urgent whisper. "I have come to save you, Caine, but not as you think. Jake Armitage and I have—"

The door flew open, and Jim Ballentree came inside, his face gone white. "Out, preacher! They're coming!"

Caine wheeled to face the preacher. "Did you say, Jake Armitage?"

Crosston was unnerved. He glanced from Ballentree to Caine and back to Ballentree again and suddenly held his Bible aloft.

"Simon Caine," he said, "if you're to be saved, it has to be now!"

He flipped open his Bible and, from its hollowed-out

center, produced a small Smith & Wesson. In the lamplight, Caine saw the glimmer of engraved initials on the butt—J.A. He knew the gun. It had been a gift from himself to Jake Armitage years before.

If Jake was here, there was hope. More than hope, for he and Armitage, had dodged fate more times than he could remember.

The preacher cocked the pistol and thrust it into Ballentree's face. "The original idea was for Caine to do this, not me, but under the circumstances, I must improvise. Caine and I are leaving. Unlock the door."

Ballentree's face clouded. "Montrose sent you."

"No. I represent myself. *Unlock the door!*"

Ballentree did, and Caine charged out of the cell.

Outside, the mob nearly had reached the jail. Some of its members wore flour-sack masks. A few carried torches. All were armed.

"Turn your back, Marshal," Crosston said.

"Don't kill him, friend. I mean that," Caine said.

"I've no such intention."

He pounded the pistol into Ballentree's skull. The marshal collapsed.

Outside, someone shouted for the marshal. There was a blur of cursing and dogs barking, and the general roar of a lynch mob.

"Damn, there must be twenty of them," Caine said. He pushed aside Ballentree's limp body, and he and Crosston moved into the jail office, crouched and scuttling along.

Torchlight streamed through the windows above the half curtains. Caine went for his rifles and bags. He loaded both weapons and tossed the Spencer to Crosston. He threw his saddlebags over his shoulder and donned his battered hat.

"Don't know who you are, friend, but I hope you shoot as good as you play preacher."

The group outside, taken aback by the lack of response from inside the jail, surged forward cautiously.

"The outside window?" Crosston queried.

"No. They'd kill us before we were halfway out. There's only one thing to give a group like this—" Caine strapped on his gun belt, put on his coat " —and that's what they don't expect. Preacher, it's time to get mean as old Satan himself."

With a startling shout, Caine leaped forward and flung open the door, leveling his Henry at the same time. The Henry roared, flame and smoke gouted in the darkness, and men screamed.

Unseen by Caine and his companion, a stunned Jim Ballentree let his newly recovered Winchester slip from his hands as he fell unconscious once more. Caine had been in his sights a good five seconds, but he had not squeezed off the shot.

Earlier, Caine had handed him his life. Now he had handed it back again. Right or wrong, he did not know. All he knew was he could have done nothing else.

Like dry leaves caught by the wind, the would-be lynch men drew back. Three fell wounded. A few attempted to return fire, then ran. One wheeled and leveled a shotgun. Caine gritted his teeth as he drove a slug through the man's shoulder.

Crosston stood behind Caine and watched, awestruck by his fury. He understood now how Caine had become the legend he was, why he was so feared.

In the urgency of the moment, though, Crosston's awe was short-lived. There was an escape to be made, and that could be done best by running, not fighting.

"Into the alley!" he shouted. "Horses in the shed behind!"

"Not just yet, friend," Caine said.

Caine sent a slug straight toward a man who thrust his head around the corner of a nearby building. The man ducked aside as lead ripped through wood only inches from him.

Except for the four men who lay wounded in the dirt, the street was now deserted. Dropped torches cast an eerie glow upon one of the wounded men as he tried to crawl away. Caine went to him, kicked him over, and hefted him up by his collar. The man whimpered.

"You tell William Montrose something for me," Caine said. "Tell him my quarrel up to now has been with his brother, not him. He's changed all that. Tell him I don't forget, and I don't forgive, and give him this." Caine dropped the man and dug into one of the saddlebags on his shoulder. He found the scalp lock and dropped it on the man's bleeding chest.

"He'll know what it is."

Still whimpering, the man nodded.

"Caine, move?" Crosston yelled.

This time he did respond. He ran to the alley where Crosston waited, and together they moved to the rear of the jail. Along the street, bolder members of the scattered lynch mob reemerged. One followed the fugitives into the alley. Caine spun and fired. The man grunted and fell, clutching his stomach.

Behind the jail was a weeded lot and an abandoned shed. Inside were two horses, one of them Caine's gray. Both were saddled.

"How'd you manage this?" Caine asked as he led the gray out.

"Bought him. It cost me a premium, being the horse and saddle of Simon Caine."

"Obliged," Caine said. Then with a raised hand: "Listen!"

They heard hooves against the street, the creak, and slap of saddles on horseflesh.

"Let's run 'em a good chase, preacher," Caine said.

"I'm no preacher."

"I figured."

They rode across a rolling field toward a wagon trail leading into a dark conifer forest. When the pursuing riders emerged into the field, Crosston and Caine were nearly on the other side. Rifles cracked, and lead passed above them like a wailing ghost.

Crosston glanced across his shoulder at the oncoming riders. Then something happened that his common sense told him was near-impossible.

The range, the motion, the darkness—all made it improbable any shot could connect. But by luck or destiny, one of the pursuers fired off a blast as Crosston and Caine entered the woods. The sound of the shot reached Crosston as he saw Caine jerk and fall across his saddlehorn. Even in the dim moonlight, Crosston could see blood streaming down Caine's neck.

Caine's mount veered off the trail. Wet branches slapped the outlaw's face, and he forced himself upright. He was alive. The bullet hadn't lodged but had cut a long furrow through his skull, stinging like fire and disorienting him. His vision danced and wavered.

He felt Crosston's hand on him, steadying him. Then, somehow, he was riding forward again, faster. His companion said something, but the words were smeared, unclear.

This much he picked out of the jumble: "Up ahead, Armitage waiting with fresh horses." Armitage. The mere mention of the name helped Caine find some reserve strength. He forced himself to ignore the pain throbbing in his skull and squinted his eyes until his vision cleared.

To the right of the trail, some yards ahead, was a small abandoned house teetering on the edge of a bluff overlooking a creek. Years of erosion had eaten away the land beneath the house, leaving the back of it hanging over empty space. Log supports had been extended from the base of the house into the bank below in a final effort to salvage it, but apparently, its owners had finally given up and left.

"Up ahead, the bluff isn't so steep," Crosston said. "We can leave the horses and let them run on, get down the slope on foot and meet Armitage." But Caine heard no more. He rode into a low-hanging branch, unseen because of blood in his eyes. Already unstable, Caine could not recover, and he fell from his mount.

They were in front of the house now.

Crosston's mind worked desperately. He grabbed the reins of Caine's gray and halted his own horse. He dismounted and unbooted the rifles, which he tossed through the open door.

He heard the riders close behind.

He slapped the horses, sending them running down the dark trail. He ran back to Caine. The outlaw had pushed himself upright.

"Come on, my friend," Crosston urged.

Caine struggled to his feet, and with Crosston supporting him, moved into the shack. Both men dropped to the floor as Crosston snaked out his hand toward the rifles.

Only a second later, the pursuers passed at a full run, following the riderless horses down the trail. Then there was nothing but the sound of their own breathing and the creek waters below.

Gently Caine shook his head, trying to clear the fog. "Good horse, you lost me just now," he said. "But you did right."

"How bad is your head?"

"Plowed me good. But I'll make it."

"We've got to get out of here. The bluff is too steep for us to climb down, especially you. But we can't go much farther without walking into the lot of them."

"If we can't climb down, then we'll jump," Caine said.

"Jump? Have you seen how high this bluff—"

"Hist!." Caine signaled for silence. "Listen!"

Horses. Coming slowly back down the trail. Caine slid to the window. Two riders, armed with rifles.

Caine said, "Always two or three smart ones in every group. They must have figured it out and decided to grab themselves a little glory."

"We'll have to shoot them," Crosston said.

"Not if we can help it. It would just draw the others back. Is there a back way out of here?"

"This house hangs out over the bluff, Caine."

The outlaw moved, stooping, to the back room. He felt the floor.

"Rotten!" he said. He began chipping away at a floorboard, then ripped out the board altogether. Through the narrow opening, he saw a ledge of earth just beneath, the drop of the bluff, the creek far below.

Crosston got the idea. He joined Caine and began pulling away floorboards with tense enthusiasm.

The riders approached cautiously.

"We'd better split up," said one. "I'll go in, and you go around the back. I think I hear something in there."

"Be careful."

"Don't worry. I know who we're dealing with."

Inside, Caine and Crosston made the hole big enough to accommodate themselves. Crosston slid through, and Caine handed the rifles to him. Then Caine dropped lightly through the hole, stopping to reach back inside to replace the floorboards.

"Caine!" Crosston whispered. He pointed toward the side of the house.

One of the men was coming on foot. At the same time, the house creaked as the other entered and walked from room to room.

Nothing to do but shoot. Caine reached for his Navy Colt.

He never fired. Above, near the rotted area through which they had torn their exit, Caine heard footsteps. His next move was instinctive, performed with the grace of a man for whom life had been one fight for survival after another.

Caine holstered his Colt and lunged upward. He burst through the hole, sending rotten wood flying. With an animalistic yell, he closed his arms around the knees of the horrified man above and pulled him down through the opening. With a twisting heave, Caine threw the man over the ledge. He writhed as he fell, uselessly groping air until his body crashed against rock and water fifty feet below.

In the meantime, Crosston rolled out from beneath the house and leaped to his feet. He flipped his rifle as he moved and caught it by the barrel.

He swung the rifle like a club into the skull of the man who had approached from the side. The man fell, limp as a corpse cut from a noose.

Caine came to Crosston's side, smiling with approval. Crosston smiled back. Suddenly blood flowed anew from Caine's wound, and he staggered. He might have fallen had Crosston not caught him. A wave of nausea struck Caine, then a burst of fever, and he felt horribly weak.

A rifle blasted, a slug plowing the ground at their feet. The riders were back. The fugitives were caught in the open with nowhere to run.

"We've got to jump," Caine heard himself say.

The moments after that were forever unclear to him. Somehow he managed to make it with Crosston to the edge of the bluff. Whether they jumped together, whether he pushed Crosston or Crosston pushed him, he could never recall. But together, they spun out into the darkness, bodies plunging to strike the slope about halfway down. From there, they crashed painfully over rock outcrops, protruding roots, and dead timber until they splashed into the creek.

CHAPTER 5

Two men, *a nation* apart, were bent to their tasks.

The first was old, his sallow skin, long untouched by sun or wind, almost as gray as his patchy hair. He sat at a desk in a huge, drafty house in Boston, putting words on paper in a rushed scrawl. Books and manuscripts surrounded him, old parchments and fragments of scrolls musty with age. Charts and maps and drawings hung haphazardly about the room, tacked to walls and furniture.

Beside the old man's hand lay a pistol and a torn-out newspaper story.

The room darkened as the sun set, and finally, the writer paused long enough to light a lamp on his desktop. It cast a small globe of light around him as he wrote. Occasionally he would pause to pick up the crumpled piece of newspaper and read.

When he was finished, he folded the papers and placed them in a brown envelope. He wrote a name and an address on it, and sealed it, then pushed back his chair and walked to the door.

He did not open the door but called through it.

"Lawrence!" His voice echoed, hollow and weak, in the room.

An aging black man came to the door and tried the latch. "It's locked, sir."

"Here," the old man said. He knelt and pushed the envelope beneath the door. "See that it is mailed at once."

"Sir, is something wrong?"

"Go!" commanded the other.

Troubled, the servant left the house, huddling in his coat against a cool breeze. He took many backward glances at the house as he walked until, at last, it was out of sight.

He was too far away to hear the single gunshot, the faint echo of which was lost in the clatter of a passing buggy.

At the same time the old man pulled the trigger, far away in the Bitterroot Mountains, another man knelt in a rabbit run and retrieved a rabbit from a snare. Swiftly he snapped the neck and carried his next meal with him to the mountain ridge where he lived.

On the ridge, he stopped and looked skyward, mentally sounding a prayer that had no words.

———

Music in the Ram's Head Saloon was barely on key, but it was enough to satisfy the pointedly unmusical patrons. Two dozen flaring coal-oil lamps swung from the rafters, stained facets casting a multitude of colors against the ceiling.

The saloon was big and boasted a stage with a real lady singer and an orchestra of piano, fiddle, and banjo. Around the area, the common view was that the players sounded better the more they had drunk, or failing that, the more their listeners had.

Sam Mulhaney, the portly, calf-eyed man who owned the Ram's Head, was normally jovial, but tonight he was reserved, quietly but cautiously observing. He watched a man in the corner, an auburn-bearded fellow matching Mulhaney's own impressive girth, but much more solid. His name was Cordell Brannigan, and he had come in a quarter-hour earlier, declaring himself ready for a celebration of nothing in particular and everything in general.

Cord Brannigan in a celebratory mood usually meant good business, and for that, Sam Mulhaney was glad. But it sometimes meant trouble as well, for Brannigan was a hard man to control when he had liquor in him.

"That Cord Brannigan back there?" a customer asked.

"It is," Mulhaney replied.

"Reckon he hasn't heard?"

"Heard what?"

"Don't you know? His brother got himself shot dead two days ago up in Henley. They say Simon Caine did it, then busted out of jail, shot up some more folks, and headed into the mountains."

Mulhaney shook his head. Obviously, Brannigan had not heard, if his grin was any indication.

"Lord's sake just don't say nothing to him while he's in here," Mulhaney said.

Just then, the saloon door opened, and two men stepped in from the darkness. They were covered with trail grime and blinked in the brightness of the room. Cord Brannigan, who had just whispered in a plump saloon girl's ear, roared out a laugh and drew the attention of the newcomers.

After a mutual glance, they strode toward Brannigan.

Mulhaney, smelling trouble, spat a curse.

Brannigan saw the pair coming. His smile remained, but he shifted his attention to them. Locals had a tendency to lay claim on certain saloon girls, and Brannigan assumed the two were coming to defend their proprietary interest in this one.

He whispered again to the painted girl. She glanced at the approaching men and shook her head, then left Branni-gan. She laughed as he feigned an attempt to pinch her thigh while casually slipping his other hand down to the pistol on his hip.

One of the strangers took off his hat and held it in front of him like a man does when meeting a woman of society or a new preacher in town.

"I'm looking for Mr. Cordell Brannigan. I was told I could find him here."

"Well, that's interesting. Why you bothering me about it?"

The second one answered. "We thought you was him."

"Was, and still am."

Brannigan noted the obvious nervousness of the pair. The first was fidgeting with the hat. A good sign: a man with thoughts of gunplay would not so occupy his hands.

"Sit," he invited. "Have a drink."

"That's mighty friendly, Mr. Brannigan." The two pulled up chairs and sat down. Brannigan reached to the next table and gathered two used glasses. He tossed the dregs to the floor and poured drinks for the pair.

The two accepted the drinks despite the secondhand glasses. The first gulped his drink; the second sipped his.

"This here is Rodney Jeffers," said the gulper, pointing at the sipper. "I'm Johnny, his brother."

"Pleased. Now, what do you want with me?"

"First off, let me tell you how sorry we are about your brother."

"What do you mean?"

Color drained from two faces.

"You don't know?" A swallow, a strained voice: "Your brother—he's dead."

Brannigan frowned at first and then shook his head bemusedly as if the idea of a dead brother was more novel than sad. "Dead, you say?"

"Yes sir. He was shot down by Simon Caine."

Brannigan leaned back and laughed heartily. "Now,

that's one I would have never figured! Imagine old Clinton trying to bring down Simon Caine! Why he wouldn't be fit to wad Caine's shotgun!"

"We're awful sorry about it, Mr. Brannigan."

"No, you're not. Clint was no good to nobody, and he's no loss. I won't waste my time pretending to cry for him." He tossed off a drink. "Simon Caine. Now, there's a hellion. I heard he always stayed in the mountains. Why'd he come down to Henley?"

"Nobody knows. But a young buck helped spring him from jail. Folks figured Caine was getting ready to pull a robbery somewhere."

"Folks are fools. Simon Caine ain't a robber. He's a vengeance rider, and that's all." A realization struck him. "Henley—ain't that Will Montrose's town?"

"Yes."

"Hah! I'll wager old Montrose wasn't too tickled to see Caine ride in under his nose and back out again."

"He wasn't. That's why we're here."

Brannigan pondered the man as understanding dawned. "So Montrose wants me to hunt down Simon Caine for him?"

"Don't rightly know."

Brannigan laughed. "Well, I think I'll have a talk with Mr. Montrose. But I'm bringing some friends with me."

"Friends?"

"The Greenleaf's, and Artemus Frye. You heard of 'em?"

"Yes. Mean as sin."

Brannigan raised his glass. "Here's to you, Jeffers brothers. And here's to Will Montrose and Simon Caine—and old Clinton, too, may his soul putrefy in peace."

Glasses clinked and smiles beamed, and on the other side of the room, Sam Mulhaney thanked the fates for good fortune this night.

———

Two nights later, a party of horsemen led by Jim Ballentree plodded wearily into Henley. Ballentree was solemn, his face whiskered from inattention over four days of riding mountain trails. The band of riders dispersed slowly behind him, heading for their homes until only Ballentree remained. He rode to the jail and dismounted. Charlie Bradley met him on the porch.

"No luck?"

"No luck. No sign."

"Things have been quiet here. Your family will be glad to see you." Charlie fumbled with the badge on his shirt. It was Ballentree's, worn by the deputy while the marshal was in the mountains. "Here's your badge, Jim."

"Keep it. I don't want it anymore."

"What?"

"I did some thinking out there. About this town and the way so many were ready to string up a man just because Will Montrose wanted it. I'm quitting, Charlie. Turning the badge over."

"Lord, Jim. I didn't expect this. What will you do?"

"Don't know. I'll find something somewhere."

Ballentree scuffed his boot on the porch. "You know, when Caine was busting out, I had the chance to..." He never finished, and Charlie did not ask.

"Take care of yourself, Charlie. I'll be down in the morning to clean out my things."

"Good night, Jim. Good luck."

Ballentree mounted and rode away. Charlie Bradley turned the badge in his fingers, then pinned it back on his shirt. He watched Ballentree's form dissolve into the darkness, then looked up at the house of William Montrose. He could make out six horsemen riding up the hill toward it.

CHAPTER 6

I n a way, it was the dreams that finally brought Caine the
fever. For many nights he had lost sleep to them; for
many days, he had felt himself slipping closer to sickness.
The dreams horrified him, for they were ominous and silent,
bearing a message that was never quite clear.

Tonight, though, his dreams were not really dreams at
all, but memories.

He was back in his old homeplace in the valley of the
Calfkiller River. Nancy's arm was around him, the boy
sleeping in his little room at the back. He remembered the
smell of Nancy's coffee, the taste of the biscuits she baked
him every morning, the warmth of her by him every night.

Tormented by fever, Caine relived in his mind the most
terrible two days of his life.

A band of Confederates rode by his farm. A loose horse-
shoe brought an offer of help, and that was expanded by
Nancy into a supper invitation. The hungry soldiers quickly
accepted.

Simon and Nancy did not know at the time that at
Sinking Cane, the Confederates had just murdered a Union
colonel who happened to be a close friend of the famed

Captain Montrose. Neither did they know that a lone federal had seen the rebel fighters enter their home and had ridden to Montrose to give word.

The Confederates soon traveled on, riding around a bend in the road and leaving behind only stories of wives and girlfriends and plans for when the fighting was done.

For a day, life was what it always was—farming and trading and passing a few moments with Jake Armitage when he rode by in his wagon. Then, at sunset, a drunken and crazed Robert Montrose came charging around that same bend and, without warning, gunned down Caine and his son, then ran Nancy through with a saber. Young Marcus Caine, crying, pulled himself toward his mother's body and was cut down by the same saber that had felled her. Caine passed out then to the sound of his own screams.

He awakened to pain in his forehead and salty sweat dripping onto his lips. Leering above him, Robert Montrose was attempting to take his scalp. He passed out again as the blade butchered his flesh. He waited for death, but it did not come.

In his fever, Caine reached to the line of scar tissue at his hairline.

"Should have died," he said.

Jake Armitage came to his side. He pulled away the groping hand.

"Easy, Simon. It's all right."

Caine heard his voice and was calmed.

Jake. With him through it all. Caine remembered how Jake had come to him and told him that together they would make it right, and then the disappointment slowly building as he realized a war-torn government would do nothing to prosecute, much less punish, Robert Montrose, the Union hero.

Nancy had never cared much for Jake. It was Jake Armitage, after all, who had persuaded Simon to take an occasional drink, to make a few bets from time to time. She saw him as a bad influence and was, at best, coldly polite to him. If Jake ever had noticed, he hadn't shown it.

Others in the community pulled away from Caine afterward, treating him strangely, keeping their distance. Not Jake. He only drew closer, making Caine's burden his own.

Jake was with Simon Caine when he killed the first man in an alleyway in Murfreesboro. Jake was with him through all the others, too—the methodical slayings that wiped out the band that had murdered Caine's family.

Appropriately, Robert Montrose was the last to die. He ran hard from the phantom who pursued him, and when he was caught, he died pitifully, whimpering until his heart stopped. Then Caine took his scalp as Jake watched.

Caine and Armitage threw in with the Confederacy when that was done, fighting with bushwhackers and guerilla pistol-soldier bands from Middle Tennessee on out to Missouri. Armitage never left him. He was a brother in arms of infinite loyalty.

Caine moaned and stirred. He opened his eyes. Jake was there.

"You've been dreaming, Simon. You got shot coming out of Henley. You picked up a fever, worst I've seen you get since the time you cut your leg with that poleax. Remember?"

"I remember." He looked around. "Where are we?"

"Old hunter's camp in the mountains. They won't find us. Crosston is on the ridgetop, watching."

Again the fever rose within him. Present faded to past, and in his delirium, he saw Jake again, only younger now, as he'd been years ago.

"They offered me a pardon," Jake was saying.

"Take it. You got to."

"All the old Confederates are being pardoned, Simon. All except—"

"I know. Except ones like me."

Jake looked away. "Been some good years, in their way."

"Hard years, Jake."

"What will you do? They'll never stop looking for you."

"Then I'll never stop running."

"But where?"

"Mountains, somewhere out west. I can be safe in the mountains."

"Going to miss you bad."

"We'll ride together again someday, Jake. Someday we will."

———

"It's a scalp lock, Mr. Brannigan. Taken from my brother."

William Montrose took a sip of fine whiskey as the stocky bounty hunter fingered the rough scrap of hair and flesh. Brannigan studied the gruesome trophy with great interest but no apparent revulsion.

"You can see why I am so determined to settle accounts with Caine," Montrose said. "A man who could do such a thing is a savage. He deserves punishment, not only for what he did to my own brother but now yours as well."

Brannigan spoke as if he had been only half listening. "You know, I never saw one of those taken from a man. I hear they come off with a right loud pop."

Montrose looked peculiarly at his visitor.

"Must be as mean as they say he is," Brannigan said.

"Absolutely. A beast, a devil—but a human one. He is as mortal as you or I, no matter what stories people like to throw around. He can be stopped by the right man."

"And you figure that's me?"

"I do. You are a capable man if your reputation is merited. And that reputation—if I may say so without disrespect—far outshines that of your late brother."

"You can say so with or without disrespect. Makes no difference to me."

"I take it you are interested?"

"If the price is right." Brannigan reached for the whiskey bottle gleaming amber in the firelight.

"Five thousand."

"That's a pretty sum."

"And the equal amount available from the federal reward on his head. Success in this venture could make you a wealthy man, Mr. Brannigan."

The bounty hunter watched the leaping flames. "How will I be paid?"

"Half in advance, half when you bring him in. I prefer alive, but I'll accept him otherwise."

"You're willing to lay out twenty-five hundred dollars and let me ride off with it into the hills? How can you be sure I'll come back?"

"I can't. All I can assume is you will like the feel of that cash in your pocket enough to want more. Bring back Simon Caine, and you'll have it."

Brannigan sipped his whiskey. "I won't do the job alone. Them boys I rode in with, they'll go with me. Any objections?"

"Certainly not. You may hire whoever you—"

"Wrong. *You'll* hire them. This is your job, not mine. You don't give me the tools I need; I walk."

Montrose fingered his glass. "My, but you do like to display your brashness," he said coldly. "Well then, who are they?"

"Artemus Frye, for one. You may have heard of him. He'll need, say, two thousand for a job like this. Then there's Morgan Greenleaf and his boy, Billy. Morgan's a good man in the mountains and as stout as they come. The boy ain't worth much, but Morgan won't ride without him. Morgan'll take two thousand, the boy maybe five hundred."

Montrose said, "You're pushing pretty hard."

"You want Simon Caine; you pay the price. We'll need your best mounts, plus supplies and ammunition. That's the only deal I'll cut."

Montrose tossed the dregs of his drink into the fire, making it hiss and spit. "You've got your deal, Mr. Brannigan. But hear me—if you cross me, if you run out on me, then you're life is over."

"You'll get what I promised you. I don't go back on my word."

Brannigan drained his glass and stood. He slipped his hat on with one hand and extended the other. Montrose shook it, his own hand soft against the burlap roughness of Brannigan's.

"I'm going to enjoy working with you, Mr. Montrose. First thing we'll do is head to Cleek's Station. Old man Cleek knows them mountains better than any, and he'll know where they are if anybody does. I'll be 'round in the morning to see to supplies."

When the bounty hunter was gone, Montrose picked up the scalp lock. His lip twitched. He crumpled the knot of hair and skin in his fist and squeezed it until his fingers were white.

CHAPTER 7

As the fever passed and his clotted head wound began to heal, Caine renewed his friendship with Jake Armitage. For the first day, that renewal mostly involved looking at Armitage, getting used to seeing his face again.

"What are you staring at?" Armitage finally asked.

"Something ugly."

"That's mighty rude, Simon. Nancy wouldn't have liked you talking rude to your neighbors."

"She thought you were ugly too."

"Reckon she was right. You were a handsomer catch than I would have been. There was a time I thought of courting Nancy; you know that? Figured to make her my woman."

"I didn't know that." He paused. "But you didn't know Nancy until after I married her."

"That's right."

Caine grabbed the dipper from the water bucket and threw it at Armitage. Both laughed, and years of separation and growing apart disappeared. It felt good to laugh together again, and for a moment, they felt as they had years before.

"You know it wasn't supposed to work out like this, Simon. The word got to you wrong. We were going to meet you outside Henley, not in it. We should have never trusted a drunk redskin as a messenger boy. When we found out what he told you, we about died. When I found out you were in jail, I thought I was going to die."

"For a while there, I thought I was too," Caine said, but the way he smiled let Armitage know it didn't really matter, that he had already put it behind him. "What's this all about, Jake?"

"Crosston will tell you."

"Why the mystery?"

"It's the way he wants it, and besides, I don't really know the whole story."

"Who is Crosston, anyway? And where?"

"Who he is, is a man who will make you richer than you've ever been before. He's out scouting around and guarding, looking for anybody on our tail."

"I didn't thank him properly for what he did. Took a big risk getting me out of that jail."

———

That night Caine did thank the young Englishman, but Crosston let the words roll past, for he had other things to discuss. In the lamplight, he sat on the fireless hearth and told his story and his proposal.

The light cast his face half in gold, half in black; one eye veiled, the other a jewellike glitter.

"I sought you out for a reason, Caine. There is something I am trying to do, and unless you help me, I won't be able to do it.

"There is something in these mountains that I must find —something lost long ago. Not really lost but stolen—from my father. He has searched many years for it, and for the last few, I have helped him. Now we've found it. I've come to reclaim it."

Caine asked, "What is this thing?"

"Something valuable. A treasure if you will. But I can't fully describe it to you, for reasons I hope you will understand. Let me start at the beginning.

"My father is a wealthy man, a native Englishman who has built an empire along America's east coast. Imports, exports, shipping, international marketing in precious metals and jewels, he's done it all, and quite successfully.

"He and my mother separated after only a few years of marriage. He came to this country then, leaving her behind. It was as much her choice as his. But my father did not know I had been conceived. He learned of it only after my birth and sent for my mother then, asking her to come live under his care. She refused. She raised me alone until I was fifteen, then became ill and died. I joined my father, and I've been with him ever since. Though we were strangers for so many years, we drew close upon that first meeting. Today I love him more than any other.

"As I grew, I began working with him, and he taught me a great deal. I also became involved in his hobby—the collection of various antiquities, particularly those of a... well, unusual nature.

"When he finally found it necessary, he told me of something that had happened to him several years before I came to America.

"In the course of his researches, he came across a very covert line of evidence concerning a particular item that had been his chief fascination for years. The bulk of the evidence came from old documents recovered in southern France and shifted into my father's hands by a rather strange series of accidents and coincidences. Other evidence came from ancient British writings and oral traditions handed down through the Freemasons and others.

"He followed that evidence, piecing it together in ways most others had not, and worked himself into the unimaginable position of being able to purchase the very object he had studied for many years. That this should even be possible was a bizarre claim on its face, but my father had reason enough to believe it true. He made the purchase at enormous expense, even for a man of his wealth.

"Few knew of it. It was not the sort of thing one could publicize. There are those who would kill to own it—in fact, many have. There was a time when wars might have been fought over this.

"That, in a way, is what is so ironic about its theft. The culprit was no collector, no secret society—it was my father's own hired man. A gardener. A very unusual man—with arthritis, a sickly wife, an oversized son who was totally deaf. He took it one night from the place it was kept and simply vanished with it. My father never knew how he had come to understand what it was.

"I lived with my father several years before he told me of this. He told me for a reason; he had found the thief's trail and wanted me to follow it. You see, his health is failing. He couldn't make the search himself. The trail was not quite complete, so it would take work to follow it up, and my father had grown too old, too ill. I was to complete the trail, find the treasure, and return it to him.

"I agreed, began my search with the few facts we had, and added to them. A death record in Dakota showing when the thief's wife died, a bill of sale showing a rifle purchased in Virginia City—that sort of thing. But I never could get close enough. I became frustrated. I began keeping a journal just to ease the tension—it's a habit I now can't break.

"Then, at last, I found the final piece of the puzzle.

"It came from an unexpected source: an Indian legend told mostly among the Crow and the Flatheads. I heard it first from an old Crow warrior who begged for scraps and liquor outside a fort. It seemed only the vaguest hint at first until I began examining it, talking to others who know these mountains and their lore.

"It tells of a strange being of some sort—a very large, bearded white figure—who the Indians say guards a treasure in the high Bitterroots. What the treasure is supposed to be varies with whoever is telling the story, but one thing they all agree on: it is somehow sacred and mystical, and supposedly given to its guardian by a spirit, a manito, who revealed himself only as—listen to this—a diseased old man with twisted fingers and joints 'knotty like an old tree,' as my old Crow storyteller said.

"Of course, I immediately linked the legend with the treasure's theft: an oversized white man, a smaller one with an apparent case of arthritis, a mysterious treasure they guard—it all fit. But, obviously, if the legend predated the theft, no matter how well the details fit, they couldn't really relate. So I investigated further and found the story isn't old at all but relatively new. I knew then I had my answer. The thief had taken the treasure into the mountains, and along with him his monstrous son—no doubt quite an impressive figure to superstitious Indians and the probable inspiration for the legend.

"Eventually, with the help of an old mountain man, I developed a map to the area where this white 'god' supposedly lives. It's a good map, quite detailed.

"I have it with me today. I believe it shows where my father's treasure is hidden. It also shows that I need your help, Mr. Caine."

"I don't follow you," Caine said.

"The treasure is in a cave above Sam Ten Pennies' valley."

Caine understood. "Protection," he said.

"Exactly. If I ride into his country alone or with any guide other than you, the half-breed will have my scalp on his belt within a day. I can't reach my destination without crossing his valley, and I can't cross it unless I'm with one of the few men he calls friend. That's why I searched you out, Caine. That's why I involved Mr. Armitage. Only with his influence could I hope to gain your assistance."

"You're wrong on one thing," Caine said. "Ten Pennies is no friend of mine. He's let me be, and me him, but friends we're not."

"If he leaves you alone, that's enough for my purpose," Crosston said.

"He's going to pay us ten thousand apiece, Simon," Armitage said. "Five thousand up front, five thousand when it's done."

"That must be a right valuable treasure," Caine said. "What makes you think I won't just trounce your head once we get it and take off with it myself? And what is it, anyway?"

"You answered your first question with your last one," Crosston responded. "If you know what the treasure is, its value is immense. If you don't know, you could sell it for pocket change, perhaps, but no more. That is my ace, so to speak, my protection."

"And what if I stick my pistol up your nose and ask you to let me in on the secret?"

"I'd tell you to go ahead and shoot. I'm doing this for my father. I'll die before I betray him."

"Ten thousand dollars, you say?"

"That's right."

Armitage leaned forward. "Will you do it, Simon?" Caine did not answer. Instead, he stood, opened the cabin door, and walked into the night.

———

Armitage found him leaning against a spruce, smoking. He cut himself a chew and settled it in his jaw.

"The boy didn't know what to make of you running out like that, Simon."

"I don't know what to make of him," Caine said. "That's quite a tale. But I don't trust a man who wants me to help him but won't tell me the whole story."

"That mean you're saying no?"

"A lot depends on you, Jake. You given thought to turning him down?"

There was a long pause before he answered. "I can't."

"Why not?"

"The truth is, he's already paid me—even the pay I wasn't supposed to get until the end. I owe it to him to finish up."

"Just give the money back."

"It's gone."

Caine frowned. "You spent ten thousand dollars already?"

"It was spent before I got it. Gambling debts. The kind of people I owe make this Ten Pennies look like a Sunday school teacher."

"I never would have figured you for a fool, Jake."

"No sermons. I don't want to hear them."

Caine drew on his cigar. "Well, I can't let you ride under Sam Ten Pennies' nose alone. I guess that's all there is to it."

Armitage cast down his eyes, ashamed. But he said: "It's going to be good riding with you again. Just like the old days."

"Like the old days, Jake."

FROM THE JOURNAL OF JOHN CROSSTON

I should *be* asleep, but it would be useless even *to try; I'm far too excited. As I write by the fire,* Simon Caine is sitting on a deadfall, smoking, and *Jake* Armitage already is snoring in his bedroll.

Caine has agreed *to help me*, more out *of his* friendship with Armitage than anything else, I believe. Perhaps he feels *some* obligation to me for what I did in Henley. I shudder *to* remember that. But I am eager for what is ahead.

Soon it *will be* in my hands. I *will be able to* give back *to my father the* thing around which so much of his life has been centered. *I am* beginning *to realize just how close* I *really am.*

Caine is bothered by my secrets. He has said nothing, but I can tell. He thinks *it a fool's* venture, and for that, I can hardly blame him. The time *will come,* though, when he *will see.*

Caine is a strange man, strong, very cold. From time *to time, there are* glimmerings *of what he* must have been before. Particularly when he smiles, which is seldom.

Armitage is *awake*—Caine *is* laughing *at* him, waking himself up with his own snoring. *Now* Armitage is watching me write, *as he has done so often. I must guard my packet carefully.*

Tomorrow *we will reach Cleek's Station.* Caine told me just a little *of it, and I* gather *it is a* grim place, quite dangerous. But *we* must *have supplies, and that is the only place they can be found.*

I must rest now. Tomorrow I will be another day closer. *Be well and safe,* Father. I will bring it back to you, no matter *what I must do.*

CHAPTER 8

Cleek's Station was a brown scab on the land, an outpost for trading, drinking, gambling, hide-selling, and, whenever proprietor Ezra Cleek had some cast-off Flathead maiden, whoring. Beyond the station lay only the tangled wilderness and dark Bitterroot trails.

Caine stayed away from Cleek's, usually, for several reasons. Rumor had it that many who entered to spend the night at five cents a bed never came out again. Furthermore, it was an occasional haunt of bounty hunters and disreputable lawmen. The mountains drew those on the run, as they had drawn Caine twelve years before, and both worthy and unworthy agents of the law naturally followed.

"I'm a fool for coming here, Jake," Caine said from the ridgetop overlooking Cleeks. "I've got as much a place here as a bastard at a family reunion."

"Then let me ride down, and you stay."

"No. A man gets tired of hiding out all the time." They began a descent toward the jumble of unpainted buildings that comprised Cleek's Station. The place looked much like an oversized lumber pile or scrap heap, the kind where rats live. "Hold up a minute," Caine said, sniffing the air.

He reined his mount leftward and slightly back, descending now at an angle opposite the Station. At last, he led his companions to a wide sinkhole tangled with vines.

"What's this, Simon?" Armitage asked.

Caine dismounted without answering and walked to the sinkhole. He pushed aside the tangle of brush and peered inside. Both Crosston and Armitage caught the stench, a putrid smell on the breeze.

"Some dead critter," Armitage said.

"Here's your critter," Caine responded. He pointed into the hole. The others dismounted and came over to look.

A body was there. The torso was split open and filled with rocks. The obvious intent of whoever had killed the man was to drop him out of sight into the hole, but the body had caught on protruding roots and was suspended in the rocky mouth of the pit.

Crosston went pale. "Who would have done this?" he said.

"Ezra Cleek, son. This hole has swallowed more dead men than hell, and we'd best take care not to become the next ones." Caine removed his cigar from his mouth and tossed it into the hole. "I know that one down there. One-Eyed Charlie Dreyfuss. Injun trader, some of the worst scum in these mountains. Most of the ones Cleek gets don't know better. One-Eyed, he should have."

Caine scouted about until he found a large rock. He hefted it, staggered to the edge of the hole, and dumped it on top of the corpse. The body folded and fell into darkness. Crosston turned away.

Caine shook his head and gingerly touched his wounded scalp.

"Shouldn't have done that, Jake. Made me dizzy. Next corpse is yours to sink."

By the time the trio had descended the ridge, Ezra Cleek was standing on the porch of the Station's main building, which served as a general store, saloon, and dining hall for those with sufficiently strong stomachs. He smiled broadly, a welcoming host. Crosston and Armitage eyed him warily, and Caine remained poker-faced. Ezra Cleek scanned the men as they dismounted; his gaze lingered a bit longer on Caine than on the others, but his expression provided no obvious evidence of recognition.

"Gentlemen," he said.

"Howdy," returned Caine.

"Pretty day," the old man said. His head was tilted slightly, and his eyes sparkled. Armitage thought of a blue jay. "You pilgrims bound for the high mountains?"

"We're in need of supplies. And something to drink." Caine's eyes narrowed as he noticed that a young man had come around the corner of the building and now stood gaping at them. It was obvious that he suffered some substantial mental impairment, and on his filthy shirt were bloodstains drying from red to rust.

Cleek noted the questioning stares of Armitage and Crosston.

"Don't mind him," he said. "He's my son. He's short—up here." He tapped his forehead. "He can handle your horses, though. Come inside, and I'll pour you drinks."

Armitage looked to Caine. The latter stood by his mount for a moment, considering. Then he turned the reins over to the young man and stepped onto the porch.

"We have visitors inside already," Cleek said.

Armitage slid to Caine's side. "Simon—"

Caine cut him off. "I can't dodge every stranger I run across."

The two inside were nondescript enough. One was a huge man, bearded and gap-toothed, dressed in a buckskin shirt and fringed hide trousers. He had a rusting cap-and-ball Colt thrust beneath his belt and a long Bowie on his right hip. As he looked over the newcomers, Caine caught the egg-white gleam of a dead eye. The other man, sipping whiskey from a beer glass, was older, with squirrely, squinted eyes and white wisps of hair. He wore filthy store-bought clothes and a derby hat that had been white a decade before. He slid his eyes over the three who entered; they came to rest on Caine.

The interior of Cleek's Station stank of mold, dust, spilled beer, smoke, even animal excrement. The darkness inside was oppressive, particularly in contrast to the bright sun outside, and the lanterns that swung from the ceiling had to be lit even in the day.

In one corner, a hound slept amid a cloud of fleas. In another, a fat Indian girl sat peeling onions and wiping her nose. Flies buzzed throughout the low, wide room.

"A truly remarkable place," whispered Crosston in a sarcastic tone.

"When you got no competitors, you offer what you got, and somebody's bound to take it," Caine observed. He walked to the bar, a rough lumber contrivance, as Cleek circled it and pulled from a wooden crate a corked bottle. Cleek dusted it on his sleeve and sat it before Caine, along with three beer mugs.

"I'm afraid my shot glasses are all dirty," Cleek said. "The Crow girl yonder has been here three weeks, and I can't get much work out of her. She's too ugly for other uses and too smelly to sell. If you see somebody half blind and noseless, looking for a woman, send him my way, if you please."

Caine sipped his whiskey with the respect the hot liquor merited. The doorway darkened. Henry Cleek entered and slid onto a stool by the door.

Caine gestured toward the bloodstained shirt Henry wore. "Right early in the year to butcher hogs, ain't it?"

Cleek's expression hardened for a moment, then softened again with his fake smile. "That's dog blood. Henry's favorite got into it with a cur earlier today, and Henry held it to his chest as it died."

There was motion at the other end of the bar. The two men there edged a foot closer to Caine and his companions.

"We'll have a pot of stew cooked up in an hour or so," Cleek said. "You are welcome to stay and share it. The afternoon's getting on, anyway—perhaps some beds for the night?"

"Reckon not," Caine said. Crosston sighed in obvious relief. "It's not smart for a man to buy stew where a dog's been killed."

Armitage smiled around the rim of his glass. A faint chuckle came from one of the two at the end of the bar.

"I don't like this place," Crosston whispered to Armitage.

The dead-eyed man at the bar stepped forward, and Caine turned to meet him.

"I know you, Caine," the man said.

"Too bad."

"Will you come without us having to kill you?"

"Reckon, you already know the answer to that."

"Yeah." He went for his gun.

Caine's Navy Colt glinted in the lamplight, then boomed twice. Two men fell back as if one, the little one dead instantly, the big one writhing for a moment before he expired. Caine turned back to the bar and holstered his pistol. Henry Cleek clapped and laughed by the doorway. The Indian girl kept peeling onions.

Ezra Cleek's first reaction was to thrust out his tongue in a peculiar way and chew on it, making faint squeaking sounds in his throat. Then he squinted and leaned across the bar.

"What's on 'em and in their bags is mine," he said. "Horses too. It's my place, and that's the rules."

"Fine by me," Caine said.

Crosston watched a pool of red spread across the floor.

"We do need us a packhorse, Simon," Armitage said.

"That's so. Cleek, you sell one of these gent's mounts to us?"

"Oh, you don't want what they rode. Cheap bounty killers, cheap horses to match. I've got a good pack animal in the stable. Bought him off a one-eyed trader in here earlier."

"You're a sharp trader, I hear. He probably came out in the hole on that deal," Caine said.

Cleek's lip twitched spasmodically as his mind worked rattishly to assess the comment. After a moment, he resumed his usual facade.

Caine negotiated for the packhorse, plus supplies for a long mountain journey.

When they were gone, Cleek had his son drag the bodies to the door and dump them outside. Then the Cleeks and the Indian girl sat down to their stew.

FROM THE JOURNAL OF JOHN CROSSTON

A long ride *today. We've left Cleek's Station far behind, yet not so far as it seems, for we have* moved *slowly. The terrain* is upward a part of *the way, and the* horses are considerably strained. The air here sometimes seems so thin you *would think a* match couldn't burn in it. Already I gasp *for* breath, but we *will* go much higher before this is done.

The sky has been clouded *today, and there has* been a general grim overcast about the land. *I've felt restless and* disturbed. *It* began *at Cleek's* Station, with those *two* men and the utter calm *with which Caine* dispatched them. *It was fearful, as on the* street *at Henley, when he left the scalp lock for William* Montrose. *I heard Caine tell* Armitage today he would go back *to* Henley someday and even *the score with Montrose. Caine lives on* vengeance and memories.

Nonetheless, seeing Armitage and Caine together, I am inclined to call Caine *the more becalmed, the less troubled of the two.* Caine has his obsession and his torment, but Armitage has a manner that suggests many regrets haunt him. Certainly, he has largely wasted his *life. He told me earlier he had* never gambled until after he and Caine were separated. Now *that they are reunited,* Armitage seems happier, though *still* haunted.

A peculiar thing about *Armitage*—he seems *to* define himself in terms *of Caine. He* seems to have nothing except a connection *to* a man more substantial, more solid, than himself. Caine is his anchor, his point *of reference.*

I had an interesting talk with Armitage *today when Caine was out of hearing. I asked* him if he had ever been frightened by Caine's viciousness and coldness.

His response was a bit more insightful than I would *have anticipated. Yes, he said, he has often* been afraid *of* him but never has feared *that Caine* would hurt him. "I've *felt a fear of* Simon like you might *feel* about a ghost—it's not what he will do to you, but what he is."

There is a powerful bond between those *two. Caine* would die before letting harm come *to* Armitage, *yet Armitage has that fear of* him. Another thing Armitage said might explain *that: "I'm afraid* sometimes of *who he is, and what he* is because *I* helped make him that *way."*

That, I suppose, is the phantom that follows Armitage.

Caine also has phantoms. They come out in his dreams. I have heard him *call his wife's name* in his sleep, and I think he often relives her death. There are other dreams too. I heard him trying *to* describe one *to* Armitage only *today.* He couldn't frame the words. The dream bothered him intensely, and he could not describe *it.*

My own dreams are not quite as frequent anymore— thank God. I had no choice, *yet it bothers me. If there had* been any other *way . . . but the* priest *was a threat.*

I did it for you, Father, though I pray you *will* never know *of it.*

CHAPTER 9

The mountain man rode in great pain. The jolts of his mount's hooves hitting the trail stung him with dull jabs of suffering. Blood dripped from two burning holes in his back and a jagged exit wound above his stomach. Somewhere inside him, a bullet was lodged, and it moved each time he moved, gnawing away at his insides like a mouse.

Not far beyond, he could see a fire. Whose it was, he had no idea; perhaps a band of hunters, trappers, maybe Indians —or the half-breed who this afternoon had tried to kill him; who had succeeded, just not as swiftly as intended. He knew he would be dead soon. That is why it hardly mattered whose fire it was. If that of enemies, they could do him no further harm. If friends, then they could take his final message to Opequon, his lady.

Only a short distance, yet it seemed far. He groaned, blacked out for a moment, then caught himself as he began to slide from the saddle.

He pulled himself upright, squinting at the pain. Just a little farther.

It was too late. Darkness spread across his vision, dimming the yellow flicker that had been his mark. Silently the tall man slid from his saddle and collapsed, eyes shut and mouth open. Even his beard was clotted with blood.

His horse nosed his body. The mountain man did not move. The horse's breath came in steamy gusts against his face, but he did not feel it.

After a time, the horse wandered farther into the woods and stopped by a little stream to graze.

———

Four horsemen rode down the dirt trail toward Cleek's Station. Henry Cleek stood outside, alone except for a small kitten that played at his feet, sniffing and pawing a rusty circle in the dirt where two bodies had laid through a cold night, a warm day, and another night—until at last the stench and the flies grew so obnoxious that even the insensitive Ezra Cleek could put off disposal no longer.

At the lead of the four riders was Cord Brannigan, his heavy form swaying in the saddle, as deadweight as a sack of grain. Behind him rode two blond men, both baby-faced but one considerably older than the other. That they were father and son would have been instantly obvious to anyone with a mind slightly more able than Henry Cleeks. They were Morgan and Billy Greenleaf.

The fourth man had a leathery, sunken look. His tiny black eyes hid beneath heavy brows. This was Artemus Frye; few knew more about him than his name, and fewer dared ask.

The four stopped a few yards from Henry Cleek. Brannigan, chewing a twig, studied the young man and immediately perceived the slowness of his mind.

"Howdy, boy," he said.

"'Lo," Henry said.

"Where's your pa?"

"Up over the hill puttin' 'em in the hole."

Bill Greenleaf gave a childish laugh. "What's he talking like that for?"

"Can't you see, boy?" the elder Greenleaf said. "He's a half-wit."

"Putting what in the hole?" Brannigan asked.

"Them that's dead and been laying here stinking. Pa took 'em to the hole."

Brannigan sighed. "Where is this hole, then?"

Henry pointed up the ridge. "On t'other side."

"And your pa's up there putting dead critters in it?"

"Not critters. Men."

The four riders exchanged wary looks.

"Men?"

"Yeah. Shot with a pistol."

Brannigan then noticed the blood on the ground. "They were shot right here?"

"No, inside. Pa said it was Mister Simon who done it." Henry Cleek knelt, stroking the kitten. "My kitty, she like the blood." He picked up the kitten and held it to his chest.

Brannigan smiled broadly. "Thank you kindly, boy. We'll go see your pa now."

The four turned their mounts and rode toward the ridge. As Artemus Frye rode past Henry Cleek, he reached down and scooped the kitten from his arms.

"My kitty!" Henry yelled. "Gimme my kitty!"

The riders paid no attention. Henry Cleek scrambled up the trail after them. Frye held the kitten high over his head, twisting the flailing little animal to further torment the retarded young man. Henry Cleek began to cry.

Ezra Cleek had just dumped one body when the four rode into view. Frowning, he eyed his shotgun standing against a tree. He had enough sense to keep away from it, though, and as the band drew near, he put on his phony smile and assumed the attitude of a house servant patronizing his master.

"Cleek? My name's Cord Brannigan."

"I've heard of you, sir. Yes, I'm Cleek."

"My kitty! Pa, he got my kitty!" sobbed Henry.

"We're looking for Simon Caine," Brannigan said.

"Indeed."

"The boy there said he's been here."

Cleek smiled, the face of a senile old minister at a tea party. "Sir, I'm a simple merchant and must sell what I can for my living."

Brannigan fished out a coin and tossed it at Cleek's feet.

"My kitty, Pa!"

"Caine was here," Cleek said. "Two others with him, one older, one a good deal younger and with a strange way of talking."

"When?"

Again the placid smile. Another coin fell in the dirt.

"Day before yesterday, in the afternoon. Caine left a mess behind. I'm only now cleaning up."

"So I see. Which way?"

Cleek waited for his coin. Henry was on his knees by Frye's horse, and Frye looked down on him with an almost demonic grin.

Brannigan tossed no more coins, and Cleek figured he had better not press the issue.

"That way," he said, pointing north. "Carrying supplies for a long journey. I know the trail they are likely to follow." Cleek outlined the route, hoping the riders would quickly be on their way.

"Obliged," Brannigan said.

"Pa!"

"Here's your cat, boy," Frye said. He held the kitten toward its owner, then tossed it to Brannigan. Cursing, Brannigan batted it away with his arm, and it arched into the sinkhole where Cleek had tossed the corpse.

"My kitty!" Henry pitched forward, face in the dirt.

Frye laughed convulsively.

Henry raised himself and looked around at the group.

"Someday, somebody going to hurt you. Someday some-body'll put you down in a hole like you done, my kitty!"

Frye's laughter stopped. He reached for his sidearm.

"Leave it be, Artemus," Brannigan said.

Frye turned to Cleek. "You need to keep better control of your half-wit, old man."

The four rode on. Cleek gathered his coins, bit them, and slid them into his pocket.

"Come on, boy," he said. "Help me dump this last one."

Henry Cleek did not rise. He continued to cry.

"All right, then. I'll do it myself." Cleek was more patient than usual because of the new jingle in his pocket. He hefted the stiff body, grunted, and tossed it into the hole. It disappeared into the darkness and death stench below.

Ezra Cleek said nothing to comfort his son. He walked alone back to the trading post. Henry Cleek cried more, then finally slept in the weariness of grief.

He did not waken until he felt a rough little tongue against his cheek. Cleek's last corpse had been a ladder out of hell for the kitten. Henry swept up his pet and poured out upon it all the love he could muster.

The rider wore a long cloak that flapped behind him in the stiff breeze and a black derby noticeably inappropriate for these rugged mountains. He progressed slowly, his weary horse fighting both gravity and wind on an upward trek. The rush of chilly air made the man squint and tugged at his impeccably groomed beard.

The man looked big but wasn't. His face, upon first impression, appeared aged and weathered, yet the prematurely gray whiskers hid skin that was childishly smooth and rather fair.

The trail gradually widened into a road that led into Henley. The rider looked over the little town as he passed through it; the conglomeration of low buildings and false fronts was as ugly as the last time he had seen it. Why William Montrose insisted on living here, he could not imagine. He contradicted the thought immediately. Of course, he knew why: William Montrose lived here because, in Henley, his power was unquestioned. The rider felt a swell of familiar contempt, but he squelched it. William Montrose, he might secretly despise, but the man's money was something else again.

It was dusk, and light from Montrose's windows streamed out high above the town. The rider's horse pulled to the left, wanting water from a nearby trough, and the man let it drink. "Old Will can wait a minute more, I suppose," he said to the thirsty animal. His voice was soft but very deep.

He knew he was watched. This was a town of eyes that peeped from behind curtains and shutters, of whispers and suspicions and all other such things that thrived in the shadow of oppression. While the horse drank, the rider swept his gaze across the town, reconfirming his hatred of it.

He moved on again, riding slowly up the hill to Montrose's house. At the stable, Rodney Jeffers met him and took the horse's reins.

"Evening, Mr. DeGuere."

"Hello, Rodney. Is he inside?"

"At his desk."

Morrison DeGuere dismounted. "The horse could use some oats," he said as he turned the gelding over to Jeffers. "Fact is, I could stand a feeding myself." He pulled his cloak tighter around him and walked to the house.

Montrose met him at the door. The sallowness of his

face and the unusual intensity in his eyes struck DeGuere at once.

"I'm displeased, Morrison. I expected you last night," Montrose said.

DeGuere smiled. "Good evening to you, too, William." He took off his cloak and hung it over his arm. "Your message arrived late, and the ride was hard. I came as quickly as I could."

Montrose wheeled and walked into his study. DeGuere followed. A fire blazed in the fireplace. On the desk sat a half-empty bottle of whiskey and an uneaten meal.

"Have you dined, Morrison?"

"I haven't."

Montrose waved his slender hand over the food.

DeGuere sat down and neatly tucked a napkin beneath his beard. He emptied the plate speedily yet daintily. When he was done, he carefully wiped his fingers on his napkin and poured a glass of whiskey.

Then he looked at Montrose and said, "I understand Simon Caine broke free from jail here."

Montrose smiled bitterly. "Word does travel. He broke free, yes—with help. A young Englishman who told our marvelously ineffective and stubborn marshal that his name was Crosston."

"Crosston," DeGuere repeated, mentally filing the name. "Is he the one I'm after, or Caine?"

"Caine is already taken care of. You might have heard of a bounty hunter named Cord Brannigan. I've hired him."

"Oh yes," DeGuere said. "A capable man, I'm told."

"We shall see. Your only concern is the Englishman. I want you to trace him down, learn everything there is to know where he came from, what he's done, his relationship to Caine, his plans. I want to know his shoe size and the number of hairs on his hand. Caine escaped me because of him, and I want him."

"You know nothing more than his name—if that is his real name at all?"

"Other than the fact he posed as a clergyman to enter the jail, no. But what more does Morrison DeGuere need, eh? A detective of your skill could do the job with even less."

DeGuere despised Montrose's patronizing but responded only by raising his glass and taking another sip. "I'll do my best, William." He finished his drink and stood, taking up his cloak. "Crosston—an Englishman. There's something vaguely familiar in that, though I can't quite recall..." He paused, slipped on the cloak, then shrugged. "Oh, well—if it is there, I'll find it. What is my time situation, William?"

"Work as quickly as possible. Keep in contact with me— hire a courier at my expense if need be. I want to become very familiar, very soon, with young Mr. Crosston."

"May I assume the usual hotel arrangements still hold?"

"No charge for you, Morrison."

DeGuere said his thank you and went to the door. Montrose called to him, and DeGuere turned.

Montrose looked darkly at him. "Do not fail me."

The detective's perpetual loathing for Montrose surged, but as always, he hid it. "I won't," he said.

"Good." Montrose turned his back on him, and DeGuere walked quickly out the door.

CHAPTER 10

Simon Caine raised his hand to halt the others when he saw the riderless horse. A chill swept him.

"Jack's horse," he said.

"What do you reckon, Simon?" Armitage said.

Caine didn't answer. Instead, he dismounted and slid the Spencer from its boot. Looking about, he walked to the horse and patted its neck. Then he went farther on, searching the ground as he proceeded.

Before he had gone a hundred feet, he found the mountain man lying still and pale on the ground where he had fallen. He was alive, but his chest shuddered with pain every time he breathed.

"Jack. Good Lord."

The eyes, amazingly, fluttered open. The injured man gave forth a weak smile. His voice came in a whispered rasp: "My prayers answered. Simon."

"What happened, Jack?"

"Ten Pennies." Then he fell unconscious again.

Caine called Armitage and Crosston over to him. "Who is he?" Armitage asked.

"Jack Whitaker. Old North Carolina fellow, from off the

Yadkin. This old boy's seen every inch of country between here and there. Just kept coming west with his squaw. She's a Cherokee, name of Opequon."

"You talk like you know him well."

"I do. He's been the only friend I've had since I came to the mountains."

"Who did this to him?"

"Ten Pennies."

Crosston looked sharply at Caine.

Armitage said, "We should build a fire to warm him up."

"No. I don't know where Ten Pennies is. If he's close, I don't want to draw him."

"But Ten Pennies wouldn't hurt you, would he, Caine?" Crosston asked.

"I wouldn't have thought so, but he's never hurt Jack before, either. We may have been dealt a whole new hand."

Caine examined his friend, who was trying to fight his way back to consciousness. He had bled heavily, apparently for a long time.

Armitage shook his head. He had seen many gunshot wounds during the war, and these were severe. "It doesn't look good, Simon."

"I know."

"Why would Ten Pennies do this?"

"I don't know."

Jack Whitaker opened his eyes. "Opequon," he said.

"Don't worry about her," Caine responded. "I'll get you to her."

"No... you won't."

Caine knew it was true.

"I'm hurting bad, Simon."

"Why did he do this to you?"

"He's out for white blood—mostly out for Charlie Dreyfuss. Dreyfuss killed Ten Pennies' woman a few days back, and Ten Pennies has been trailing him since.

Somehow I got in the way. I was shot before they even got a good look at me... I think Ten Pennies took me for Dreyfuss."

"Dreyfuss is dead now, Jack."

"Dead?"

"Ezra Cleek."

Jack Whitaker laughed at the irony, but pain choked the laughter away.

"Simon, stay away from Ten Pennies. Get out of the mountains and take Opequon with you."

"I'll see to her, Jack."

The mountain man was breathing hard. The effort of speaking had exhausted him. He closed his eyes.

Caine stayed at his side until he was dead.

————

They buried Jack Whitaker, where he died, piling stones on top of his grave. When it was done, Armitage sang an old hymn in his rough baritone, and Caine stood remembering the time Jake had sung that at the funeral of his wife and son.

That funeral had been a time of inward battle when old values of peaceful living and forgiveness had struggled with a raging desire for revenge.

That day in the church graveyard, the latter had won easily.

His brother, James Brice Caine, had presided over the funeral. The time would not be long before he would deny his kinship to Simon Caine and even change his name to avoid the stigma of being associated with him.

Standing now by Jack Whitaker's grave, Caine wondered what other changes would come.

"He was a good man, Simon?"

"Surely was, Jake. I learned the ways of the mountains from that old buzzard. Never even thought about him dying.

He seemed the kind that would stand as long as the mountains did."

Crosston came to Caine and shook his hand. "I'm sorry about your friend, Caine. But we're losing time. We have a long way to ride."

Caine glared back at him. "Didn't you hear what Jack said? Ten Pennies is on a death spree, boy, and there'll be no riding into his country until it's done."

Crosston was incredulous. "We can't possibly give up now! You don't understand, Caine— I have to go on and recover my father's treasure."

"Well, you can forget about it for the time being," Caine returned. "Besides, I got to go to Opequon."

Crosston's temper flared. "I paid you, Caine."

"What's money worth to a man who'll be running the rest of his days?" Caine said. "I'm doing this for Jake, and I'm going to Opequon for Jack Whitaker. If you want me to help you find your treasure, you'll do it my way."

Crosston assumed a haughty tone. "Consider it this way, Caine. If you no longer, as you implied, are protection from Sam Ten Pennies, then perhaps I should just go on without you. The risk would be the same either way."

"You want to go on, then you go on. But Jake stays with me."

"Oh no. Jake is in this to the end, whether he likes it or not, and whatever you think about it."

There was a long, tense pause. Finally, Caine said, "You talk about Jake Armitage like that, and he's liable to kill you. And if he doesn't, I might."

Caine wondered, though, if what he had just said was true. Jake, right now, seemed deflated and old. He had taken Crosston's bossing without response. It wasn't something he would have done in the earlier days.

"We'll say no more about this right now," Caine said. "I'm going to Jack's lodge to tell Opequon what happened.

You can come with me or ride on—but I advise you to come with me."

Caine's calmer tone soothed Crosston a bit. "Very well. I'll go. But we'll discuss this later."

"That we will."

Caine went to the packhorse they had bought at Cleek's and took off its burdens. As best he could, he redistributed them on the horses they rode and put some on Jack Whitaker's mount. He slapped the rump of the former packhorse, sent it running.

"We can't use this horse no more," he said. "If Ten Pennies recognizes it as One-Eyed Charlie's, that might just set him off."

Caine mounted, and the little band rode off in silence.

CHAPTER 11

C aine stopped the group shortly before they reached the clearing where Jack Whitaker's lodge stood.

"Something's wrong," he said.

"What do you mean?" Crosston asked.

"Son, someday you'll learn that when Simon Caine feels something wrong, you'd best listen," Armitage replied.

Caine dismounted and unbooted the Spencer. "I'm going in close. You two stay put until I give the word." Then he slipped into the woodland and was gone.

Jack's lodge was a beauty, roofed with dirt and solidly built. Caine had always believed a man's work showed his character, and if that was so, Jack Whitaker had left behind a fine memorial.

At the moment, though, Caine was not thinking about such things but was instead studying the horses tethered outside the lodge. Saddled and lathered, they had been ridden only minutes before.

Caine dropped behind a deadfall, debating what to do next.

Suddenly a gunshot blast came from inside the lodge, then a shrill scream. The door fell open, and a young man tumbled out, screaming again in the same high shriek. He was blond, very boyish, and his chest was a mass of blood.

He rolled in the dirt, arms clutched around himself, giving one screech after another. The shotgun blasted again; a shutter blew outward from the window and showered the wounded boy with shards of wood. Three men came running out the door, dragging with them articles of clothing, boots, weapons. They obviously had been half undressed when the shooting began, and now they looked like surprised lovers exiting a back door as the husband arrived unexpectedly through the front.

Two of the men fairly leaped astride their mounts, but the third man, blond like the wounded one, stopped long enough to heft the latter onto his shoulder and then onto the rump of his horse. Blood streamed down the horse's flanks.

The blond man mounted the horse and put one hand behind him to steady the wounded boy. The others were already riding away by the time the blond man spurred his own mount. At the same time, Opequon came to the door, a shotgun in her hands.

She raised it and fired. The blond man ducked as a shot patterned over his head.

When the riders were gone, Opequon leaned heavily against the frame of the door. The shotgun slid to the ground.

She tensed and stooped for it when Simon Caine stepped into the clearing. Then she saw who he was. He thought he saw tears in her eyes—but Opequon never cried.

It made Caine dread all the more telling her the news he had brought.

———

She accepted it with her usual stoicism, this beautiful Cherokee woman, far from the land of her fathers, in mountains they had never seen. She had come a long way for the love of Jack Whitaker, but now, as Caine asked her if she understood what he was saying, she simply nodded and rose to boil coffee.

When the cups were filled and distributed, she told of what had happened before.

"They came from the forest and entered my lodge. I did not know them. The big one held me while another, a boy, tried to force himself on me. They laughed when I fought them. But I broke free and reached the shotgun. They did not laugh then. They ran like cowards. The boy will die."

"Did you hear any names?" Caine asked.

"The big one's name was Brannigan."

Caine leaned forward in his chair. "Cord Brannigan?"

"He kin of the one you downed in Henley?" Armitage asked.

"Brother."

"Lordy, Simon. That means he must be looking for you."

"Montrose sent him."

"Why do you say that? Might just be because of family."

"No. I know a little about that pair. All but hated each other. It's got to be Montrose. He's hired Cord Brannigan to bring me back."

Crosston sat in silence, bitterly knowing his hope was fading ever faster. Caine was sure to back out. Not only was Ten Pennies a far greater threat than first anticipated, but now they also had hired killers on their heels. Caine would never expose Armitage to such risk.

Only with effort did Crosston restrain himself from smashing his coffee cup against the wall.

Later, Caine spoke to Opequon of Jack's wishes for her.

"He made me promise while he lay dying," he said. "He was worried about what Ten Pennies might do. With these others roaming about now, there's even more cause for concern. They might come back."

"But I don't want to leave."

"I understand that. But I promised him."

"Very well," she said.

They spent the rest of the day at the lodge. Opequon busied herself in minute tasks. Armitage cleaned his weapons and made a repair on his saddle. Caine wandered about the lodge, smoking, thinking, feeling the peculiar emptiness of the mountains. It was hard to believe his old friend was not out there somewhere.

Wagh! We had shinin' times, Simon. Some rough going, but *that's how the stick floats. Aye?*

Simon Caine smiled to himself. Jack had been a mountain man to the core. Knew no other life, wanted no other.

Inside, Crosston fumed silently. He found a corner and sat down, knees up, journal propped in front of him. He wrote furiously, in wide strokes, and his pen often tore clean through the paper.

Opequon had been packing her meager possessions in an elk-hide sack. Now she went to the huge fireplace her husband had built and took from its mantle hooks a gleaming Hawken he had loved. Jack had retired it from use two years before and had always kept it shining clean.

The men slept that night in the lodge, but Opequon was restive. She lay awake, staring at the ceiling beams and listening to the soft snores of Jake Armitage, the clockwork breathing of Crosston. She also heard the moaning and stirring of Simon Caine, who seemed lost in some horrible dream.

She rose in utter silence and took up the Hawken and the supplies she had packed. Without so much as a glance behind her, she slipped out of the lodge and was gone.

CHAPTER 12

Billy Greenleaf was alone when he died. Chest ripped open, the boy cried out to his father, his mother, and Jesus as life drained away.

Morgan Greenleaf left his boy because Brannigan had given him two options: "Stay with him and lose your cut, ride with us and keep it." He rode.

The next day, after a night of torment inflicted by what remained of his fatherly love, he mounted and rode back to where he had left his son, hoping to find him still alive.

Billy lay in ivory stillness, eyes half open. Moisture lay in droplets on his white face and in his hair. Mist rose around him in the little grove.

Morgan Greenleaf dismounted and walked stiffly to the body. Kneeling, he stroked back the sodden hair from the boy's forehead.

"I'm sorry, Billy. God, I'm sorry." He gathered up the cool form and held it close.

As if he had come to a decision, he laid the body back in its place and closed the eyes with his fingers. He went to his horse, brought back a slicker, and laid it across the blood-caked chest.

The sun rose above the treetops, sending scattered rays through the forest. A fly buzzed and settled on Billy Greenleaf's face, and the father waved it away.

Finally, Greenleaf bowed his head. "God, if God there be, let me pay for what I've done."

He reached, trembling, for his pistol. Sliding it from the holster, he studied it, turning it in the dappling sunlight, looking at its contours and the gleam of the oiled metal. When his courage let him, he raised the pistol to his head.

He closed his eyes. The hammer went back, and his finger began tightening on the trigger.

He couldn't do it. He had never been able to do what was just and right. He cursed himself. In a burst of anger, he threw his pistol into the brush.

"To desert one's own flesh is a great crime."

In one motion, Greenleaf stood and turned.

The man who had spoken was a dark man, almost as black as a Negro. His hair was long and flowed down both sides of his face. With high cheekbones and a narrow Roman nose, he had a distinctly Indian appearance. A hawk's feather was tied to the bright cloth around his head.

Greenleaf stumbled backward. He tripped over his son's body and fell. Quickly he rose again, staring into the face of the stranger, his own face pale as his dead son's. His hand brushed over his holster before he remembered he had tossed away his gun.

"The fear left him before he died," the stranger said. "He died as a man should."

"Who are you?"

"I am Sam Ten Pennies."

Other forms emerged from behind trees and underbrush. Twelve of them in all.

"It is only the greatest of cowards who leaves his own son to die alone," Ten Pennies said.

Greenleaf backed away another two steps, then realized he was surrounded.

"Please, sir, listen!" he pleaded. "I can lead you to others who have money, lots of it. Here—I got some too. It's yours." He dug into his pocket and produced the advance William Montrose had paid him.

The half-breed said nothing. Greenleaf tossed the bills aside. They floated down atop the corpse of his son and scattered throughout the grove.

Ten Pennies gave a signal. The others moved back to their waiting horses and mounted. The half-breed retrieved his own mount from the brush and slid into the worn saddle.

"You may run."

Greenleaf held out his hands. "Please, let me take you to Simon Caine. I can track him down for you. There is a big reward on his head."

Ten Pennies nudged his horse with his heels and moved forward.

"Please don't hurt me! You can have anything you want."

Still, the half-breed edged forward. The others followed.

Morgan Greenleaf broke and ran. The two behind him made no attempt to stop him. Ten Pennies did not increase his speed. For a moment, Greenleaf thought they were letting him go. Then he realized they were toying with him, giving him a lead before running him down.

As he struggled through the underbrush, sticks and thorns tore at his face each time he tripped over a tree root. But each time, he pushed himself frantically up and continued. Ten Pennies and his men were still behind but moving around the thicket rather than trying to penetrate it.

Greenleaf came to a hill and climbed. Rocks scattered underfoot, and he slid down. He tried again, and this time reached the top.

Ten Pennies now was galloping his mount, leading the

others up a clear expanse toward the hilltop. Greenleaf ran on.

He found a narrow gully and dropped into it, running down its course until a deadfall blocked his path. He picked his way through the branches of the fallen tree and found himself in thicker foliage on the other side. He turned. No sign of his pursuers.

Another hillside. He climbed again until it became so steep that he could not go on. He stopped, looked around, and found another gully; this one apparently carved out of the mountainside by the spring rains. Using protruding roots for handholds, he proceeded to the top.

Still no sign of the half-breed. He took several deep breaths and began running again, inhaling in gulping double gasps, saliva pooling in the corners of his mouth and blowing back to dry on his cheeks.

Trees and brush became sparse, the land more rocky. He picked a path between boulders and conifers, and soon the land tilted up once more. He climbed again, for a long time, then found a cool area behind a boulder and fell into it, panting in the thin air. He closed his eyes.

When he opened them again, he was cold. The shadows lay at different angles. He had slept.

Disoriented, he rubbed his face and stood. He looked straight into the face of Sam Ten Pennies.

Just as before, the half-breed began edging slowly toward the terror-stricken man. Greenleaf wheeled and ran. A sharp stick gouged a hole above his eye. He wiped away the blood and continued.

Then it struck him: Ten Pennies was alone. The others had not ridden to the top. Whether that was the half-breed's design or not, it gave him hope. It was one against one now.

Greenleaf swept up a dead branch from the ground. He turned, crouched like a primeval man-beast, snarling and even faintly growling. But Ten Pennies had moved.

A rustle behind him. He turned; Ten Pennies was there, still mounted. Greenleaf yelled and swung at him with his club. Ten Pennies pulled an Army Colt and put a .44 slug through Greenleaf's leg.

The half-breed holstered his gun and edged forward again.

Greenleaf stood, gritting his teeth against the pain, and tried to run. Limping badly, he pushed into a narrow crevice between two massive rocks. Dead branches and scrubby undergrowth blocked his view beyond the end of the crevice. But above, he saw sky, clouds, perhaps another open area where he could run lay ahead.

He pushed through the brush. For a moment, he faced a panoramic view of the Bitterroots that spread out for miles. He turned and saw the barrel of Ten Pennies' Colt. He pushed forward.

The land beneath his feet suddenly disappeared. His stomach knotted as he realized what he had done. Sky and mountains became a whirling blur as he fell off the sheer cliff he had not even seen.

Sam Ten Pennies dismounted and walked to the edge of the cliff. He looked at the crumpled body below, then threw back his head and sent forth a throbbing cry that echoed through the Bitterroots.

CHAPTER 13

It could not be, yet he had seen her clearly.

Sam Ten Pennies had seen his slain mate, alive once more, astride a dun and looking at him.

But she was dead, slain by the one-eyed trader.

The half-breed rubbed his eyes, shook his head. But what other woman would follow him and watch him as she had? He knew his own mate, did he not?

Perhaps he was going mad, as Indian and white men alike had claimed. But if this was madness, it was better than a sanity that left him without his loved one.

He believed in spirits and visions, yet he was not quick to accept them. But if this had been a vision, perhaps it bore a message. If so, it had probably been sent by the one entity Ten Pennies considered worthy of his worship.

He stood alone, thinking. In a rugged way, he was a handsome figure. Half Crow, half black, Ten Pennies stood out among all categories of men. His life had been one of separation, hatred, and violence.

He had been born through violence. An escaped slave had raped the woman who became his mother by blood, though never by action or love. When he was born, she left him on the doorstep of a hunter's cabin. The hunter, a griz-zled old fellow with a slow mind, managed to keep the infant alive on goat's milk squeezed from the corner of a rag. At the first opportunity, he had taken the boy to a trading post and sold him to a freight runner for three dollars, chortling to the man when the deal was done that the boy wasn't worth "ten pennies, much less three dollars." So it was he got his name.

The freight runner, named Lomax, was married to a sad-eyed woman who gave the boy all the love she could, though repeated beatings from her husband left her unpredictable and sometimes cold toward all around her. As best she could, though, she raised young Sam. He grew up on the fringe of white society, rejected for both his black and red heritage.

Like the woman who served as his mother, Ten Pennies was often beaten by Lomax until finally, he had had his fill of it. He walked into their little cabin one morning with a shotgun and blasted Lomax in the back. From then on, Sam Ten Pennies was on the run.

He lived a few years in the Black Hills, then helped herd cattle near Bismarck. There, a brawl over a woman resulted in the killing of two men. He ran to the mountains far west-ward, drawing ever closer to the Bitterroots. By now, his name was becoming known. At least one dime novel rolled off the presses in New York, detailing the cruelties of a char-acter based upon the half-breed.

Ten Pennies fell in with some Crow renegades and at length became their leader. He had shifted northward along the Bitterroot Range by this time and had claimed a broad valley as his own—a claim he enforced with his scalping knife. It was there that he found the closest thing to happi-ness in his experience, as well as the one thing he had always craved: power. He also found a mate and then a god he could worship, a figure known only by him and a few others.

He had seen him for the first time upon awakening one morning when the land was bathed in light and mist. That was part of the reason, perhaps, that he believed he had seen a being somehow deified. It was tall, broad, with dark eyes that looked deeply at him. The half-breed had felt no inclination to defend himself, though normally he would have attacked with the first available weapon anyone who came so unexpectedly upon him. He knew, somehow, that this monumental being would not harm him, and so the half-breed merely marveled at him, wondering who he was and why he was silent. But the figure just turned and walked away into the mist.

He saw him twice after that, both times at distances far greater than that first encounter. The last time, one of the renegades with whom he rode saw the figure, too, and that calmed one quiet fear Ten Pennies had suffered: that this strange figure was an illusion and that he was, indeed, insane.

It was from this companion that he first heard the legend of a large white being who guarded a treasure in the mountains above the valley now claimed by Ten Pennies.

What kind of treasure? Ten Pennies wondered.

His companion did not know. None had ever gone near enough to the white one to find out.

Ten Pennies thought much about the legend and slowly came to the conviction he had found an object of worship peculiarly his own. Gradually he developed his own notions about the white being of the mountains and about his relationship to him. Perhaps he himself was some sort of secondary guardian, charged with protecting the one who protected the mysterious treasure. Ten Pennies thereby created a divine sanction both for his possessiveness of the valley and his killing of most of those who invaded it. He was protecting the One who guarded the secret even Ten Pennies did not know.

There were some who Ten Pennies did not disturb, men such as Jack Whitaker, who had lived long in these mountains and who was no threat to the half-breed. Ten Pennies even now regretted wounding Whitaker earlier on, having mistaken him for another momentarily.

Simon Caine, too, he left alone, for Ten Pennies had heard the stories of how Caine had fought the government of the nation from which he, himself, was estranged. Caine, like Ten Pennies, was an outcast and also a great warrior, and for that, he was left unmolested.

Ten Pennies caught a flicker of distant movement. Her again, almost out of view, now gone among the trees.

Was this a vision? Was his god trying to speak to him? Ten Pennies determined to go alone into the mountains and seek the answer.

Alone in the night, Sam Ten Pennies finally surrendered to the mental illness that had seemed ordained for him since birth. That he was of unsound mind had long been clear to most around him, but he had clung to rationality as best he could, and with his will, had fought back the advancing madness.

But the loss of his mate had robbed him of that will, and the visions of her since had put an even greater strain upon him. Now, as he let what remained of sanity twist away like a wind-driven leaf, he felt a great unburdening and release. Madness did not seem what it was. Rather, it seemed an answer to the questions raised by the visions of his mate.

He now knew that his god was speaking to him through visions, wanting her death avenged, just as Ten Pennies himself did.

The half-breed arose, his determination made. He would stalk and kill, seeking guidance from his deity through the visions. When understanding was needed, it would come.

He walked higher into the mountains until he came to a pinnacle overlooking spined ridges and valleys deeper than canyons. As when Morgan Greenleaf had died, he sent forth his reverberating cry. It rang through the darkness and echoed back, heard by those who haunted the isolated Bitter-root lands.

Simon Caine heard it and looked up as the echoes faded. Jake Armitage heard it too.

"What in blazes is that?" he asked.

"That's Sam Ten Pennies," Caine said.

"Mighty eerie."

Caine thumbed toward John Crosston, who was asleep, his head on his closely guarded packet. "Too bad he didn't hear it," he said. "It might put a little sense into his head." He looked at the packet. "You ever wonder what he's got in there?"

"Many times," Armitage said. "The time might come when I'll just find out."

"You thinking of taking a look?"

"I am. I want to read that journal he keeps. A lot of answers in there, I'd wager."

"Jake, I've given a lot of thought to it, and there's only one thing I can do if he insists on pushing this thing. I've got to find Ten Pennies myself and see where I stand with him. And I've got to learn how bad this Brannigan wants to find me. I can't let him endanger somebody else just trying to get to me."

Armitage shook his head. "I can't let you do that, Simon. You need me with you."

"Hang it, Jake, the whole reason is so you won't be with me. Fact is, you're stuck in this until the end. Brannigan is going to hunt me whether I'm alone or not, and Ten Pennies is going to do whatever he takes a shine to no matter what any of us does."

"And if things don't work out?"

"Then I'm dead, or they're dead."

"One man don't stand a chance against the kind of odds you'd be facing. There's no way you could survive."

"There's no way I could have survived all these past years, but I have."

"And if I let you ride out alone, knowing what you'll face out there, what kind of a man does that make me?"

"One with sense. Look, Jake, if you and Crosston lit out after that treasure tomorrow, you know I'd be right beside you, probably in just as much or more danger than if I was alone. If we do it my way, one man is endangered instead of three. Besides, I believe I can work out a safe passage for us. Maybe I can get Brannigan or his bunch lost or steer them toward Ten Pennies and let one end of our problem take care of the other. And if there's a chance to talk to Ten Pennies, I might be able to make a deal with him."

"Reckon there's no point in arguing with you."

"Nope. With Opequon gone, there's nothing keeping me from going out and clearing the way the best I can."

"You think she went after Ten Pennies?"

"I can't figure anything else."

Armitage shook his head. "What chance does a woman stand against a whole band of renegades?"

"Don't underestimate her. She just might wind up with Ten Pennies' scalp. She's as good a tracker and mountain traveler as I've ever seen. I just spent a whole day looking for her sign, and there's no trace."

Crosston stirred and rolled over, drawing their attention.

"You want to wake him up and tell him now?"

"No. Tell him in the morning. That's good enough for him."

FROM THE JOURNAL OF JOHN CROSSTON

I have accepted Caine's proposal. Ten days Armitage and I are *to wait* here, while Caine goes alone *to deal in* whatever way he can *with Ten* Pennies.

His concern for *the* safety *of* Armitage is remarkable. The *two are like* brothers. *It was difficult for Caine to restrain* Armitage this morning when he *left. Jake* insisted, despite *the agreement, that he go* along *as well. Finally, Jake* relented, but if Caine does not arrive back here *well* within *the ten days, I may have trouble keeping Jake from going after* him.

We are *at* Caine's own cabin now, not far from that *of the Indian* woman who vanished. Caine did not seem surprised when *that* happened. I doubt we *will* see her again.

Though hidden *away* in this cabin, *Jake and I are not fully safe. The* bounty hunter might come here—maybe even the half-breed. There is every possibility none *of* us *will* survive this quest.

Yet *it* is *worth the risk.* Already *what* we are seeking has cost one life I did not wish *to take. There may be* others *yet to come.* But *I will* return to my father *what is his, and if blood is the price, then so it shall he.*

Ten days I will wait. But no longer.

CHAPTER 14

It had been six days since Caine had left Jake and the Englishman, and in that time, he had found only the most meager traces of the half-breed. Caine was beginning to feel the pressure of time. If he was not back in the designated period, Crosston would take Jake in tow and strike out alone, and there would be little probability of survival for either.

Jake, you old coot, leave the fool and get back to safer territory. Don't get *killed just to save your* pride. Caine barked out the commands in his mind, knowing the words wouldn't have been more useful had he shouted them in Armitage's face. Jake was a prideful man; he felt he owed Crosston, and nothing would dissuade him from paying his debt.

Before he had left, Caine had considered using his own cut to buy off Armitage's debt, but he had never made the offer because he knew it would hurt and humiliate Jake. There was only one recourse, and he was taking it now, though with little success so far.

He caught some sparse sign and followed it through a ravine. Caine picked out the trail as he thought about his years with Jake Armitage.

He remembered the skirmishes they had fought, with handfuls of men dodging in cover and shooting in sporadic bursts. He remembered bigger battles, hordes of gray and blue moving in waves upon each other as cannon roared and the Confederacy sent out a collective rebel yell.

But the war was past. Now, all that mattered was the need to find Ten Pennies and, somehow, clear the way for himself and the others.

He rode on, the trail becoming more clear. Ahead, a rumble of thunder called to him.

———

Caine rode in a hard rain that beat craters into mud and streaked erosive trails down rocky bluffs. It slanted in silver-gray lines and hazed his vision as he dropped from his horse and crouched behind a deadfall, wondering who had just taken a shot at him.

Water gathered in the brim of his hat and sluiced down his back and over his face. His capote diverted some of it, but not all. His feet were soaked, and he was chilled. And he could see nothing to give him a clue of who fired the shot.

Another shot spanged off a rock behind him. He ducked, then came up and fired at the spot where the flame had flashed. There was movement, then silence.

Caine looked around and above. His position, safe enough from straight-on fire, was poorly protected from above. To his left ran the trail he had been following, narrowing around the side of the mountain until it was a mere ledge above a steep bluff. A similar ledge was behind and above Caine, accessible from several points. He had to move.

He also had to forget about his mount. It was gone, frightened by the shots. Moving on foot was better at the moment, anyway.

Another shot rang, and a voice shouted something indiscernible. Caine ducked lower and thought out his plan.

Ahead, where the path narrowed, was a crumbled heap of rock. The bluff extended above it but offered no obvious perch along its face from which a gunman could threaten him. It was no final solution but a safer option than staying where he was.

Movement above—Caine wasted not a second. He threw himself over the deadfall and lunged for the tangle of rocks. At the same time came a thunderous sound as an eroding bank, strained by spring rainwater, gave way. The mountain vomited a white flood that tore Caine's feet from beneath him and swept him down the slope.

Daylight vanished, and the roaring of water suddenly became a dull rumble around him. He could not breathe.

Just as suddenly, the torrent lifted him back to the surface in a mass of white foam and brown mud. His face broke into air, and he could breathe again. He had been swept into a mountain stream far below where he was before.

Inches above him was a dark mass, moldy and dank. Daylight streamed in weak rays through some sort of openings. Caine moved to grasp the branchlike projections above him. He pulled air into his lungs and coughed out muddy water. Only then did he realize he still clutched his pistol. He holstered the weapon while clinging to the roots with the other hand. He then used both hands to get a better grip and let the water float his body as he tried to assess where he was.

He finally realized he was beneath a tree, a huge one rooted in the bank. Above half, the root dug into the dirt, and the other half reached out like a gnarled hand over the water. He was beneath that portion now, and the dark surface above was the base of the tree.

Water rushed to Caine's chin, splashing into his nose and eyes. He realized he was fortunate to have washed up where he had, for he was hidden from whoever had fired at him. Fortunate, that is if he could avoid drowning.

He resolved to stay there as long as he could. Let them look for him until they decided he had washed downstream.

There was a noise above him. Some of the light streaming through the root mass was dimmed. He looked. A foot rested directly above him. Someone was standing on the root and looking into the water beyond him.

Water rose to Caine's nose, and he had to pull a half-inch upward.

"See him?" Cord Brannigan asked.

"No," said Frye.

"Keep looking. If he washed on down, he'll probably snag up on that dead tree yonder."

Thunder rumbled. The noise of rain pounding the water was intense in Caine's dank niche. The water rose once more, and Caine had to strain to stay above it.

"What's *that*?" Brannigan said. Caine thought he had been spotted. But Brannigan didn't move.

"I didn't hear nothing."

"Look?" Brannigan whispered.

Caine had one option. He reached to his knife and drew it. Clinging to the roots with one hand, he slashed the blade upward through the water toward the foot above him.

The foot moved, and Brannigan was gone in a wild rush. Caine's blade probed emptiness, then the water rose past his eyes and hammered his ears.

Caine lunged downward and outward. He came up in the middle of the stream and kicked toward the bank. His foot struck land, and he stood. He opened his eyes and shook away water in time to see a Crow renegade, one he recognized from Ten Pennies' band, kicking at him. The foot knocked the blade from his hand.

At the same moment, an ax rose and fell, blade upward. Caine dodged the worst of the blow, but his head wound, still raw and tender, was burst open. Blood gushed down his face, and he fell senseless.

The Indian flipped the ax blade downward and raised it again. A bronze hand caught his arm.

The Indian turned, puzzled, and looked at Ten Pennies. The half-breed clung to his arm but stared into the forest. He had seen her, just for a moment.

"Do not harm him," Ten Pennies said.

The renegade grunted a protest and pulled his arm free. Ten Pennies as quickly grabbed it again, his eyes blazing angrily.

"Do not harm him!"

Moments later, they were gone. Simon Caine's blood drained into the water. Silent as the vision Ten Pennies had taken her to be, Opequon came to his side.

———

In the darkness, Crosston stirred and awoke. Only a dim flicker lit the hearth, but in it, he saw Armitage, his face masked by shadows.

Crosston also saw the journal in his hand and said, "You read it?"

"Is all of this true?"

"You read it!"

"Is it true?"

Crosston was silent.

"God help us," Armitage said.

CHAPTER 15

"You killed a priest?"

"I had no choice," Crosston said. "He would have published his own findings before my father had completed his. The only thing that mattered to him would have been snatched away. And then the Church would have tried to claim the treasure and take that too. I couldn't let that happen."

Armitage spoke wearily. "So all this scheme is something you dreamed up to put your father's treasure back into his hands so he could publish a book? You killed a priest and are letting Simon risk his scalp for the sake of a book?"

"Don't be a fool, Armitage. Can't you see the value of this? The significance? The risks are worth it, even if some have to die."

"Why didn't you tell us about the priest?"

"Damn it, Armitage, I was as honest with you as circumstances would allow. I didn't want you to find out what the treasure was, for just as I told you, its value lies in knowing what it is. You can see that now for yourself."

"Yes." Armitage fingered the journal in his hand. "Why did the hired man steal it? No one ever would have believed him if he had told them what it was. How could he have hoped to profit?"

"He wasn't looking for profit. He didn't steal it for what it is worth but for what it is. He was a zealous fellow, all wrapped up in delusion and superstition. He even left behind a note, written in that arthritic scrawl of his, saying he had been called to guard the thing. That's why he came to a place as remote as these mountains. Protection, for himself and for his treasure."

"Could he still be alive?"

"Impossible. He was old and infirm even when he stole it. He must have died years ago."

"And his son? Gideon?"

"He must be dead too. He had the size of two men and strength of three, but he was deaf, very withdrawn. He probably starved after his father died. A hard death, I'm sure. One his father can take credit for."

Armitage shook his head. "This is all a little too incredible to believe."

"But it is true. There are books, very ancient, that I possess. Books referred to in the earliest poetry written about the treasure and long thought lost. They are not lost. And they confirm its authenticity. We obtained them from a reliable individual who also was the broker in the actual purchase.

"I understand the incongruity of it all, Armitage. But is it really that surprising? This thing has followed a path through many nations, to France, to England, and, for a time, to Rome. There are parts of the trail missing, but it can be followed. My father finally found the thing in Spain. He brought it to the United States, and here it will remain after I have recovered it."

"Back in your father's hands?"

"Yes. And then mine, when he is gone. But I care little

for it, though you may not believe that. I'm doing this for my father, not for the treasure or the glory."

"You killed for your father, then?"

"I suppose I did."

"Does he know?"

"No. He must never know."

"But now *I* know. How will you shut me up? Will you kill me too?"

"You are a fool," the Englishman said, glowering.

————

Caine's eyes fluttered open. He saw dim morning light, a network of branches against a pale sky made cloudy by his vision. Pain raged in his head.

Opequon knelt beside him and looked into his face. "Be silent," she admonished when he tried to speak. "You reopened the wound. Rest, and I will take care of you."

How long have I been out? Caine wanted to ask. Hours? Days? But the words never formed, and he dropped away into deep blackness again.

He was in motion when next he awoke. It took a long time to make sense of it, but finally, he realized he was on a travois, a makeshift litter slung between two drag poles. Opequon had found his strayed horse, and it pulled him now through the mountains to where he did not know. He slept again, for a long time.

Moisture against his lips awakened him. Opequon was giving him water. It was night. He felt as sick as he had after the brutal escape from Henley. He was feverish once more, and as he dropped back into sleep, the dream came again.

It started as always. He and Nancy were together in their farmhouse. He held her close, and she was so vivid and real that he could smell the scent of her hair and feel her in his arms.

Then he heard drums in the distance, growing closer. He peered out the door and saw a funeral procession marching slowly around the bend. They stopped near him and laid a coffin on the earth.

The men who bore it wore hoods, but they threw them back, and he saw their faces. These were men he had killed: Robert Montrose and his band, others he had felled in battle, and now some new faces, Clinton Brannigan, and the two men who had died on the floor of Cleek's Station.

In the dream, Caine asked who was dead. One of them stooped and threw back the lid.

Usually, Caine saw the bloodied corpses of his wife and son in that coffin. But now, the dream was different. In the coffin was Jake Armitage.

Caine struggled to awaken, but sickness would not let him. He writhed on the travois, and as always in the dream, something hammered the back of his mind, trying to make him understand a message he could not grasp.

Opequon took Caine to her cabin, and the day after they arrived, the outlaw's fever broke, and he was back on his feet. He was weak and dizzy, not really well enough to be up, but he was convinced that Jake was in danger. He tried once to saddle his horse but collapsed in the effort. His fever came again, and Opequon put him in bed once more.

On the ninth day since he had left Armitage and Crosston, he was well enough to move about. He would leave the next morning, the last morning before Crosston would ride out for the treasure on his own. But Caine felt sure he would reach his cabin in time.

He reminded Opequon of his pledge to Jack to take her out of the mountains.

"I know you want to do for me what you said, but I'll not leave," she said.

"Why?"

"Because of what I must do."

"Kill Sam Ten Pennies?"

"Yes."

Caine shook his head. "It's not the way, Opequon. God knows I'm the last man who has the right to say that, but I also know it's true. Let it go. It's what Jack would want."

"I can't."

Caine did not argue further.

The next morning he rode toward his own cabin, fearing much for Jake's life. He had dreamed again of Jake in the coffin, and though he was not one to believe in premonitions, he could not shake the image, nor the conviction that Jake needed him.

Near his cabin, he stopped. There were marks on the earth all about—unshod horses, many of them.

Ten Pennies.

The marks were maybe a day old. Caine mounted and spurred his horse at a run toward the cabin.

———

Morrison DeGuere, to all appearances, was sleeping. He sprawled across a bench outside a telegraph office, enjoying the shade of the roof overhang. His bowler rested low across his eyes, and his fingers were linked across his chest, which moved up and down with the steady rhythm of slumber.

But the detective was not fully asleep. He hovered in a mental twilight between sleep and awareness. DeGuere seldom slept more than three or four hours a night. Half naps such as this one provided the balance of his rest. It was an unusual pattern, but it suited him. Along with a coon dog tenacity and logical mind, it was part of what made him one of the best detectives from the high plains to the Mexican border.

Even in semi-slumber, DeGuere's mind was busy, sorting and thinking through the things he had learned these past days. Amazing things, even to an old cynic who had seen too much for too many years to be easily impressed. But this John Crosston was fascinating, though DeGuere had not yet decided if he was clever or just very deceived. In either case, he definitely was ruthless—a characteristic DeGuere admired in any man, himself most of all.

He became aware of someone beside him. He opened his eyes and tilted back his bowler. It was the telegraph operator, with a paper in his hand.

"Your associate just wired in, sir," he said.

DeGuere took the paper. "Thank you." The wire operator re-entered his office, and DeGuere read the lengthy transmission.

Then he smiled, folded the paper, and nodded. "As I suspected," he muttered. "Just very deceived."

He thrust the paper into his pocket and walked down the street whistling.

CHAPTER 16

Inside the cabin was only darkness. No light, no fire. They were gone.

For a moment, a hope arose: perhaps Ten Pennies, too, had found the cabin empty. Maybe the impatient John Crosston had not honored the pledge of ten days' wait and had gone on.

When Caine struck a match to light a lamp, though, the hope disappeared. The cabin was ransacked. His meager furnishings were scattered, and most of the food was gone, as were his extra guns and ammunition.

And here, at his feet, was blood.

He had no doubt that Jake Armitage and John Crosston were prisoners or dead. And with night falling, Caine could not search for their trail until morning.

Despair tugged at his throat. He knelt, feeling the blood. It was dry and rust-colored. The raid must have occurred hours ago, maybe a day or more.

He stepped outside, holding the lamp. He examined the ground in front of the cabin. Hoofprints and moccasin tracks abounded, and more blood. Somebody had put up a fight.

Even in his sadness, Caine let a smile flicker. The thought of Jake fighting and defiant was better than the image of the weak and aging Jake he had known these past days.

But he was also afraid. Ten Pennies was showing no rationality, no predictability. That he had spared Caine's life back at the river and then had come in violence to Caine's cabin was evidence there was something unstable in his actions.

Caine walked back inside and collapsed on the floor. He was weakened and unbalanced because of his wounded head. He lay on the floor a long time, staring mindlessly at the jumble of books and papers before the hearth. It took several minutes for him to notice what they were.

Crosston's journal and the other contents of the packet he carried. Except for glimpses of the map Crosston kept stowed inside, the packet's contents had been kept from Caine throughout.

He went to the heap and sat beside it, Indian style. He picked up the journal and began to read.

From time to time, he had to look away into the dark cabin, partly to let his straining eyes rest, partly to absorb the astounding things he read.

When morning came, Caine had slept little. He set out along Ten Pennies' trail, which was very clear upon the dew-sodden earth.

Two hours later, unseen by him, two riders topped a ridge at his rear. One of them pointed, and the pair watched him for a moment before spurring their mounts onward and downward, riding in hard on his trail.

———

If Jake Armitage had ever been a coward, he was not now. Tied to a sapling, stripped of most of his clothing, hurting from the stab wound he had suffered during the raid, he spat and cursed at his captors, particularly the hard-gazing half-breed who led them.

He had overheard the fate they were planning for him and Crosston, and it roused a fury that pushed fear aside.

"Come here, 'breed! Cut me loose and see what I can do to you! Coward!"

One of Ten Pennies' renegades came to him and struck him hard in the stomach. The stab wound, superficial but painful, began bleeding. Armitage winced, then spat defiantly into the renegade's face.

The Indian struck him again, harder. He would have beaten him more if Ten Pennies had not stopped him.

"Do not kill him," said the half-breed. "His talk of a fight is good. A fight to the death, eh?"

The renegade smiled. "I will fight him, Ten Pennies," he said. "I will see him die screaming like a child."

Ten Pennies walked to Armitage and lifted his chin. He looked into his eyes. "You wish to fight the Wolf? You think you can defeat him? And what shall we do with your young friend?"

Crosston looked at Ten Pennies and spoke for the first time since his capture: "I will tell you what to do with me. Let me fight. If I win, let me go free. Give me safe passage through your valley."

The half-breed was intrigued. "Safe passage? For what purpose?"

"So that I may reach the place I must go."

Not an answer, but Ten Pennies did not pursue it. He was thinking. "So you, too, wish to fight the Wolf?"

"No," Crosston said. "I will fight my friend."

Armitage blurted, "Are you loco?"

Ten Pennies was very interested now. "A fight to the death, with the winner to go free?"

"Yes. With a horse and weapons."

"Crosston—"

Ten Pennies chuckled. "You will fight each other. The one who lives has my word—no harm will come to him in my country."

Armitage twisted his neck to look at Crosston, unbelieving. Crosston evaded his eyes as an Indian cut their bonds.

Lashed together at the wrists, Armitage and Crosston were given knives. The band of renegades gathered in a wide circle around the two men, grinning and whooping. Armitage was grim. Crosston, despite his bravado, could scarcely hide his fright.

Ten Pennies spoke: "Fight."

Neither moved. The half-breed walked to his horse and there found a long whip. Returning, he lashed the shoulders of Armitage, leaving a long bloody gash.

"Fight!"

"No."

The lash came down again. Armitage bit his lip but did not cry out.

"We have no choice," Crosston said. He gave a tentative wave of his knife.

"We had one," Armitage said. "This was your idea, not theirs."

"And it was your idea to pry into affairs that didn't concern you," Crosston said. "I cannot afford to leave you alive."

Armitage stood and looked at his blade, still unwilling. But Crosston swung at him again, almost cutting him a second time.

This time, Armitage slashed back.

———

Caine dismounted at the foot of a slope and tethered his horse. With rifle in hand, he climbed, gritting his teeth against the pain of it, until at last, he topped a high ridge looking across a narrow valley.

They were there, below. The renegades gathered in a circle. Caine heard their shouts and laughter. Armitage and Crosston were fighting, slashing at each other with blades. There was blood on Armitage's back and chest.

Caine lay on his belly and sighted down the rifle, putting the bead on Ten Pennies' head. His finger began a slow squeeze on the trigger.

There was a sudden thud. Something like fire shot across Caine's vision, and he went numb. The rifle dropped, his eyes fluttered, and he fell unconscious.

"Kill him now, Brannigan?" queried Artemus Frye.

"No. I want him alive for a while. Look yonder, Art. What a fight, huh?"

———

The renegades became frenzied, thrilled by the new vigor of the combatants. For his part, Armitage was raging mad that Crosston, a man he once had trusted, even liked, was trying to kill him.

Armitage finally understood Crosston as he pivoted and jabbed with his knife. Crosston cared only about one thing —recovering his treasure hidden to the north. Nothing else mattered, not promises, not the life of any other man. It was clear now, but the realization came too late.

It was neat and convenient, Armitage had to admit. Fear of Sam Ten Pennies was the sole reason Crosston had hired him and Caine, to begin with. By winning this fight, Crosston could obtain the safe passage he had sought all along. He would no longer need either of them.

The older man slashed at Crosston and noted how tired he was beginning to feel.

Crosston lunged and thrust his knife into Armitage's

shoulder. The other grunted and pulled away, jerking the blade free as he did so. Blood streamed down to the pounded dirt at his feet.

The old Civil War veteran snarled and swung his knife in a wide arc. Crosston gave out a shrill scream and pulled back. Blood ran down his hand. His little finger was nearly sliced off.

"Let's make a run," Armitage said as best his strained lungs would let him. "Let's try to live."

"I intend to live," Crosston responded.

His knife sang through the air and drew blood once more, bringing a loud cheer from the renegades. Ten Pennies alone showed no emotion; he merely observed.

Armitage jerked suddenly on the cord binding him to Crosston, unbalancing the Englishman. His knife came down as Crosston slid past him like a bull swiping a matador, but it inflicted only a minor cut to Crosston's bicep.

The younger man pivoted and slashed, barely missing Armitage's gut. The latter jerked the cord again, but this time Crosston was ready. He jerked back simultaneously, and it was Armitage who stumbled. Crosston's knife came down and plunged deep into the older man's back.

"Simon!" The name burst from Armitage instinctively.

He was terribly weak now and hurting. He bled profusely, and Crosston's image wavered before him like a heat demon. He poked with his blade and nicked Crosston's arm, but his fight was gone. Armitage realized his hope for survival was gone too.

He dropped his knife and slumped forward. Crosston moved in and put his blade through his opponent's heart.

CHAPTER 17

Caine came to and found himself tied to a sapling. His head throbbed like a hammer-struck anvil. About twenty feet away, Brannigan and Frye sat eating jerky and crackers. Brannigan smiled broadly at him.

"Howdy, Simon Caine!" he said. "Pleased to make your acquaintance. My name's Cordell Brannigan. You've never met me. You met my brother in Henley, though. You recall him?"

"Where is Jake?" Caine said. His throat was scratchy, and his voice was like a rasp against wood.

"Was he fighting in the Indian camp?"

"Yes."

"Well, the old one's dead as a rock. The boy stuck him."

Caine leaned to one side and was sick.

"They turned the boy loose when it was done. Even give him a horse. We watched it all from the ridge, me and Artemus, here. Artemus Frye."

"Good to meet you, Caine," Frye said around a mouthful of cracker.

"Artemus here will be the one to end your earthly existence once we get near Henley," Brannigan said. "He's partial to his machete, and besides, we'll have to prove to Montrose that we really got you. Your head will do real fine."

"Are you sure the older one was dead?" Caine asked.

"Deader than John Quincy Adams's great-grandma. He was a friend of yours, huh? Bet you'd like to get your hands on the boy what killed him. He the Englisher who busted you out of jail?"

Caine, his head in his hands, did not answer.

"What were you doing here, anyway?" Brannigan asked.

Caine too numbed to do anything else, answered truthfully. "Looking for a treasure."

The broad, mirthful face went serious. "What?"

Caine said, "You heard me."

Brannigan gave an uncertain chuckle. "Say now, you wouldn't josh an old boy, would you?"

Caine looked up through bleary eyes. "What you are I don't josh with. I smear it under my foot."

Brannigan's eye twitched at the insult, but Caine had caught his attention. Brannigan rose and came over to him. "What kind of treasure?"

Caine hesitated only a second, then: "I don't know."

Brannigan leaned down in Caine's face. Frye joined him. "You don't know?"

Caine spat on them.

Frye cursed and gripped his machete, but Brannigan caught his arm. "Easy, Frye. Maybe he's telling the truth." He turned back to Caine. "You know where it is?"

"I know."

"You know *what* it is, too—you just ain't telling."

"I told you, I don't know."

"You'll tell me. You'll sing it like a choir boy." To Frye, he said: "Artemus, we got a new hand to play here. We let Montrose wait a little longer, let Caine lead us to this treasure if there is one. He gets us to it; we just might let him go.

He don't, and we head back to Montrose, just like we planned. Nothing lost but a little time at the worst."

"What if he gets loose?" Frye countered. "Sounds to me like he's trying to save his hide."

"If he's lying, we'll find out soon enough. And he won't get loose. We'll keep him in such a shape that if he does, he won't be able to get nowhere."

Brannigan addressed Caine: "Looks like you got a chance to live, outlaw. Do what we tell you, and you'll be fine. If not, you're a dead man. But first, you talk." Brannigan punctuated his demand with a hard slap across Caine's jaw.

Caine relaxed to ease the sting of the blow, but he had to struggle to retain his consciousness, for his head still ached as if squeezed in a vise.

"Only the boy knew what the treasure was," Caine said. "He never told us."

Brannigan drew back his hand, then dropped it. Muttering, he moved away and talked covertly to Frye. He came back and wordlessly cut Caine's bonds.

They lashed Caine to the horn of Brannigan's saddle, using a long rope. Packs were set and guns checked, and Brannigan and Frye mounted.

"You walk out front. Head for that treasure. You fall, and I'll drag you. I get a notion you're leading us to nothing, and I'll drop you where you stand. You understand me?"

"I need water," Caine said.

The answer was a jerk on the rope. Caine staggered forward, dizzy and sick. He blinked and shook his head, trying to clear his vision.

He walked a long time, heading north. He thought about John Crosston. Where the treasure was, there Crosston would go. Caine generally knew where that would be, for he had seen Crosston's map a few times at the outset of their venture. In a cavern overlooking Ten Pennies' valley. But which cavern? Could he find it?

The sun grew hot as they traveled. Brannigan was relentless, pushing him on like a mule.

Caine concentrated on the trail, on Crosston, on the treasure. One thing he had to confess to himself: all the subtle points Crosston had made about the treasure made sense now that Caine knew what it supposedly was. No wonder Crosston had been willing to pay such a high price for protection.

The money. Crosston had paid him five thousand dollars, a sizable wad of bills Caine had kept in his trouser pocket. But now it was gone, and that was a puzzlement. Brannigan didn't seem the kind of man to find such a sum and not crow about it. Yet he had said nothing.

That could mean two things: either Brannigan had taken the cash and was trying to hide it from Frye, or Frye had taken it and was trying to hide it from Brannigan.

On they plodded, Caine losing track of the hours, Frye intoning an old hymn somewhere behind him. His head pounded to the staggering of his feet.

The day wore on. Since this morning, Caine had been given nothing to eat or drink. When darkness fell, though, they made a camp, and Brannigan offered him water. Caine drank it lustily.

He was surprised when Brannigan built a fire.

"You ain't much worried about Ten Pennies, are you?" he said.

"That the 'breed? I ain't afraid of him," Brannigan said. He had occasionally been sipping from a bottle all day and was sufficiently intoxicated to throw aside caution.

Frye was busy sharpening his machete. The long black blade threw back the firelight. "I understand, Caine, you have a brother who is a preacher," he said.

Caine looked at the darkening sky, silent.

"What does he think about the life you lead?"

"Not your affair."

"Doesn't like it too much, I would suppose."

Brannigan laughed. "Get used to it, Caine. Frye's getting ready for one of his religious talks. He knows that Bible from Genesis to Revelations."

Eerily, Frye moved to where Caine was tied and touched the tip of the machete to Caine's hand.

"The hand of a gunman," he said. "A hand that has killed many men. 'If thy right hand offend thee, cut it off.' What do you think, Caine? Would you like to be free of the killing hand? 'Without the shedding of blood, there is no remission of sins.' Better to enter heaven without a hand than hell with all your limbs. Shall I free you of your killing hand, Caine?"

Caine stared into the crazed face, unspeaking.

"Leave him be, Artemus," Brannigan said. "Your time is coming —unless Caine is really telling the truth about that treasure."

"I don't believe he is. I believe he's leading us up the path."

"Speaking of treasure," Caine said, "how did you divide my five thousand dollars?"

Brannigan looked up sharply. "What five thousand?" Frye's features stiffened, his lip curling back a half second in a snarl worthy of a beaten cur.

"Paper money, right in my pocket," Caine said. "You must have taken it."

"What do you know about this, Frye?" demanded Brannigan.

"Nothing. He's lying again."

"Is he?"

"Course he is. I don't know nothing about no money."

Brannigan started to say something else but didn't. He sat back and relaxed. "Reckon you just dropped it somewhere, Caine. Too bad. I've killed men for less bounty than that. A whole lot less."

They roasted a rabbit and gave Caine a little. Not nearly enough, but a little.

That night Caine slept without dreams.

He awoke to the smell of coffee, sunlight in his face. Brannigan was pouring two steaming cupful's. He brought one to Caine. The outlaw accepted it, cupping it between his bound hands.

Brannigan was actually jovial.

"A little accident last night, I'm sorry to say," he said. "I can't imagine how it happened."

Caine looked at Frye's bedroll. The man was on his back, eyes tightly shut. His machete was thrust through his chest and into the ground.

Brannigan walked away, whistling. He patted his bulging pocket in time to the tune.

Time for Caine slid by in hours of heat and exhaustion, thirst and hunger, and pain from the scab-clotted wound on his head. Moving ever northward, they at last penetrated the valley of Sam Ten Pennies.

Caine struggled to remember the details of the map Crosston had shown him. Though uncertain, he never faltered, for to do so would have invited a bullet from Brannigan.

The valley was vast, wide, and green up to the timberline. They traveled through it several hours, Caine heading for a ridge where he knew there were caverns similar to those marked on Crosston's map. Darkness came, and he passed another night of deathlike sleep. The morning broke, and they moved again in the same monotonous way.

As they moved up along broken land, Caine found the tracks of an unshod horse. Later, where a jumbling of the tracks indicated the horse's rider had dismounted to let the beast graze, Caine found boot prints, small English boots like Crosston's. He knew then he was near the mark.

The tracks were old, though. And later, he found fresher ones heading the opposite direction. Either Crosston had gotten lost and doubled back or had found his treasure and begun his return home.

Caine said nothing of this to Brannigan, for it would not do for the bounty hunter to believe the treasure was removed. Brannigan himself never noted the tracks, for he was always drinking, throwing aside both caution and attention. Caine silently observed his captor's behavior and waited for his chance.

As they moved up a narrow ravine that broadened to a rocky slope, the bounty hunter dismounted because of the steepness and trudged heavily along behind Caine. They climbed until the valley was far below, and then Caine made his move.

Near the top of the slope, he pivoted, leaping down toward Brannigan. His foot pounded into the soft pillow of the fat man's belly. Wind bursting from his lungs, Brannigan tilted back and rolled down the long slope in a jumble of dust and bruises.

Frye's blood-caked machete, kept by Brannigan as a souvenir, was keen and made quick work of Caine's bonds. He was free even before Brannigan had stopped rolling.

Brannigan had slung Caine's Spencer and his gun belt to his saddlehorn, and now Caine loosened them, along with a cloth sack full of ammunition, as Brannigan staggered to his feet at the base of the slope. There was no time for Caine to load.

Brannigan had lost his rifle as he rolled, but his pistol was secure in its holster, held by a leather thong. He drew the weapon and fired at the outlaw.

The shot sang high past Caine but spooked the horses. They angled down the slope and vanished into the woodlands.

Caine scrambled upward and cut across a bare rock face. He topped the crest of the slope, then turned left and darted through a conifer grove. A few yards beyond, he found a dry streambed that led farther into the forest.

More rocks ahead; he ran for them. Risking exposure for a moment, he climbed over the face of a massive boulder, then found his way back into the forest. Dodging along an uneven path, he ran where the ground was rocky and would leave no tracks. Coming to more broken land, he darted among boulders and rock slabs. Then, head throbbing, he dropped to the earth beside a small stream, immersed his face in it, and drank.

He splashed water through his beard and across his face and slowly raised himself. Then he saw a track.

It was the biggest he had ever seen, longer by a good three or four inches than the average man's foot. Whoever made it wore moccasins, the depth of the track indicating he was quite heavy.

Caine stared at it, amazed, then through his mind flashed words spoken by John Crosston at the beginning of the journey and other words written in the journal.

"So you didn't die after all," Caine muttered.

He rested a long time until he was sure Brannigan was not near. Then he stood and began following the tracks, curious and eager to see if at the end of the trail he would find Crosston's treasure, and maybe Crosston himself.

He doubted he would. The hoofmarks he had seen suggested Crosston had come and gone. Then again, if the treasure's keeper was about, maybe Crosston would not have been able to get past him, especially if he was as big as these tracks indicated.

But knowing well how far the young Englishman was willing to go, Caine was unsure that even a man as big as this one could keep Crosston back. Jake had paid the price for Crosston's zealotry, as had a priest back in Boston, according to the scribblings in Crosston's journal.

Caine moved on, following the massive footprints.

Meanwhile, Brannigan also was moving, cursing with every step. Caine was gone, and the bounty hunter had not even a horse to carry him out of these mountains. At least he still had his weapons.

Brannigan scanned the Bitterroot land around him, keeping watch for Caine as well as the half-breed Caine had called Ten Pennies. Thinking about it, Brannigan recalled some dime-novel folklore about such a half-breed. He supposedly was a particularly vicious hater of whites. Now that he was alone in these mountains for the first time, Brannigan felt a shiver of fear. He thanked the heavens for his rifle and sidearm.

For nearly an hour, he followed the curve of the valley until it gave way to hills, then to rocky country. Brannigan had hoped to encounter a stream by now, but so far, no luck. No sign of the lost horses, either.

He climbed a slope because the land's contours left him no choice. It was for the best, anyway; from high up, he could gain a good vantage point of the whole valley.

He went on until he could go no farther. He sat down in the shade of a juniper and let his pounding heart calm itself. The shade was cool. He closed his eyes.

When he opened them, some time had passed. He stiffened, for below, he saw the lost horses. But the half-breed and his band were there too.

They did not see him yet. He sat there, ludicrously exposed, watching the renegades examining the horses and pilfering the saddlebags and pack.

They mounted and rode away, taking the horses. Brannigan closed his eyes and exhaled.

He headed farther up. At the top of the ridge, he was exhausted and desperately thirsty but heard running water not far away. Following his ears, he headed down the other side of the ridge until, at last, he saw a stream running out of the mountainside. It flowed from a sizable cavern. He ran to it and drank. When he had finished, he stood and looked directly into the cave. All was blackness, enclosed and dank. Brannigan feared nothing more than darkness and enclosure. He turned away.

He heard the horses before they came into view, and that saved him. Ten Pennies again. He and his band had doubled back around the ridge and come up the other side. Brannigan wondered for a panicked moment if they were after him. Then he saw that the dirt at his feet was trampled flat. He had stumbled upon one of Ten Pennies' watering holes.

The only escape route was into the cave. Brannigan entered and picked his way along in the darkness. He thought about stopping and holding still until Ten Pennies was gone, but the oppressive cave and his fear of the half-breed kept him moving. He could not bear to be still in this darkness. Besides, if he followed the stream, he couldn't get lost. Deeper he went.

Sometime later, he realized his feet were crunching on dirt and gravel rather than splashing water. The stream was gone. No water at his heels, just bare rock.

He moved within the span of a few feet. Nothing.

He had wandered out of the stream, and now he couldn't find it.

Someday somebody is going *to* hurt you. Someday some-body'll put you down in a hole *like* you done, my *kitty!* The voice of Henry Cleek came clearly to him.

"Get hold of yourself, old boy." The sound of a human voice, even his own, was comforting, so he said it again. "Get hold of yourself, old boy."

He stood, breathing deeply, clutching the stock of his rifle. Deliberately, carefully, he moved forward, feeling his way along.

Though he tried to remain calm, despair was overcoming him. It would have been best to have hidden just inside the cave's mouth until Ten Pennies was gone. Too late now. He sank to the floor and longed for sunlight and space.

Then, against the background of pure night, he saw a spot of lightness. Not really light, just lightness. It was so dim he thought it might be an illusion.

Keeping his eyes on it, he stood again and crept forward. He ignored the abrasions of the rocks against him. The farther he traveled, the more sure he was—the lightness was really there and becoming brighter.

It was an opening, a downward hole at his feet. Below he could discern only more rock, but the light had to come from some outside opening nearby. He sat on the hole's brink and let his feet dangle in, then hesitated. What if his eyes were fooling him? How far down were those rocks? The idea of falling into the heart of a mountain was too horrible to consider.

His gun. He could drop it and see how long it fell. He did, and the rifle clattered against stone only a few feet below.

Brannigan slid through and dropped in a heap at the base of the passage.

The light came from behind him. Picking up his rifle, he moved toward it. It grew brighter. A gust of fresh air struck him deliriously, and he almost cried.

Here the cavern widened, and the light was bright enough to illuminate the walls. He rounded a bend in the passage and stopped, frowning and looking around him.

"What kind of place is this?"

On the floor of the cave lay furs, cast about in a seemingly random way, along with assorted trash, bones, ragged pelts, handmade tools, flints, and wood stacked beside a heap of black ash where repeated fires had been built. The smoke residue was thick on the walls.

He slowly stepped through. He caught a glimpse of something, someone, against a wall.

He raised his rifle, then saw it was not a man who looked back at him.

It had been a man once, but now it was only a skeleton, crumbling, dressed in a parchment-dry bearskin robe that hung on it, a decayed shroud.

Brannigan looked more closely. He noticed the curving of the fingers, cupped together on the lap, but holding only empty air.

He remembered Caine's treasure story and wondered but discounted it. The outlaw probably made it up to save himself. He was a fool to have listened.

The lure of treasure gone, the memory of being lost in the darkness shadowing him, Brannigan wanted nothing but to be free of enclosing walls.

He blinked in the afternoon light as he emerged. Scanning the landscape, he looked for evidence of human presence and found none. Then his eyes dropped to his feet and grew wide.

"God a'mighty! Like a bear in moccasins!"

The entire area fronting the cave was trampled and marked with huge tracks. Bigger even than Brannigan's own large feet. He cocked his head and frowned. Nobody was this big.

Finally, he found a recess in a hillside and slid behind a tangle of brush. His hand slid to his pocket, and he suddenly realized he had lost his roll of bills. Funny—after being lost in that cave, it hardly seemed to matter.

He lay down and quickly fell asleep.

CHAPTER 19

Caine stood at the mouth of the cave, rifle ready. The tracks had led him here, and now, mingled among them, he saw more sign that John Crosston had been here before him. The treasure, probably, was in his hands.

If the treasure really was what the journal said, there was something wrong about Crosston having it. It was like a rat with a jewel in its mouth. Crosston wasn't worthy of it.

No more unworthy than me. Caine resisted the idea. *Everything I've done has been* for the sake of justice. But the thought had a hollow ring.

Caine looked into the cavern. If the occupant of this cavern had resisted Crosston, Crosston might have shot him. If so, he would likely be inside somewhere, dead or hurt.

Caine stepped into the darkness, waited for his eyes to adjust, then went forward. He could hear his own heartbeat. The air was close and tight.

When he found the skeleton, he stood before it a long time, looking into the eye sockets.

"Hello, thief," he said. He glanced at the cupped, empty hands. "You kept watch over it a long time, old man."

He walked on until the darkness was too dense for him

to see. He lit a match, and as the yellow flare burst, he caught a whiff of decay. Something dead.

He looked about, expecting to find the body of the one who had left the tracks. What was the name written in Crosston's journal? Gideon, he recalled.

But Caine found no body. A heap of animal carcasses was the source of the stench. It appeared to be composed largely of ground squirrels and rabbits— even a few hawks and a buzzard. They were just bone and ragged meat, as if they had been gnawed raw and tossed aside. The match fizzled out.

Deeper in the cave, unseen, a hulking form shifted in the darkness, a whisper of movement Caine could not be sure he had heard. He quickly struck another match and peered about. All was still. He saw strings of something hanging from a crude rack of sticks near the cave wall. He touched it. Dried venison.

He turned back toward the cave entrance. He felt something, invisible and unheard, looked back again into the blackness, but couldn't see anything.

He emerged into the sunlight.

"Caine!"

The voice came from somewhere close beside him. He wheeled.

It was Brannigan. "Right good to see you again, Simon Caine! You just hold still while I scramble your brain like an egg."

He was shapeless against the sun, with his rifle raised and aimed squarely at him. "Drop your rifle," he said, and Caine did. "You'd best pray if you know how," the bounty hunter said. "This time, I'm taking no chances. It ends here."

As Brannigan spoke, Caine edged backward and around. Brannigan moved with him step for step. Caine slid his hand to his gun belt.

"Don't think about it!" Brannigan stepped in front of

the cave. "Your time has come, Caine." He sighted down the barrel, squinting.

For a second, Caine imagined it was a piece of night that emerged from the cavern and engulfed the bounty hunter. The creature that took Brannigan in its grasp was nearly seven feet tall, a Goliath of a man.

He dwarfed Brannigan as he wrapped his arms around the bounty hunter's chest. He squeezed until Brannigan's eyes rolled up in their sockets. The giant then tossed the body aside; it rolled down the slope into the brush, the rifle rattling down after it.

The mountain on legs turned to Caine.

The outlaw responded reflexively. He drew his pistol and fired a shot into the fur-clad bulk before him.

He saw the eyes as the bullet struck. They were as childish as those of his son, staring up at him from a trundle bed on the banks of the Calfkiller River.

Gideon turned, whimpering, and ran back into the cavern. Caine dropped his pistol, squeezed shut his eyes, and in an instant, he understood the truth that his nightmares had been trying to convey to him for so many nights now and also knew from where it came.

It came from himself, or himself as he would have been if he had left vengeance to the heavens those long years back. It was simple: There must be an end.

He looked into the cavern, thinking all the wrongs he had done seemed small compared to what had just happened. He had shot Gideon simply because it had become his way to hurt and kill. Suddenly it seemed absurd.

Caine entered the cave and searched for the one he had shot. He did not find him. He also searched for Brannigan and—strangely—could not find him either. He returned to the cavern mouth and sat alone until sunset reddened the sky and darkness followed.

————

Sam Ten Pennies also sat alone, his head buried in his hands. The malady that ate away his sanity had caused his band to abandon him at last.

He lifted his face when he heard someone approaching. His mental illness robbed him of perception, so he saw not the face of Opequon but that of his slain mate. He extended his arms, welcoming the miracle without question.

Opequon stopped. She moved as if to raise Jack Whitaker's old Hawken rifle but did not. Finally, she turned and walked away.

This was the one abandonment Sam Ten Pennies could not endure. He rose and followed her, but she moved swiftly and with an elusive skill that kept her always a flitting, distant ghost. Finally, he lost sight of her.

He ran to the top of a ridge and looked across his valley. He shouted her name, and the echo called back, but she did not.

When the sun grew hot, he ceased calling and sat down. He leaned against a boulder and waited, but she did not come. When night fell again, still he waited, and on through the next day and night, until many weeks later, the renegades who had abandoned him found his body slumped against the rock, his dead eyes still gazing across the valley.

————

Ezra Cleek did not know what had made him awaken. He sat upright and saw a tall figure standing beside his bed. He drew in his breath. A cold voice said to him: "I want a horse."

He recognized the voice as Simon Caine's. The old man's heart pounded.

"I— What are you—"

"Don't sit there stammering. Get me a horse."

Cleek nodded. He rose, trembling, and pulled dirty clothing over his even dirtier body. Caine remained beside him, face hidden in the darkness, and that made him seem particularly threatening.

But even frightened, Ezra Cleek was a businessman. He said, "I've got nothing very good right now, so your price will be low—"

"You're going to give it to me," Caine said.

Cleek chewed his tongue. "Yes. Of course."

He walked, stooped from the stiffness of his aging bones out to the horse pen. Caine followed. The tall Confederate studied the handful of horses and pointed to one.

"A good choice, Mr. Caine," Cleek said. He opened the pen and fetched the animal. "Enjoy him."

"A saddle."

"A saddle. Yes." Cleek shuffled off to a shed and came back, puffing beneath the weight of an old saddle. Caine took it, threw it across the horse, and cinched it.

When he looked at Cleek again, the old man was pointing a derringer into his face and smiling.

"It appears I've got you, Mr. Caine."

Caine walked to him, wrenched away the derringer, and grasped Cleek by the neck in one steel-trap hand. He pulled the little man up to his tiptoes and drew his face to his own.

"I'd snap your scrawny neck except for one reason, and he's sleeping in your station yonder. God knows he deserves better than what he's got for a pa, but I'll not rob him of what little he has." He shoved Cleek to the ground, mounted, and rode away.

Later that night, another man came to Cleek's Station, and this time it was Henry Cleek who heard him, or, at least, sensed his presence. The young man rose, picked up the kitten that slept beside him, slid out his window, and looked about in the moonlight.

He saw the man approaching. He was amazingly big, like a huge shadow in the moonlight. Silently he came to Henry Cleek and stopped.

For several moments, the two looked at each other. Then Henry Cleek smiled and held up his kitten.

CHAPTER 20

HELENA, MONTANA TERRITORY

Deputy Jim Ballentree, the newest member of the staff of the town marshal of Helena, stood in the afternoon sunshine, cutting a long chew of tobacco from a plug, and pondering his own happiness. A long-skirted woman passed him with a rustle and teasing scent of perfume, and he tipped his hat. He settled the chew into his jaw and walked slowly down the boardwalk. It was a daily afternoon ritual for him now, one he liked. There wasn't much about this job he didn't like, except the low pay. It was a world away from Henley, and he was satisfied.

His wife also seemed happier here. Ballentree had realized now that the days in Henley had been hard ones for her. She, more than himself, had sensed the oppressive shadow of William Montrose on the town. Ballentree had feigned a lot of independence in those days, but he never really had been free to be the kind of marshal he wanted to be.

Ballentree leaned over, spat a dollop of tobacco, adjusted his hat, and turned the corner. The building that marked the end of his daily rounds was the Montana House, a three-story hotel with its own dining room and stable, plus an authentic Chinaman to pour water over you in your own ten-cents-per-half-hour enameled bathtub. It was a popular hotel, and its owner, Benjamin Landers, was a well-off man.

Ballentree liked Landers, who was a few years older than he. Landers had taken on the task of making the new deputy feel welcome, and the pair enjoyed their daily conversations at the end of Ballentree's rounds. It was usually no more than a two-minute exchange, after which Ballentree returned to the office to do the standard least-seniority job of paperwork. Indeed, this task was the symbolic end of the day for him, for it was immediately followed by the ride home to his wife and the aroma of the waiting supper.

Ballentree entered the Montana House lobby and removed his hat. Delicious smells wafted across from the dining room, putting him in mind again of the supper he anticipated. The lobby was a beautiful work of architecture and craftsmanship, by western standards: fine mahogany paneling, imported from Chicago; fancy brass lamps, all enveloped in a burnished-gold atmosphere enhanced by sunlight through the west-facing windowpanes.

Ben Landers stood behind the lobby desk, his thumbs hooked in his vest pockets. "Afternoon, Jim."

"Ben."

"All well with you?" It was his standard afternoon query.

"Fine."

They went through their usual banter; then Landers surprised Ballentree with a supper invitation for three nights hence. He accepted, agreeing with the hotel owner that the visit would give their wives a chance to meet and maybe strike a friendship.

A young black man stepped out of the dining room, balancing a tray covered in a checked cloth. He swept up the stairs in straight-spined dignity, wearing the red velvet jacket Landers required of all his employees.

Ballentree watched the waiter disappear around the land-ing. Landers, having just lighted a cigar, waved his smoking matchstick toward the stairs.

"Funny thing," he said. "We have us a hermit of sorts living here. He's been here nearly three weeks, and he's stayed in his room since he arrived. He walked in one day, rented out a room for a night, and picked up a letter that was waiting for him. He took it upstairs, and since then, he's been a fixture. He rented out his room a month ahead and started taking his meals up there, and he's ordered, God knows how many bottles of whiskey. He never comes out. Must slip out in the night to empty his chamber pot. He signed in as Williamson."

Ballentree said, "Has he given you any trouble?"

"No. He just stays up there, all alone."

"Figure he's waiting on someone?"

"If he is, he's never said." He paused, then spoke more solemnly: "You know, it's crossed my mind that we'll find him up there some morning, dead."

"You want me to check him out?"

Landers considered, then shook his head. "Not just yet."

"Just let me know, then. Williamson, you say?"

"Yes."

"I'll check our records and see if he might be wanted. What was the first name?"

"John, I believe."

"John Williamson. I'll see what I can turn up. But for now, I'd best be going."

"Good evening. Don't forget that supper date." "I won't." Ballentree slipped on his hat and headed for the door. Jim.

"Yeah?" He turned back to Landers. "He's not Ameri-can. Sounded British to me." Ballentree hesitated for a second and then continued out onto the porch. On the hori-zon, clouds had gathered, and thunder rumbled. Just like that night in Henley, he thought. Feeling disconcerted, he headed for the office to flip through wanted posters.

———

Gideon's pain grew worse with every step. He had been able to overcome it so far and keep his head, but now he was beginning to despair.

His struggle to keep up with the tall man who he had followed from the cavern had been difficult from the beginning. Gideon had managed to do it as long as the man was on foot. But when the man had gotten a horse, Gideon lost him. Now he had reached a place where windows glowed here and there on the mountainsides at night, and there were cattle and roads and people.

He was hungry; here, he found less of the roots and berries and animal flesh left by the mountain carrion birds that had sustained him—barely—up until now.

He was bleeding again, too, and the wounds, when he dared look at them, were horrible to see. So he made himself not look at them and concentrated on his mission.

He prayed for guidance, though without words. Unhearing, Gideon had never learned to speak. But as best he could, his father had taught him of the thing they guarded, their duty toward it—Gideon's duty alone, now—and of the God they served in fulfilling that duty.

Below Gideon lay a valley. He saw lights. There was a house, a barn, fences, and a chicken coop with hens and roosters scratching around it in the twilight. He recognized none of these things as such but knew the birds would be food.

Breathing heavily, Gideon stumbled into the valley as night descended.

———

Old Bailey, they called him. First name, last name, which it was, nobody knew or cared, least of all Bailey himself. Too many years washed away by whiskey had wiped out all such trivialities.

Bailey was on hard times at the moment. No money, no liquor, and nobody needing a saloon swept or a stable shoveled clean. He hadn't had a drop since last night and had been shaky all day. He huddled against a shed wall on a side street, knees pulled against his chest and his arms wrapped around his calves. It was dark, a storm was blowing up, and he was cold. But the need for a drink was all that really concerned him.

He heard a noise and looked up to see a rider gazing down at him. "Hello," the stranger said.

"'Lo."

"Where could a man find a hotel in this town?"

"You want good or cheap?"

"Good. The ones a man would go to if he had money and was used to spending it."

Old Bailey thought it through. "The Montana House is where I'd go if I was such a man. I ain't, though. I'm just a broke old drunk who they wouldn't let in the back door."

Simon Caine studied the old man silently. He dug a hand into his pocket and produced a greenback, the one bill the bounty hunters had not found when they robbed him. He let it flutter to the ground. "Thanks, old man," he said.

Old Bailey watched him go, then picked up the bill. A ten-dollar note. He stared at it, disbelieving, then kissed it. He looked up at the cloud-roiled sky.

The rider must have been an angel, straight from heaven's gate.

CHAPTER 21

The Montana House lobby was empty except for Landers' cleaning boy when Simon Caine entered. The boy stared blank-eyed at him, then went back to sweeping. Caine walked up the stairs.

He reached the second level, turned down the hallway, and stopped. He believed Crosston was here, somewhere, but he had no proof and no idea which room he would be in. He thought of asking the cleaning boy, but with the purpose, he had in mind, such advertising might be unwise.

Caine leaned against a wall, thinking about what to do. Why had he been forced to argue with himself all the way here from the Bitterroots, firming his conviction by day and watching it dissolve at sunset?

A door opened and closed. A man in a derby fumbled with his key three doors down. When he finished and came toward Caine, the outlaw touched his arm. The man stopped.

"I'm looking for a young Englishman. You know what room he'd be in?"

"Did you ask at the desk?"

"No one there."

"Well, I heard there was a foreign man in 312. I don't know if he's English."

"Obliged." He let the man go and climbed to the next level.

At the door of room 312, he stood in silence. At his feet was a tray of dirty dishes still scrapped with fragments. He raised his fist, hesitated again, then knocked.

"Just take the tray," came a voice from inside. It was Crosston's, but it was different than he remembered it.

Caine tried the latch. It was locked. He stepped back and kicked open the door.

Crosston lay on the bed. He was unshaven, his hair matted and dark with sweat. The clothes he wore obviously had not been changed in weeks. The stench of stale liquor permeated the room, which was lit by two lamps, one attached to the wall and another on the night table beside Crosston.

The young Englishman barely reacted to the crashing of the door. He turned bleary eyes toward Caine, showing neither surprise nor fear. Caine had seen the same look in the faces of mortally wounded soldiers on bloodied battlefields.

For a time, neither man spoke. Then Crosston pushed himself up on one elbow and said, "Hello, Caine. Pardon me if I don't get up, but I'm very drunk." He looked away toward the dresser across from the foot of the bed.

"Well, there it is. That's what I've spent years searching for, what I broke you out of jail for, what I've killed for. It's beautiful in a rather simple way, eh?"

Caine's gaze followed Crosston's to the dresser.

A chalice stood there, shining in the dull light of the lamps. It was wide at the flange, tapered toward a round base, and appeared to be made of bronze. It was unembellished. Just a plain chalice, apparently very old.

"Do you know, Caine, why a man would do all I have for such a meager thing as that?"

Caine said, "I read your journal in the cabin. I know what it is."

"Ah, do you? No, Caine, you don't. No more than I did."

Caine did not understand the remark and did not respond. But something from Crosston's journal came to his mind, and he said: "Carried by Joseph of—"

Crosston nodded and cut in: "Joseph of Arimathea. Brought by him to Britain, then by the Magdalen to Marseilles. From there, it has traveled far, possessed at various times by Knights Templar, Albigensian heretics, and the Church itself. It has been stolen and traded and smuggled and sold, and the men I killed were not the first to die because of it. So goes the story of the long-sought Holy Grail." He paused, then sadly continued: "But as it pertains to the chalice you see there, a story is all it is."

"What do you mean?"

"It's a fraud. A lie. If the Grail survives today, as I believe it does, that is not it."

"How do you know?"

Crosston reached to the table beside his bed and picked up a crumpled letter. He tossed it toward Caine; it drifted down to his feet.

"From my father. I had told him he could reach me here when all this was done, and I gave him the name I would use. What that letter tells me is that all these years of searching have been a waste. My father was duped. The broker who sold the cup to him was a swindler. He played on my father's obsession, knew enough facts to convince him the cup really was the Grail. My father now knows the truth about him. And about the cup. The years and devotion he spent, the money and the danger—just to be duped by a swindler."

"I don't give a damn about your father," Caine said. "Are you telling me that Jake died for absolutely nothing at all?"

Crosston laughed bitterly. "So he did. Isn't that irony for

you, Caine? But Jake wasn't the only one. I killed a priest because of that cup. I felt I had to. Somehow he learned the location of it; he might have reached it before me. Funny. He was swindled too. Probably by the same man who cheated my father."

Caine drew his pistol and aimed it at Crosston. The Englishman smiled faintly. "So you're going to kill me? I don't really care, you know. My father is all in this world that has ever mattered to me. More than anything, I wanted to do something important for him, something to show him how much— but it doesn't matter. I've failed. Kill me if you've got to. If you don't, I'll probably just do it myself."

Caine sighted down the barrel and clicked back the hammer.

————

Gideon ran from the farmstead, frightened by the hot flare of a shotgun blast that had fanned his head. Even though he wasn't hit, his clumsy efforts to save himself had further torn his previous wounds.

He went far and fell to the ground. He was lost, badly hurt, and was beginning to fear he would never see his treasure again. He would, instead, die here alone, far from his cavern and the presence of his father.

Being alone did not frighten him, but this distance from all he knew, and the separation from the sole item of importance in his life, was unbearable.

The thunder crashed again, and rain came down at bullet speed, driving into the earth and his skin. At length, he arose, strength almost gone and began wandering randomly.

CHAPTER 22

Jim Ballentree stood, knocking over his chair. He read the paper in his hand again, speaking the key parts: "Ian John Crosston . . . England . . . murder of a priest . . . speaks with noticeable accent. . ."

He folded and pocketed the notice. He slid on his hat, drew his pistol, and checked the loads, then left the office. He walked fast through the darkness, heading for the Montana House, splashing puddles and smelling the pungency of the just-passed storm.

Inside he climbed the stairs and moved stealthily down the dark hallways, hardly breathing, listening to silence. He rested his right hand on the butt of his pistol. Curse his pounding heart—the Englishman would hear it; it beat so loudly.

Up the hallway, he saw a door ajar. He slid forward. The door was open just a few inches. The lock was shattered as if kicked in.

Something at his feet drew his attention. A dark line was running from beneath the door and across the hall. Ballentree knelt and touched it. It was blood.

Ballentree drew his pistol and pushed open the door. Warily he looked inside.

On the bed lay the Englishman he had encountered in Henley. His face was pale, and his eyes half closed. His left arm dangled over the side of the bed, a long, ragged cut gaping open from wrist to elbow. Blood drained from it in a thinning stream, pouring into and overflowing a shallow metal cup into which the fingers dangled. Beside the cup lay a bloodied piece of a broken bottle.

Ballentree holstered his pistol and rushed to the bed. He raised the bleeding arm. Crosston's dull gaze lifted to him, and the coated lips moved slightly.

Ballentree pulled a handkerchief from his pocket and knotted it around the slashed arm. The flow of blood diminished, then stopped.

Crosston's lips moved again, whispering words Ballentree could not hear.

"Why did you do it?" Ballentree asked, expecting no answer.

But John Crosston's good arm came up, and he weakly grasped Ballentree's wrist. He spoke with effort, and this time Ballentree understood: "He didn't kill me."

"Who?"

"Simon Caine."

Crosston's eyes closed, and his lips parted. He fell unconscious, leaving Ballentree wondering if he had heard correctly.

"Did you say, Simon Caine?"

Crosston could not answer. Ballentree laid his ear against his chest; a heartbeat was there.

The deputy hefted Crosston onto his shoulders. Grunting under the weight, he moved toward the door. His foot slid in blood; he staggered and had to step back to balance himself. In the process, Ballentree kicked over the cup. Blood drained across the floor in a livid scarlet flood.

The deputy suffered an assault of squeamishness and had to close his eyes for a moment. Then he carried Crosston's limp body out the door and down the hallway, balancing Crosston as he made his way into the street. He brought the Englishman to the office of an aging doctor named Seward, whom he roused with kicks against the door.

A half hour later, Dr. Seward, white hair askew and backlit by a coal-oil lamp perched nearby, was half finished with the stitching of John Crosston's arm. Ballentree watched from the corner.

"This one meant business," Seward said. "Good thing you found him when you did. Otherwise, he would be dead by now."

"Will he make it, Doc?"

"Can't say."

"Strange to run into him again," Ballentree spoke like a man thinking aloud.

"You know him?" asked the doctor.

Ballentree flushed; suddenly, he was embarrassed. "In a way. I met him once before I came to Helena."

"I see. You were where? Oh yes. Henley, up in the Bitterroots."

"Yes."

"I hear you had some interesting times there. Even met Simon Caine."

Ballentree mumbled: "Yes, I met him."

"Now there's a murdering heathen if ever there was one. You're lucky he didn't scalp you, Deputy. I hear tell he's done that a time or two."

"He has."

"Tell me, what's he like?"

Ballentree had to stifle a burst of anger at the doctor's gossip mongering.

"I don't know what he's like," he said. "I spent a few hours with him in my jail, that's all. Now, if you'll pardon me, Doc, I need to get back over to the hotel and look over that room. If your patient there wakes up, let me know. By the way, he's wanted, so watch him."

The doctor turned. "Wanted? For what?"

"Murder."

Ballentree left the office and returned to the Montana House. The place was astir, its residents awake and talking about what had happened. Ballentree mounted the steps and entered the room where Crosston had been, angrily ordering out two gapers who had come inside it.

Landers appeared at the door. "May I come in?"

"Come on," Ballentree said. He was looking at the blood on the floor, the shattered bottle, and the overturned chalice.

"I can't believe this," Landers said. "Nothing like it ever has happened in my hotel. My business doesn't need this sort of thing."

Ballentree stooped and picked up the bottle fragment by the bed. "Ripped his own arm open with this, Ben. Not just a little cut, either. All the way up his forearm."

"Why did he do it?"

"That I don't know. He sure wanted to die."

Ballentree picked up the bloody cup. He raised it and eyed it curiously.

"What's that?" Landers asked.

Ballentree shook his head. "Evidence. That's what you call it when you can't say what it is."

The deputy swabbed out the blood with a corner of the sheet. "Don't give me that look, Ben. Sheet's bloody, anyway. Close up this room and don't let anybody in. And don't you think about cleaning it yet. We'll be back."

Ballentree wandered alone onto the street. He moved slowly back toward the doctor's office, not wanting to hurry. He needed to think.

He paused on a porch and leaned against a rail. He sat the cup at his feet, then cut a cud of tobacco and settled it into his jaw. Sucking at it, he let the strong taste burn tongue and throat.

Simon Caine, if he was nearby earlier tonight, where was he now? In some shadowed corner, a throw's distance away? Ballentree frowned. God, he didn't want to see that face again.

It wasn't out of fear, strangely, though Ballentree knew Caine would kill him without hesitation if given cause. But that was the point. Caine hadn't killed Ballentree, even though he had had two good chances.

It was a funny thing. All the stories said Caine was a man without a heart, utterly compassionless. But in Ballentree's case, it had not proven so. And that had nagged at the lawman ever since.

The dime novels and the saloon storytellers portrayed Caine either as a heroic figure—, if the storyteller was an unreconstructed southerner—or as a murderer devoid of any worth or kindness.

I'll bet you're not either one, Ballentree thought. I'll bet you're just a man who stumbled into hell and lost his way trying to get out again.

Ballentree spit tobacco and shifted his foot. Accidentally, he kicked over the chalice, and it rolled off the porch into the street.

CHAPTER 23

William Montrose heard the slow plodding of a weary horse that drew near outside his house. He picked up a derringer, palmed it, went to the door, slid back the cover of a small view hole, and looked out. Montrose dropped the derringer into his pocket and threw open the door.

Brannigan looked like a nearly dead man on a nearly dead horse. His face was almost gray, and his eyes were wild with pain. Leaning forward, he gripped his right arm tightly across his chest. It was obvious that every breath brought suffering. Bloodstains crusted his shirt and his beard.

"Montrose, help me," he said. He fell from the saddle and hit the ground with a hard thud.

Montrose looked down at him, his lip curled. He shook his head, laid his finger across his nostrils to block the stench of the fallen bounty hunter, and shouted for aid. Two of his men came at a run.

Brannigan would have slept a long time on the feather tick upon which they placed him, but Montrose would not allow it. The bounty hunter wakened with a cry of pain as Montrose shook him.

"Where is Simon Caine?"

"Where he always will be."

"Talk straight to me, or I'll kill you right here."

"You'll never catch Caine," Brannigan said. "Nobody will ever catch him."

Montrose pulled away for a second, then his eyes sparked, and his lips went tight. He drew back his fist but did not follow through. Instead, he wheeled and walked away. Pausing by a bookshelf, he reached up and took the scalp lock of his brother. He fingered the stiff hair, the parchment like flesh. When his temper had cooled, he turned.

"What happened to you?" he asked quietly.

"I don't know," Brannigan said. "Something got me. Something from a cave."

"What? A wolf, a bear—"

Brannigan shook his head. "Something else." He paused, then said: "The redskins say there's a spirit or a devil or such up there."

Montrose looked at him intently, then laughed. "A spirit? I sent you to get Simon Caine, and you come back telling me ghost stories?"

"I saw it. More than saw it—look what it did to me! Cracked my ribs, threw me over a bluff. I crawled away, finally found a horse, made it back here."

"And what of Caine?"

"I had him, but the... thing—it protected him. The man can't be taken, Montrose. Leave him be."

"What about the others?" Montrose said. "Where are they—and the money?"

"Dead. All of them dead. The money's lost."

Montrose glowered and nodded at two men who stood near the door. They went to Brannigan. One struck the bounty hunter across the mouth. The other pounded his elbow into his cracked ribs. Brannigan screamed and passed out.

One of the men dug into Brannigan's pockets but found nothing.

"Get rid of him," Montrose said in disgust.

They hefted up the broken, senseless man and carried him back to his horse. They threw him over the back of the unsaddled animal, brought out a rope, and lashed him down.

One man drew his pistol and pointed it to the sky. "Wait," the other said. "It seems right cruel to send him off like that in the shape he is. Wait a minute."

The man re-entered the house and half a minute later came back out with a paper in his hand. He attached it to the back of Brannigan's shirt. The other read it aloud: "This man needs a doctor." He laughed and fired the pistol. The horse ran down the hill, through the town, and vanished into the forest.

———

Caine heard the voice of a child slice through the murk of his sleep. He moved, feeling the roughness of the straw tick against his back. His eyes opened just enough to see morning sunlight shafting in at a familiar angle. He heard the child's voice again. Marcus, up early for a Saturday morning. Simon Caine reached across to Nancy.

He opened his eyes and, for what seemed the millionth time, suffered the stab of reality. He was not on his bed back in Tennessee but on his blanket spread atop loose hay in a barn loft. The sunlight that poured in came not through his bedroom window but through a ventilation hole in the barn wall. He closed his eyes and wished he could sleep again. In sleep, it was, sometimes, as if he were with them. Awake, he always was alone.

"Mister, I said wake up."

The child's voice again. Caine sat up. A red-haired boy with his hands wrapped tightly around an old percussion-cap rifle looked up at him, his freckles spangled across a scared white face.

"You just sit still. My pa, he'll be here in a minute with the others."

"Son, I've intruded in your barn, but I meant no harm. You just lay down that rifle, and I'll be gone."

"No sir. My brother's run to get Pa and the others, and they'll be here directly."

Pa and the others was a group Caine was not eager to meet, but he couldn't ignore the boy's rifle.

"How old are you, son?"

"I'm near twelve. Man enough to shoot this thing if that's what you're getting at."

"I'd say you are. You know, son, I had a boy once. He was a handsome young fellow, just like you."

In truth, the redheaded little rifleman was quite homely, but Caine's compliment seemed well taken. The boy eased his grip on the rifle just a trace.

"What's your boy's name?" he asked.

"Marcus," Caine said. "We called him Mark. Like the man in the Bible."

"Yeah. Is he somewhere around here?"

"No. My boy's dead. Died years ago, even before he was old as you."

The boy didn't seem to know what to say to that. Finally, he asked: "He get sick?"

"No. He got.... hurt. Hurt bad enough to die."

"I'm sorry, then. But I'll still shoot you if you move."

"Reckon you would."

Outside Caine heard horsemen. He looked through a knothole. There was a small army approaching out there. Cattlemen, from the look of them, armed and looking frightfully serious.

The boy grinned. "I told you they'd be here."

The riders moved around the barn, and five or six

dismounted. They came into the barn, guns ready, and surrounded the boy.

"You did a brave thing, Clarence. I'm proud of you," said a man whose hair rivaled the boys in brilliance. He gazed up with pinhole eyes, twin islands in a sea of freckles.

"Mister, you just sit still," he commanded. "Shadrach, is this the one you seen?"

Another appeared, a bald man with a head round as a billiard ball. He squinted at Caine.

"No," he finally said. "No way, this is the one. I told you, Will, he wasn't no regular-looking human being. He was half bear."

The redheaded man lowered his gun and his brows at the same time. "Who you be?" he demanded of Caine.

"A traveler. I needed a place to sleep, and I figured I'd be out of everybody's way in this loft."

The man shrugged and chewed his lip. "It's my barn and my loft, and I don't run it for no hotel, but there's no harm done. Sorry about the ruckus, friend. There's been trouble last night, and me and Shadrach and these here others have been out looking since sunup. When my boy here"—he indicated a slightly older version of the first lad— "come saying there was somebody in the barn, we just kind of got nervous. You're lucky it was us that found you and not the one we're after, though."

"Why?"

"We're not sure it's really a man. I know that sounds crazy, but Shadrach seen him and swears that . . . well, you just heard him yourself. He saw this . . . thing in his chicken pen, just ripping open a live hen like it was a bread load. Ate at it all raw and bloody. Something bad wrong with a man who would do that if it is a man."

Caine recognized the singular description, but Gideon? The giant he'd seen, the one mentioned in Crosston's journal? He didn't let the others see his reaction.

"I'll be getting out of your barn now. I'm obliged for the use of it."

"What's your name?" came a voice from below. Caine's heart raced. Mentally, he began mapping out a plan—who would take the first shot, who the second, which way would be the best to leap from the loft. . .

"Robert Cole," he said.

"Would you mind moving into the light where I can see you?" Caine moved to the edge of the loft and looked down.

"I've seen you before, Mr. Cole. Can't recall where. Ernest, you recognize him?"

Another man scrutinized him, then shook his head. "Don't reckon I have," he said.

The other man frowned, still suspicious. "Just can't put my finger on it," he said.

"Why don't you just go on, Mr. Cole," said the red-haired leader. "But if you're traveling alone, I suggest you be careful. The one we're looking for is big and likely to be mean. If you want to join us, you may. We're going into Helena to get the law."

"Thanks, but I'll just ride on."

Caine recovered his mount from the meadow where he had hobbled it and rode away, feeling their eyes on him.

———

"One man, but that's all," said the marshal to the cluster of men in his office. "One's all I can spare.

Why are you so worked up, anyway? Crazy man tears apart a chicken, and you expect me to deputize the whole population?"

"First a chicken, then maybe a child, Joe," said the red-haired man. "We told you, this was no ordinary man. He was big as a mountain. His track was wide as my head, and that's no lie. Maybe it's not a man at all, but some kind of animal that nobody's seen yet."

"Aw, get off that foolishness," the marshal said. "You get your bowels in an uproar over every little thing. One man's all you're getting. That'll be you, Ballentree."

Jim Ballentree looked reluctant. "Marshal, with the prisoner over at Doc Seward's, I think—"

"We can watch him just as good as you, Deputy. You're the new man, so you chase the chicken killers. We'll make sure your Englisher stays put."

"Yes, sir." Ballentree turned to another deputy, who was smiling his seniority. "Wilbur, if you would—"

"I'll tell your wife you won't be on time again," the other said.

When they were out of town, Ballentree had the riders take him to where the big man had been seen. When he saw the footprints in the mud, the mission suddenly didn't seem so trivial.

The print was huge—not as big as the man had implied back at the office, but definitely bigger than any Ballentree had seen before.

"One thing we can know: it is a man," he said. "That's a moccasin track."

One of the others asked: "What kind of man would do this?" He gestured at a scattering of bloodied feathers on the ground.

"A very hungry one, I suppose," Ballentree said.

"Well, we'd best find him. There's good tracks here. Why didn't you follow these on your own?"

The leader looked sheepish. "Got a little skittish, I admit. Started out after him, then decided we'd best get the law. We never found anything but a stranger in my barn."

"A stranger?"

"Tall fellow. Looked like a mountaineer. He said his name was Cole."

Ballentree was thoughtful a moment. "Let's get started," he said.

They rode through the late-morning light, following a trail that seemed to lead nowhere and often circled back upon itself. It was the track of a man lost, wandering.

They paused for a bite at noon, then continued. The trail led into high, rocky country. Then it disappeared along a dry streambed. Ballentree dismounted and searched the ground. Nothing.

"He's gotten away," he said. "We'll never find him in these high rocks."

He stood, slapping dust from his hands, staring up at the ridgeline. "We could try circling and...." His voice caught in his throat.

High above, silhouetted against the sky, was a rider. A distinctive, lean form of a man. Though the distance was too great to let him discern the rider's features, Jim Ballentree knew who it was.

The rider on the ridge turned his mount and was gone.

"What is it, Deputy?" one of the others asked.

"Nothing," Ballentree said. "We'd best turn back."

CHAPTER 24

Gideon hardly walked now. He merely groped his way through the rocks, moving on only because he could find no place nor reason to stop. The pain he had endured so long was almost unbearable. He finally fell, dropping to his hands and knees, then onto his face. He rolled onto his back, grimacing at the sun.

He was unconscious when Simon Caine's shadow blocked the light from his face. The outlaw knelt over the fallen man.

"Did you think I could bring it back to you? Is that why you followed me?" Caine felt for and found Gideon's pulse, then nodded. "It's going to be all right now," he said.

————

Back from his fruitless search, Ballentree sat alone in the doctor's office, staring into the corner. His duty was to guard John Crosston, but his mind was not on it. He remembered the image of Simon Caine against the sky and mulled over this unexpected repetition of the past.

The chalice stood at his feet. He had been toying with it

since this morning. After yesterday's sighting, thoughts of Caine had stolen his night's rest. Weary today, he sat heavily in his straight-back chair by the doctor's bottle-laden cabinet, turning the cup in his hands, sometimes dozing.

The old chalice was a fascinating piece of refuse. Ballentree had picked it up at the marshal's office this morning, planning to ask Crosston to identify it, but so far, he hadn't, for Crosston had been asleep.

Ballentree's head bobbed, and his eyes drooped and shut. He began to snore.

"Deputy?"

The voice was soft, almost tremulous. Ballentree awakened with a start and stared into the eyes of John Crosston.

"May I have it?" the Englishman asked, extending his hands. His face was of an almost ghoulish pallor, his hair matted and eyes red. He shook where he stood.

"What are you doing up? The doctor said you couldn't even stand."

"I hardly can," whispered the other. "But I need the cup."

Ballentree handed it to Crosston, who smiled feebly. He cradled the chalice gently.

Crosston glanced up at Ballentree. "I know you," he said. "From the jail in Henley."

"Yes."

"I'm sorry about striking you. I had no choice."

"Who are you, Crosston? And what is this thing?"

The Englishman staggered. Weakly, he made for another chair. He fell into it, breathing heavily, still holding the cup.

"What is it?" repeated Ballentree.

"Nothing."

Ballentree stood. "You need to be back in bed. Let me help you."

Crosston stood with Ballentree's help. "I'm dizzy," he said. Ballentree helped Crosston into the bed. The young man sank his head into the sweaty pillow and gasped deeply. He held the chalice across his chest. Ballentree could see the scabbed gash down his arm. Crosston looked like a corpse, but for his shuddering breathing.

Ballentree turned away, wanting to be away from the stench and pallor of this man. He returned to his chair but grew restless. He stood and walked to the windowed door. He pulled aside the yellow curtain and looked out.

He was alone in the office. The doctor had been called out in mid-afternoon; now, it was beginning to darken, and he was not yet back. Ballentree wished he would return. Being in the office with a delirious, breathing-and-pulsing cadaver was unnerving.

Ballentree turned, digging into his pocket for a match to light a lamp. Crosston stood no more than a yard away, with the doctor's heavy mortar raised in his hands. He brought it down hard, and Ballentree fell senseless.

————

A pale dawn light touched Helena's streets as Simon Caine walked slowly into town, leading his travois-burdened horse. In this early hour, only a few saw the strange pair from the wilderness—the blacksmith early at the forge, a laundryman, Old Bailey the drunk, lounging in an alley.

From the opposite end of town, a buggy rolled in, carrying the exhausted Dr. Seward, returning from a delivery of twins. He saw Caine and his cargo approaching as he drew near his office. He halted his buggy and waited until they reached him.

"Are you the doctor here?" Caine asked.

"I am. What's wrong with that. . . man?" The doctor had noticed the size of Gideon.

"He's shot. You got to help him."

"Who is he?"

"His name is Gideon."

Caine unhitched the travois, and together he and the doctor struggled with the huge body. The doctor pounded on the door and called for Ballentree.

The door creaked open, and Ballentree's face appeared. It was bloody. The deputy clung to the doorframe to keep on his feet.

Doc Seward could only shake his head. He recalled what he had been told in student days: a doctor's business was like summer rain—little for a long time, then a flood.

"He's gone," Ballentree said. "Hit me—now he's gone."

Then Ballentree saw Simon Caine. The lawman and the outlaw stared at each other.

"I'll tend to you later," the doctor said. "We've got one a lot worse right here."

Caine and the doctor carried Gideon inside and laid him on the bed where Crosston had been. The bedframe creaked under the weight. Caine laid his hand on Gideon's shoulder.

Ballentree went to his chair and sat down, cupping his head in his hands, not sure whether he was about to be sick or burst into laughter.

CHAPTER 25

The doctor, shadowed by Caine, worked on Gideon's festering wound. Gideon's broad face was calm, and he breathed steadily despite the doctor's probing.

"Who is this man?" Doc Seward asked. "Where did he come from?"

"From the mountains," Caine replied. "He's just... what he is."

"And what's that?"

Caine did not know how to answer. He watched the doctor awhile longer, then walked into the front room.

Ballentree followed him. "I'm going after Crosston," he said.

"You're in no shape for it," Caine returned.

"I'll make it. He's in no shape to get far, either." But as Ballentree stepped toward the door, he stumbled to one side.

"I'll go after him," Caine said.

"No. I'm the law here. He's my prisoner."

"I've got more cause than you to go after him," Caine said.

"You're a wanted man, Caine. I don't know your

connection with Crosston, but you might be in league with him. Or maybe you'll kill him."

"I'm not in league with him, and if I wanted to kill him, I would have already."

Ballentree straightened again but was unsteady on his feet. "I've got to stop you, Caine."

"I don't believe you will."

Ballentree drew and leveled his pistol. "I don't want to do this. But I've got duties."

Caine was calm. "I'm going after John Crosston. And you're not going to stop me, Deputy. We're not going to hurt each other."

Ballentree, after hesitation, lowered his pistol. "No, we're not."

"Was he armed?" Caine asked.

"No. He didn't even take my pistol, as you can see." Ballentree leaned against the wall and touched his scalp gingerly. "All he took was that cup of his."

"He's got the cup?"

"Yes. What is that thing, anyway?"

"Something Crosston has no right to. It's Gideon's."

Ballentree wanted to know more, but Caine walked past him and out the door, so there was no time to ask. Ballentree stood alone, marveling at the fact he again had let Caine get away from him.

There was blood on the porch. Caine had learned from the doctor what Crosston had done to himself. The blood indicated Crosston had reopened the wound in his arm and was again losing blood. He could not go far.

Caine mounted and rode slowly down the street, picking out Crosston's footprints and the rusty bloodstains coagulating in the dirt around them.

Outside of town, he dismounted and studied the ground. Finding Crosston's sign amid the pounded hoof prints and boot marks, he once more mounted and followed.

The trail became a path cutting down into a narrow valley heavy with trees and undergrowth until finally, a hundred yards away, he saw an old log house, apparently long abandoned. Outside it was a small cemetery plot with six tombstones standing crooked among weeds. Crosston was there, leaning against one of them, watching himself bleed to death as he clutched the cup.

Caine walked through the rotting cemetery gate and stopped.

"I tore it open when I got up," Crosston said, looking at his arm. "They had sewed it up, but I tore it open again." He spoke without obvious emotion. "Bleeding like ruddy hell," he said.

He pulled the chalice close. "I've got to keep the cup. I thought about it as I lay there—I know it isn't real, but maybe I can convince my father it is. I don't care if it's a lie. I want him to be happy."

Caine said, "Did you really think you could survive in the shape you're in?"

Crosston smiled sadly and shook his head. "I had to try."

Caine said, "I can't let you keep the cup. There's one who's got more of a right to it than you ever will."

"No," Crosston said. "It's mine." But his eyes glazed for a moment, and the chalice slid to the ground. "Too weak to hold it," he said, his voice scarcely audible.

"Let me take you back," Caine said. "The doctor can stop the bleeding, maybe save your life."

"Why should you care, Caine?"

"A man can't kill forever."

"It's too late for me," Crosston said. "They'd just take the cup from me."

"It's your choice," Caine said. "But I'm taking the cup."

Crosston closed his eyes and leaned to one side. His wounded arm fell limply across his thigh, blood coming out now in slow, erratic spurts.

"Crosston?"

No response. The Englishman's body slid to the earth. He stopped breathing. Caine went to him and opened one of his eyes. The orb had the luster of cold marble, and the pupil was fixed. No more blood came from his arm.

Caine picked up the cup and returned to town.

When he arrived back at the doctor's office, he found Gideon resting on the sickbed in the back room. Beside him stood Jim Ballentree and the town marshal. A third man stood back in the corner. Caine recognized him as one of the band that had questioned him at gunpoint in the barn loft.

The man looked fearfully at Caine. His dry tongue licked over his lips, and his hands trembled on the brim of the hat he clutched.

"Howdy, mister," the marshal said to Caine. "I need to talk to you."

"Then talk."

"What's your name?"

"Robert Cole."

"You sure of that?"

"A man's generally sure of his own name." Caine glanced at Ballentree; the deputy looked like he was about to pass out.

"Mr. Cole, I got a man here who says you're Simon Caine. Says he seen you in the Battle of Saltville."

"Well, if I was Simon Caine, I reckon you would be living out your last moments right about now."

The words bore a cold sting the marshal took without reaction, other than a subtle narrowing of his eyes. "We can get this straightened out easy enough," he said. "Jim, is that the man you had in your jail in Henley?"

Ballentree looked into Caine's face. In his mind, duties battled duties, instincts and thoughts tangled into knots. When he spoke, it was like hearing someone else say the words: "I'd know Simon Caine if I saw him again, Marshal."

The marshal thought for a moment. "You would at that, Jim."

CHAPTER 26

"So his father killed himself, eh?" Montrose said.

"That he did," said Morrison DeGuere. "When the police found him, he had a newspaper clipping in his hand—a story about the arrest of the swindler who had sold him the cup years before. It seems the man had been at it for years—cheating the rich with various swindles, most of them involving the sale of antiquities of supposed great rarity and value. When old Crosston found out he had been fooled, he apparently couldn't handle it. Wrote a letter, had his servant mail it, then put a hole through his head."

"A letter?"

"To his son, I suspect. My associate talked to the servant who mailed it. The servant can't read, so he didn't know who it was addressed to or where."

Montrose shook his head. He took the scalp lock from his pocket. DeGuere watched him touch it, feel it—it was becoming a habit with Montrose, though Montrose obviously didn't even realize it.

"The man was a fool—his son too," Montrose said. "The very idea of such a relic surviving all those years, being carried all this distance—it's preposterous."

DeGuere said, "So it would appear. But there's the strangest twist in this whole affair. The swindler has confessed to more than two dozen outright frauds, but he swears the Grail is real. Nobody believes him, of course."

"Of course."

DeGuere leaned back in his chair and linked his fingers behind his head. "What's next, William? Will you hire another bounty hunter to try to bring back Caine?"

"No," Montrose said. "Not a bounty hunter. A detective."

DeGuere smiled. "A good decision. But a detective on such a job would require high pay—"

"He will be paid well," Montrose said. "But only if he succeeds. I want Simon Caine dead, Morrison. Whatever you have to do, wherever you have to go—I want Simon Caine."

DeGuere said, "It might take time. The word is that Caine has left the mountains."

"You can find him."

"Yes."

Montrose poured whiskey for both of them. He raised his glass. "To the death of Simon Caine."

"Hear, hear."

And they drank.

———

Caine placed the chalice into the hands of Gideon as he slept. The big man clutched it tight as if by instinct. His breathing deepened, and he seemed to relax.

"Where is Crosston?" Ballentree asked.

"He died east of town in an old graveyard. I left him there."

Ballentree looked down at the chalice. It moved with Gideon's breathing. "What is it, Caine?"

"Just an old cup."

"But who is this man? And what's his interest in it?"

"His name is Gideon. He guards the cup. Protects it. It's his way of serving God, I think. Some of us serve. Some of us run."

Ballentree lowered his head. "What I did wasn't right. I'm a deputy, and I've got duties."

"We've all got duties. Some real, some we just dream up and spend our lives chasing after. Or letting them chase after us. I'm not sure I know much about it anymore. The older I get, the less I seem to know about most things."

"What will you do now?"

"Just keep moving."

"Talk in Henley was you'd go back and kill Will Montrose someday."

"No," said Caine. "Just don't seem worth it anymore."

"You'll go back to the Bitterroots?"

"No. Maybe I'll go find my brother if I can."

"I hope you do," Ballentree said. "A man can't run forever."

"No. But he can try."

———

Caine rode out of Helena the way he had come. Only as he left Ballentree's sight did the deputy realize he had never explained the cup.

Three days passed, then four, and Gideon still hung onto his chalice and his life. The doctor was astounded. The big man should have been dead.

On the fifth day, Gideon was much stronger, so much so that the doctor could no longer wrestle the cup from his grasp. At last, the doctor began to see there was a connection between it and Gideon's tenacity of life, and after that, he left it alone.

On the seventh day, Gideon was gone. He had squeezed out a window in the night and had taken his cup with him.

Jim Ballentree traced Gideon's sign a couple of miles. He had headed west toward the Bitterroots.

HISTORICAL ENDNOTE

The character of Simon Caine is fictitious, but his inspiration comes from a historical figure out of Middle Tennessee's Civil War years—a Confederate bushwhacker named Champ Ferguson. Ferguson was a violent, bloodletting man who, according to some reports, killed more than a hundred men during the war. Legend has it he began his wholesale killing career, like Simon Caine, in revenge for a Union atrocity.

Depending upon the source, one can find two versions of the purported offense that made Ferguson become a bushwhacker. One story claims that after the war began, eleven Unionist neighbors of Ferguson entered his home while he was away, forced his wife and daughter to disrobe and cook a meal for them in the nude, then drove the humiliated pair, still unclothed, down a public road. A more melodramatic story claims Ferguson's small son was murdered by passing Union soldiers after the boy waved a small Confederate flag at them from the front porch of the family home.

Colorful as those legends are, neither is likely to be true. A more probable explanation for Ferguson's activity is the one he gave himself: He was promised by Confederate

sympathizers that murder charges against him in a neigh-
boring county would be dropped if he would side with the
South.

Ferguson's base of operations was the Calfkiller River
valley of Middle Tennessee. From there, he led irregular
fighters into East Tennessee, Kentucky, and Virginia, battling
both regular federal troops and Union guerilla bands. A
particular foe was "Tinker Dave" Beatty, a farmer from
nearby Fentress County, who decided to fight against rather
than run from Ferguson and his like. A body of folklore
exists describing various encounters between Ferguson and
Tinker Dave.

Ferguson and his cohorts were heartless killers. In 1864,
for example, he shot to death a federal prisoner who lay
wounded in a military hospital bed. In the Battle of Dug
Hill, fought near Ferguson's home with him as a participant,
Confederate bushwhackers with Ferguson killed three
captured Union troops by smashing their skulls with rocks.
It was a cruel execution, but the bushwhackers were trying to
save ammunition.

Unlike his fictional semi counterpart Caine, Ferguson
did not evade legal reprisal for his actions. In May 1865,
federal troops arrested him at his home in White County and
took him to a military prison in Nashville. He was tried
before a military commission; the hearing lasted from mid-
July to mid-September. He was charged with being a guerilla
and with murdering fifty-three people, including the afore-
mentioned military prisoner. No one was surprised when he
was found guilty.

On October 20, guards escorted Ferguson to a scaffold in
the Nashville military prison, and there more than twenty of
the charges against him were read (one eyewitness reported
that Ferguson nodded as some of his crimes were recounted,
and at one point said, "I could tell it better than that").

Ferguson's final request was to be buried near his home on the Calfkiller.

As his wife and daughter watched, Ferguson was hanged. His family took his corpse to the Old France cemetery in the valley of the Calfkiller and buried it there. His grave remains clearly marked today.

Cameron Judd September 26, 1987

A Note from the Author

I was born in 1956 in Tennessee, the state in which I have lived all my life. I wrote my first western at age twenty-two, and now I am writing exclusively for Bantam.

My interest in the American West is just part of a broader interest in the frontier. I am fascinated by the vast westward expanses on the other side of the Mississippi, but I am equally intrigued by the original American West: the area west of the Appalachians and east of the Mississippi. I hope someday to write fiction set in that older frontier at the time of its settlement, in addition to traditional westerns.

My interest in westerns was sparked in early childhood by television, movies, and books. I love both the fact of the West and the myth of the West; both aspects have a valid place in popular fiction.

I received an undergraduate degree in English and journalism, plus teaching accreditation in English and history, from Tennessee Technological University in 1979. Since that time, I have been a newspaper journalist by profession, both as a writer and editor. Today I live near Greeneville, Tennessee, one of the state's most historic towns. Greeneville is the seat of the county that contributed one of America's original frontier heroes to the world, Davy Crockett. Greeneville was also the hometown of President Andrew Johnson and was for several years the capital of the Lost State of Franklin—an eighteenth-century political experiment that came close to achieving statehood.

My home is in rural Greene County. My wife, Rhonda, and I have three children, Matthew, Laura, and Bonnie.

CAINE'S TRAIL

CHAPTER 1

His name was Rubio. Clad in white, loose clothing and a broad-brimmed hat that clung to his head despite the wind, he ran through the bright Texas moonlight, and in his fist, he held a coin.

A hound bayed at the boy; in a nearby pen, chickens fluttered and clucked, disturbed by his passing. In the shadows beneath a porch, a prowling cat lifted its slitted eyes and watched him dart by.

Beside the gently cambered road ahead stood the imposing, solemn house where Garth Kensington slept alone on his big bed, dreaming whatever are the dreams of an old and dying man. In the moon shadow of his mansion stood a much smaller frame house. Rubio ran to the door of that smaller house, paused to catch his breath, and rapped.

Inside, Brice James bolted upright in his bed. The knocking sounded again through the dark house. Brice rose and put on his trousers, slipping galluses over his bare shoulders. He walked down the hallway, looking into the room where his son was just beginning to awaken.

Rubio was about to knock again when Brice opened the door. "Rubio?" Brice said. "What is it?"

"Señor James, there is a man waiting for you at the old tower. He sent me here to tell you to come."

"A man?"

"*Sí*. A tall man. He did not say his name. He is alone."

Brice frowned, intrigued but a little concerned. "The tower," he repeated. "Thank you, Rubio."

The boy flashed a smile brighter than the moon. "He paid me this," he said, holding up his coin, then turned and ran back into the night.

Brice closed the door. His son stood in the hallway.

"Don't go, Pa."

Brice scratched the back of his neck. "It might be important, Keelan. Don't worry; I'll be back safe and sound. You go on back to bed."

The night was chilly, in marked contrast to the sweltering heat of the day. Brice thrust his hands into his jacket pockets as he trudged down the road. He walked with the slight limp that was his ever-present reminder of his part in the failed fight for the Confederacy.

The farther Brice walked, the more uncomfortable he became. He thought of turning back but already saw the dark tower ahead, a stone spire thrusting toward the blue-black sky. The tower was all that remained of a chapel that had been part of an old rancho here. Brice trailed his gaze up its length, seeing the black outline of the old bell in the open belfry at the top—and then a shadow moved across the bell's dark face.

Someone was in the bell tower, watching him.

Brice edgily strode forward. He could not see the figure in the belfry anymore; perhaps he had not seen it at all. The night and the stark old tower could stir numinous imaginings in a man.

It was dark in the base of the tower and deathly silent. Vermin scurried nearby. The moon sailed high above and cast its light through the open door behind Brice.

Brice found a candle in a holder on the wall and lit it. Light spilled onto the stair that spiraled up inside the tower.

"Hello?" he said. No answer came.

Swallowing his fear, he began climbing. Hot wax dripped on his fingers and solidified.

"Hello?"

Still no answer. He continued up, limping more badly now. Through a tiny window in the tower wall, he saw the moonlit expanse of naked Texas landscape. The sight made him feel enclosed. "Is anybody here?"

Near the top, he stopped. The candle's feeble glow lit the shape of a tall man standing at the top of the stairs. He was lean, stood with one leg cocked slightly to the side and appeared to be looking back down at Brice, though Brice could not see his face. The iron bell swung gently in the wind behind the man.

The man's voice was soft but deep. "Hello, brother." Brice dropped the candle; it snuffed out. "Simon!" he exclaimed.

———

"So you were in the Bitterroots all those years," Brice said. "I never knew if you were alive or dead."

"Occasionally, there seemed little difference between the two," Simon Caine said wryly. He was leaning against one of the four stone pillars at the corners of the open belfry, paradoxically looking relaxed but also as tense as a wound clock spring.

"Still your grim view of the world," Brice said. "I recall when people saw you as lighthearted and me as melancholy."

"We've lived different lives. Makes us different men," Simon Caine said. He reached into his pocket and came out with a small cigar. He dug for a match, then seemingly changed his mind. From his perch, he scanned the mesquite flats below. Brice noted it and knew Simon Caine was looking for pursuers. Simon had declined to smoke because the flare of the match might expose him.

"Government still after you, Simon?"

Simon Caine nodded.

"How have you lived?"

"Off the land, mostly. I took a sort of job sometime back, guiding some folks through the mountains. But that didn't work out like it was supposed to. I got to see Jake Armitage again, though. You remember Jake?"

Brice nodded. "How is he?"

"He's dead. Got himself knifed by a young buck."

"Oh."

"You don't seem too sorry."

"It's not that. I just think Jake tended to steer you wrong sometimes."

"You sound as much like a preacher as ever."

"I'm not. I gave it up—just didn't feel right for me, somehow, after I preached Marcus and Nancy's funeral."

Mention of his wife and son's funeral sent an expression of sadness across Caine's angular features. He shifted the subject. "I heard you work for Garth Kensington now. A mighty rich man."

"Not anymore. He's stone-cold broke. There's few who know it yet, but the Kensington empire is about to fall. First Agatha dies, and now this."

"Losing a wife is a hard thing."

"You know she was Garth Kensington's daughter? That's right—I married into the family. She was pretty, sweet as she could be. Bore me a fine son. It was consumption that took her."

"Mighty sorry, James... Brice, I mean. Can't get used to calling you that."

A silent moment passed. Brice asked, "Why did you come here, Simon?"

"A man ought to see his little brother every now and then."

"Even a brother who changes his name to hide his kinship to you?"

Brice watched for Simon's reaction, but if the words stung, Caine didn't show it. "Does your boy know about me?" Caine asked.

Brice shook his head. "I never even told Agatha. She wouldn't have known how to take being the kin of an outlaw."

"And how do you take it? Have you forgiven me yet for —what did you call it? —shaming the family name?"

"It isn't me who has a problem forgiving, Simon. It's you."

"Could you have forgiven the murder of your wife and child? Could you watch a man butcher your kin and then just walk away from it?"

"But you became a butcher yourself. You murdered for murder."

"It was payback. Justice."

"No," Brice said. "It was bushwhacking. Lynching. Riding with the likes of Bloody Bill and Quantrill. That's not justice by any stretch."

The wind made the rusted iron bell hum. "Maybe I shouldn't have come back," Simon said. "I just took a hankering to see you again."

Brice spoke more softly now. "Where are you heading?"

"First to see Drew Strahan. He's hermiting out between Van Horn and the Rio Bravo. After that, Mexico. Got some business there."

Simon Caine swept his brother with a head-to-toe glance as if trying to impress his image into his mind. "Maybe I'll see you again."

Caine went to the stairs.

"Don't come back again, Simon," Brice said.

Caine stopped for a half-second but didn't turn. He descended the stairs. Brice remained in the tower for a few minutes, fighting an inner struggle. Suddenly he bolted down the stairs as best his bad leg would let him.

"Simon!"

He ran out of the dark tower into the moonlight.

"Simon!"

But there was no one there.

———

"A drunk?" Keelan said quizzically. "Why would a drunk send for you in the middle of the night, Pa?"

"It's somebody I knew back in the war," Brice said, sitting on the side of the bed and pulling off his boots. He was glad to have an excuse not to look into his son's face while he lied. "Bill Rawlins is his name. He wanted money. I gave him what I had in my pocket, and he left. Now you go back to bed."

For Brice, rest was fitful and fleeting. An hour after he lay down, he still was awake and restless.

Why had Simon come back after all this time, bringing old memories and feelings that disturbed him?

Maybe it was because Simon Caine and bad times like these always seemed cojoined in the life of Brice James, known in his earlier days as James Brice Caine.

Brice rolled over, brooding. A few minutes later, he, at last, fell asleep.

———

Years in the Bitterroot Mountains had sharpened Simon Caine's senses. He felt the rider long before he heard him, and he heard him long before he saw him. Caine veered his Appaloosa into the roadside rocks. There he waited.

Down the moonlit road, the rider came. Broad, long-haired, he was fat and heavy in the saddle; his bay's back sagged like the middle of a worn-out bed tick.

Another greasy gunman. Maybe a border bandit or a bounty hunter. Caine sat silently in the darkness. The rider passed. Then Caine's Appaloosa snorted.

The rider halted, peering into the rocks. His hand moved toward his pistol.

Caine felt a familiar tensing of his shoulders and quickening of his pulse. He felt the Navy Colt in its holster the way he could feel his feet in his boots.

But the fat rider turned away, touching rowels to flanks, and started down the road again. Caine held his breath until he was gone, then slumped for a moment, letting the tension drain from him.

He could have taken the man easily, but he was glad he had not had to. He was weary of killing and of running—the two things that had dominated his life since the long-ago day a drunken Union officer named Robert Montrose had murdered his family back in the Calfkiller Valley in Tennessee.

Caine emerged onto the road again and headed south. He hadn't slept for sixteen hours, yet he didn't feel tired. Nervous tension from the meeting with Brice, he figured—plus an intuitive sense of danger.

Caine chewed a cigar, unwilling to light it. He was looking forward to the morning when he could pull into some shady recess and sleep.

He traveled a mile and entered a region of low but rugged hills dotted with wild shrubs. When he emerged onto the road on the other side, three men, all mounted and in a line, faced him. He stopped. Six eyes bored into him in studied silence.

"Howdy, Simon Caine," said the one in the middle.

Caine shifted his shoulders but otherwise did not react at all.

"I said howdy."

"I'm afraid you've mistook me for somebody else," Caine said. "My name's Robert Cole."

"Not only a sniping *pistolero,* but a liar, too," the man said. "You're coming with us, Caine. It don't matter to me whether it's your rump or your belly in the saddle."

"Let me pass," Caine said.

"No," said the man in the middle as he drew his pistol.

CHAPTER 2

K eelan James ate silently, watching his grandfather from the corner of his eye. Garth Kensington, humped over in his wheelchair, was talking to a whispering, gesturing employee, and the old man was apparently displeased by whatever the employee was saying. Kensington's heavy brows writhed over his gray eyes like twin caterpillars.

At last, Kensington impatiently waved the employee out with his thin white hand.

The dining room door opened, and Brice entered, baggy eyes evidencing his lack of sleep. He dropped heavily into a chair beside Keelan. A black woman built like a walking cookstove bustled in with a steaming china pot and poured Brice a cup of coffee, for which he muttered thanks.

Kensington's voice was an almost falsetto squeak as he said, "Brice, there were three men killed last night, not two miles from here. Dead on the road, shot through the head. Hoofmarks showed there was only one other man there, so it must have been him that killed them. Three men gunned down by one."

Brice closed his eyes. *Simon, you carry death wherever you go.*

Kensington muttered something about dangerous times and trouble a-brewing and how it probably had something to do with that sorry desert bandit Cato Blake, all the while with knife and fork tremblingly slicing his four fried eggs into a yellow-white hash. Keelan looked away, hating to see his grandfather in his dotage. The boy sensed the old man must die soon, and that scared him. Losing his mother had ingrained in him a hatred of death.

The maid brought in Brice's plate. She set it before him and exited, but he pushed it away as the kitchen door wheezed shut behind her.

"It's getting so a man can't feel safe in his own home," Kensington muttered in his tremulous voice. He looked at Brice. "You look puny."

"Didn't sleep well," Brice said irritably.

"Drink some coffee, then. You got a pile of ledgers to go over."

"I'll drink coffee if I want it," Brice snapped. He rose and stalked out of the room. Keelan watched him, his eyes big, then turned to his grandfather, wondering how the old man would react to Brice's outburst.

But Kensington had not even noticed it. He was eating, smacking his lips loudly as little dribbles of egg leaked onto his chin.

Outside, Brice stood on the lower porch of the big house, taking in without enjoyment a magnificent view of this section of West Texas that had come to be known as Kensington, after the ranch of which this house was the headquarters. The house itself, when viewed from out on the plains, was no less than splendid. Its three stories rose from the barren landscape like a mirage. With its ginger breaded columns and two-level balcony porches, the edifice suggested a steamboat sailing across the land on shimmering waves of rising heat.

Brice missed Agatha badly at this moment. Life was so miserably uncertain right now: the Kensington financial empire in ruin, and Garth himself ready to die, leaving Brice to deal with the hopeless finances of the estate. And now, to top it off, Simon had come back again, unwelcome and disturbing as ever.

Brice chuckled mirthlessly. Fate and circumstances were imps too cruelly mischievous for him to understand. He turned and limped back into the house, feeling terribly depressed.

With great effort, Garth Kensington rolled his squeaking wheelchair through his house. Often he had to stop and cough, and every spasm wrenched and hurt.

One of his servants, a handsome and powerfully built black man of about twenty, approached. "Let me help you, Mr. Kensington." The young man took the grips of the chair. "Where to, sir?"

"The office, Orion."

Orion pushed the chair along. Kensington leaned back, resting from his prior exertion. Though he would never thank Orion, Kensington was grateful for his help. Orion was the son of Tandy Jones, who had once been Kensington's slave but now was his servant—a special one, for his long association with Kensington had carved him a notch in the family structure itself. Tandy's late wife had raised Kensington's daughter Agatha after Agatha's mother had died from consumption. When that same disease had finally claimed Agatha herself, Tandy had felt the loss almost as much as Garth and Brice. He sang a dirge over her grave when they buried her.

Orion and Garth reached the batwings that hung in the doorway of the old parlor that housed Kensington's messy office. Orion pushed the wheelchair through, and the batwings flapped closed behind him, shuddering on their hinges.

"Anything else, Mr. Kensington?"

"No, Orion. This is fine."

"Just call if you need me." Orion turned and left.

Brice was seated at a small corner table with ledgers and papers before him. His expression was somber. Kensington saw it and wilted a little farther down into his chair.

"Bad?"

"It's worse every time I go over it," Brice said.

Kensington was quiet for a moment. "Then go over it again," he said. "There's got to be something we can do."

"But I've looked at it ten dozen times already."

"Make it ten dozen and one," Kensington snapped. He coughed painfully, wheeled his chair around, and left.

Brice felt deflated and tense. He rose and went to the window. It seemed ridiculous to dig further into Kensington's records of ruin. At one time, a brilliant financier who had made a fortune in cattle, horses, and mining, Kensington had in the past five years boxed himself into a monetary prison with chancy investments Brice and others had warned him against. Any number-wrangler in the nation could investigate Kensington's books, and the conclusion would be the same: bankruptcy.

A small figure darted across the yard toward the house. Brice smiled and opened the window. He leaned out, his hands on the sill.

"Hello, Keelan," he said.

The boy grinned. His exuberance was to Brice a welcome contrast to the darkness of this closed room and the oppressive futility of this work.

"Tandy's taking me for another ride on the buckboard,"

Keelan said. "Way out on the back road. You want to come, Pa?"

"I wish I could," Brice said, and he meant it. "Your grandfather wants me to go over his books again."

"Oh," Keelan said. Books and business were alien to him, unrealities belonging to a grown-up world. "We're going right up along the creek, too."

Brice smiled. In Keelan's bright face, he saw the only remaining incarnation of his late wife, and that both pleased and saddened him. "Have a good time," Brice said.

"I will, Pa."

Keelan ran lightly across the yard toward the adobe carriage house where Tandy and the buckboard awaited. Brice faltered for a moment, almost yelling after Keelan to wait; he would come along after all. But from somewhere in the dark belly of the house, he heard Garth Kensington's rattling cough and was reminded again of his duty.

Sadly, he turned away from the window as Tandy and Keelan clattered off in a cloud of dust down the road that led to a tree-lined creek a mile to the south.

———

J. W. Fadden, a man, seemingly made of wire and whiskers, sat astride his old gelding and rolled a cigarette. Before him, stretched rolling dun-colored land, its vegetation of waist-high mesquite spaced like hairs on the head of a balding man. Fadden was staring at Kensington's mansion, an architectural majesty encircled by barns and stables like a king surrounded by attendants. Even from this far away, Fadden could smell the money this place represented—and it was a smell he liked.

Two men also mounted were with him. One of them, a thin Mexican, pointed and said, "Look. He's coming."

A rider was approaching; he was a dark speck growing

larger with a dust cloud trailing behind. Fadden and his partners watched and waited until the rider reached them.

The rider sagged like an overstuffed feed bag over both sides
of his saddle. He had been blond once; now, his hair was color-
less. A ragged mustache blanketed his upper lip and hung over
his mouth so that when he raised his dirty bandana to wipe the
dust from his lips, he had to lift the mustache out of the way.

"They're hooking up the buckboard right now," the
newcomer said. "Just the boy and Tandy the old nigger. You
cut south a mile, fast as you can go, and you can catch 'em
right at the creek."

"Mighty fine, Mr. Scruggs." Fadden produced an envelope and handed it to the man. "Count it if you want. It's all
there."

Hosea Scruggs smiled. His breath wheezed deep in his
chest. "I trust you."

He put the envelope beneath his shirt and touched his
hat. He spurred his horse with his small Mexican spurs and
galloped back toward the Kensington ranch.

The Mexican lifted a scope-mounted sniper's rifle from
its saddle holster. "Let it be, Juan," Fadden said. "The shot
might draw attention."

"But Seahorn said—"

"Seahorn ain't here. We'll do it my way. Come on,
gentlemen. Let's head for that creek."

———

The buckboard clattered along the back road. Tandy's
untrained baritone rang out an old drinking song, making
Keelan laugh because he knew he wasn't supposed to hear
songs like that. But Tandy seldom followed the rules—one of
the things that made Keelan love him so.

Tandy also drove the buckboard too fast, which

impressed Keelan even more. The fast rides always seemed daring and exhilarating to the boy, and today's was even better than usual.

They made a turn and passed a crossroads, then came to a rainwater-filled waterhole surrounded by grasses and mesquite. The hole was fed by a tiny creek a man could step across without a strain, but it provided good water for livestock except in the driest times. They heard the creek ahead, splashing along through a brake of cottonwoods that towered above the scrub brush.

They entered the cool, shaded brake. The buckboard clattered along, but suddenly Tandy reined back on the horses.

A downed tree blocked the road just ahead. It was an old deadfall that layed across the road itself now, but it had lain in the brake beside the road for months.

"How did that get there, Tandy?" Keelan asked.

The old black man shook his head. He reached to the buckboard floor and picked up the shotgun, then descended from his seat.

"Why are you getting that, Tandy?"

"You just stay put and keep quiet, Keelan."

Three riders emerged from the brake, leading one saddled but riderless horse. They positioned themselves on the road near the dead fallen cottonwood. All three looked like dusty saddle bums with dirt-stained, whiskered faces. One stayed slightly ahead of the other two; he was as filthy as his companions but had an air that marked him as their leader.

J. W. Fadden nodded at Tandy and said, "Howdy there, Toby. Got you a problem?"

"My name ain't Toby."

Fadden smiled. "Your kind's all Toby to me, and you'd best remember how to call a man sir," he said. Then Fadden looked at Keelan, almost hungrily. He touched his hat. "Hello, boy."

Keelan stared back unresponsively. Tandy remained firmly planted, the shotgun nearly horizontal before him, ready to be swung up and fired.

Tandy said to Keelan, "We'll be heading back."

"No, Toby, you won't," Fadden said. "Not until I'm ready for you too."

Keelan spoke up bravely: "You're on my grandpa's land, and he wouldn't want you talking that way to Tandy."

"Really? He likes the nigger, huh? Then I'd say this right here is really going to rile his guts." Fadden deftly pulled his pistol and fired a shot through Tandy's stomach.

But Tandy, at the last moment, had seen what was coming, and he fired off one barrel of the shotgun in tandem with Fadden's shot. Tandy's shot missed Fadden but squarely hit Juan, the Mexican, in the chest. Juan shrieked and fell from his horse.

Tandy was kicked back by the joint impact of Fadden's bullet and the recoil of the shotgun. He fell supine, moved in the dirt, then was still. Fadden turned the pistol on Keelan, who sat with his mouth open in horror.

"Get down from there, boy. The extra horse is for you."

Keelan climbed down from the seat, then ran as hard as he could away from the riders. Fadden spurred his horse forward, reached Keelan, then kicked him to the earth with the heel of his boot.

He dropped from the saddle, swept the boy up, and carried him to the reserved horse. He deposited him there, and Keelan did not resist, for he saw it would do him no good.

"Boy, I'm sorry about your nigger friend, but he's the one who came out with the shotgun. You saw that yourself."

The other rider, who had dispassionately been watching the wounded Mexican writhe in the dirt until he was still, came to the side of the buckboard. "Contero's dead," he said.

"Leave him lying," Fadden responded. "The Alianza's loss is the buzzards' gain."

Suddenly Keelan grasped the reins, shouted, and jarred his horse into motion. But Fadden's partner got in front of him and blocked the horse.

"Boy, you just ain't cooperative. Now we got to tie you up," Fadden said.

Keelan tried not to cry as Fadden's partner roughly bound his hands to the saddlehorn with a rawhide strap. Meanwhile, Fadden rode over to Tandy's body and dismounted. He knelt beside the still form, surprised to see Tandy's eyes slowly open and roll over to look blankly at him.

"You gave it a good try, nigger. Now I got one last job for you. You hang on to this," he said, reaching into his pocket and pulling out an envelope. "If you can't get back to the house, just keep it in your paw. They'll find it when they scoop up your corpse. Bye now."

Fadden stood and mounted again. By now, Keelan was well bound, and the other man had tied Juan Contero's horse at the back of Keelan's. "That ought to keep you from running off," the man said with satisfaction.

Fadden nodded his approval. "Mighty fine, then. Let's head to Serveto."

CHAPTER 3

"Tried to stop them... tried to stop them," Tandy said again and again as he lay dying. That he had made it back to the ranch house at all was remarkable, for his wound was severe, and by the time he had somehow driven the buckboard back to the house, its seat was drenched in gore.

Orion knelt by his father's bed, holding the bloody hand, tears streaming down Orion's face. "Tried to stop them," Tandy said again. He turned his face toward the wall, muttered a word in Spanish, and died.

Orion buried his face in the covers.

Brice, standing behind him, bowed his head. He still held the bloodstained note Tandy had brought home with him. All this was too much for Brice to accept—Tandy gunned down, Keelan kidnapped. And upstairs, Garth Kensington himself lay ready to die. Brice had told Kensington of the kidnapping as gently as he could, but it had struck down the old man like a hard kick from a mule. Now Brice did not expect his father-in-law ever to rise from his bed again.

Brice pulled the sheet over Tandy's face and touched Orion's shoulder. "I'm sorry," he said. He turned and walked out of the room, down the stairs, and into Kensington's office.

There he opened and read again the ransom note, written in a scrawled hand:

"Garth Kensington, we got your grandson. For one-quarter of a million dollars, you can have him back agin. Send it under a white flag by way of his pa and no other to the Serveto Mission within twelve days from now and let there be no rangers and no law at all, or the boy will be kilt at once. This is no bluff. Bring the cash money to Serveto and wait with no trickery and we will pick it up and give you back the boy safe. Send good cash money, and we say agin, let there be no law."

"Serveto," Brice said to himself. He went to the fireplace and burned the note.

The door opened. It was Felipe Espego, Kensington's gardener.

"Señor James," Felipe said, "there is a man outside to see Señor Kensington about cattle. What should I tell him?"

Blast, Brice thought. There could be no worse time for an outsider to arrive. "Tell him Mr. Kensington is ill. Tell him he has a disease that can be spread, and he has to be kept away from everyone until he is well. If he asks for me, say I am away, and let him leave a note. Tell him anything that will get him away from here and do the same with everyone else who comes until I tell you otherwise."

"Sí, *Señor.*" The servant withdrew.

Outside, the night shouldered down against the horizon.

———

They dug Tandy's grave by moonlight and buried him in a pine box.

At the graveside, Brice looked up at the lighted window beyond which Garth Kensington lay on his deathbed and pondered the peculiar twists of life: a man once wealthy and envied, with abundant power at his command, now lay near death without enough money to pay even a fraction of the ransom demand for his own grandson. The kidnappers, of course, could not know that; they doubtlessly believed Kensington could pull a quarter of a million dollars from his back pocket.

That was why Brice mentally noted; it was essential to keep Kensington's financial and physical conditions secret. The kidnappers must have no hint that anything was amiss in the Kensington dynasty, or else they might abort their plans and kill Keelan.

Brice and the little cluster of servants buried Tandy, prayed over the grave, then returned to the house. The servants were silent and tense; once inside, they looked at Brice, waiting for direction.

The meagerness of the group of servants struck Brice. Only five of them. At one time, Kensington had kept a dozen servants bustling around his estate, ordering them here and there like a gruff straw boss. No more. His crew of cow-punchers was likewise reduced, though so far, Brice and Kensington had been able to explain that away without raising substantial suspicions of financial difficulties. The process of going broke, Brice had learned, makes men into very clever liars.

Brice poured a glass of wine for each servant. He told them all to sit in the drawing room and pacing before them with his uneven gait; he addressed them.

"For the sake of my son's life, I'm counting on your silence about all of this for now," he said. "So far, no one outside those of us in this room knows what has happened, and it must stay that way. The story must be that Mr. Kensington is sick and in isolation, but in no way can we allow even the suspicion he is in danger of his life.

"The kidnapping itself must be kept secret, especially

from the law. I have read the ransom note and destroyed it. I know what it demands and how I have to respond. It requires me to leave here for a time. That means these secrets are in your hands. Felipe, I entrust this into your charge for the sake of Keelan."

Felipe nodded, then asked, "Is the ransom large? Will you pay it?"

Brice's throat went dry. He felt a strange urge, to tell the truth. Instead, he nodded and lied again. "I will pay the ransom. It is large, but we can cover the cost of it."

"Then you will need help to deliver it—guards, gunmen to protect you," Orion Jones said.

"So it would seem. Unfortunately, the kidnappers have not allowed that option."

"But if even a rumor gets out about this, somebody's going to try to steal this ransom from you before it can be delivered."

"I am aware of that. That is why there must be no rumors. None at all. You understand?"

"*Sí*, Señor Brice. We do. But what of you? How can you do this alone?"

Brice turned his back to them. He thought, if I can ride fast enough if I can find Simon, then I won't be alone, God willing.

When Simon Caine first saw Drew Strahan, he realized the man hadn't lost any of his impressive girth since the war. In fact, Strahan was significantly bigger than before. Caine had to squelch a smile as he watched Strahan spread himself like a blob of half-melted butter across the bench against a wall of his lonely adobe dwelling.

"Most times, it's hotter than perdition down here, Simon. Upwards of a hunert in the day, and then cold at night. Ain't right. Something wrong about this here country."

"Then why do you stay?" Caine asked.

Strahan swatted a fly on his neck, then studied the insect's remains on the fleshy heel of his hand. "Because it's a good country in other ways," he said. "If a man puts up with a few scorpions and rattlers, minds his own business, stay halfway honest, and don't bother the rangers or the bandidos, nobody bothers him much, neither. That's been my experience, leastways."

Strahan's house mirrored the crude and slapdash ways of its owner. The adobe structure was dimly lit, dust-filled, malodorous—yet it seemed a place where a man was welcome, where he could relax in safety and calm. A sanctuary such as Caine seldom found.

Strahan seemed an unlikely West Texas frontier dweller, with his thoroughly Alabamian accent and his lazy style of living. The broad-jowled, big-lipped man had been a Confederate irregular and sometime bushwhacker during the war and had come to Texas when it all was over.

Strahan stretched and scratched like an old hound and asked, "Where you heading, Simon?"

"Serveto. I got wind that somebody there was asking for me."

Strahan's expression became serious. "Neal Seahorn?"

"So I was told. For years I hear Seahorn is dead, then comes this letter. Intrigued me a little. I suppose that was one of about three things that led me down here."

"What are the other two?"

"Seeing you is one. The other is my brother, James. Calls himself Brice James now and lives at the Kensington spread up to the north. Him being my brother is a secret, by the way, so don't talk of it. He's always been ashamed of being linked to an old outlaw like me. And to tell you the truth, when I looked him up, he wasn't too happy to see me. But I don't want to cause him no trouble."

"That's hard, having your own kin turn on you. But I want to know more about Seahorn. How'd you hear he was looking for you?"

"It was all a bit peculiar, Drew. I was staying in a boarding house up in Wichita, calling myself Bobert Cole like I sometimes do. I'd just come off a few odd jobs and had a little money. Then I got a letter, addressed to Bobert Cole, and it's from Seahorn. What I can't figure is how Seahorn knew my false name and where to find me."

Strahan pursed his thick lips. "What I can't figure is why you'd come answering it. Have you forgotten what Seahorn did to us at Murfreesboro?"

"We never really knew he'd done it, Drew. I'm still not convinced of it."

Strahan snorted. "Well, I am. It was his job to guard for us, but he just kept quiet and let the bluebellies ride in. I believe they paid him off. We almost got killed because of him."

"He said they knocked him in the head."

"I never saw no lumps. Did you?"

"No. But don't forget, Drew—Neal Seahorn nearly took a bullet intended for me later on. I feel like I owe him at least a meeting to hear him out. He says he's going to offer me some kind of job."

"Steer clear of Seahorn, Simon. He's not to be trusted. Besides, he's tied into something big and loco."

"What do you mean?"

"I mean big crime with big connections. And folks who won't let old wars die."

Simon smiled. "That's clear as black coffee, Drew."

"Simon, think for a minute. You just now were wondering how Seahorn knew where to get that letter to you. Him in Mexico, you in Kansas—but still he traced you down. And I know how: through connections, he's got to an organization with eyes and ears all over the country. I don't know all that much about it except it's called the Alianza and is led by people with lots of money and lots more old grudges. Old Confederate supporters who never forgave the bluebellies for beating us and who figure they have the right to gouge what they can out of them now."

"Is Seahorn the leader of this—what did you call it?"

"Alianza. Mex talk for 'alliance.' Seahorn's just one grain in the powder keg. The thing is huge, Simon. I hear it goes right into the government itself. We know it was big enough to track down Simon Caine when the bluebelly government never could. Chew that over for a while before you ride in to see Seahorn."

"How do you know so much about it, Drew? You involved?"

"No, sir. I just got ears that are a little too big and hear a little too well. I'm close enough to Serveto to hear the whispers." He leaned forward. "Steer clear, Simon. When you talk Alianza, you're talking train robberies, bank robberies, kidnapping, extortion. Maybe even assassinations. You're about to get tangled up in something too loco to handle."

"Hang it, Drew. I've dodged the government and the law for years. I can hold my own. Besides, I can always just hear Seahorn out and tell him no thanks."

"Maybe not. The Alianza is like a spiderweb: touch it, and you're stuck. Anyone who learns about it is a threat unless he's part of it. So it's best not to hear anything."

"You've obviously heard about it, Drew. And nobody's slit your throat for it."

"That's because I play dumb real well. I don't repeat what I hear—except to an old friend I'm trying to keep out of trouble."

Caine thought it over. "I got to at least hear him out, Drew. I owe Neal Seahorn that much."

Strahan nodded balefully. "All right. Do what you want, Simon. You always were too stubborn to reason with. Just remember that old Drew Strahan warned you."

"That I will."

———

The top rim of the rising sun had just edged the horizon in fire when Brice put boot in the stirrup and slung himself into the saddle of Kensington's best gelding. Booted at his thigh was a gleaming 1873 Winchester rifle, and high on his right hip hung an 1878 Colt single-action Army revolver. His saddlebags were laden with provisions, and he had just finished securing the pack on a second horse he would take with him.

Brice made a final check outside the stable and mounted. He looked at the house, then across the wide plains, where the wind already was stirring up clouds of dust.

Brice was about to ride away when someone called his name. He turned.

Orion Jones walked up to him.

"Don't go just yet. I ain't quite ready."

"Ready for what?"

"I'm going with you."

Brice firmly shook his head. "No, you're not. It's my boy they kidnapped and my problem."

"And it was my father they shot down like a dog."

"I know that. But what I got to do, I got to do alone."

Orion eyed the bundle on the packhorse's back, obviously thinking it contained money. "You go alone with that, and you'll be killed."

Brice risked a little honesty. "I don't plan to be alone for long. There's a man who can help me—if he will. The best man I can think of if this thing comes down to shooting and killing. Which it will."

"Who is it?"

"Can't say."

Orion was silent a moment, his mind working. The perception evidenced by his next question surprised Brice.

"Mr. Brice, are you planning to get Keelan back without paying the ransom?"

Brice looked at the handsome black face. "Orion, can you keep one more secret?"

"You know I can."

"There is no ransom. Mr. Kensington is broke. Dead broke. If I get Keelan back, it will have to be through sneaking him out or shooting him out of Serveto."

"Serveto? That's where they took him?"

"Apparently so."

Orion whistled in awe. "I've heard whispers lately—they say the old Serveto Mission's occupied again. Bad men. Really bad."

"I've heard the same. I got to go. Don't follow me. You hear?"

Brice was about to ride away, but he stopped. "Orion, right before he died, Tandy said something I couldn't quite make out. Sounded Spanish—"

"I remember. It was *ali-* something. *Alienza,* maybe. Or *Alianza.*"

"*Alianza.* I wonder why Tandy would say that?"

"I don't know."

Brice turned the gelding and loped off. Orion watched him diminish into the scrubby undergrowth that stretched as far as he could see.

"Serveto," Orion said to himself. He turned and walked back toward the house.

CHAPTER 4

Puerta de Serveto was a narrow gap in limestone walls beyond which stood the old Serveto Mission and presidio. The former was a long-abandoned fortress of the Catholic faith, the latter a fortress for an armed garrison established to protect the mission. Together, the mission and presidio were a crucible in which the culture and religion of New Spain had been protected and nurtured a century before.

Caine was impressed by the size of the old compound. Except for its distinctly Spanish architecture, it reminded him of pictures he had seen in his boyhood of ancient European castles surrounded by the hovels of peasants.

He viewed the scene as he descended from the natural rock gateway. The mission and the presidio had been separate but now were joined by a third, middle section made of log and stone walls. The entire tripartite enclosure stood in the center of town; if town, this jumble of crude huts could be called. Numerous buildings were visible over the top of the wall—a virtual town within the town. Somewhere inside this old enclosure, Caine expected to find Neal Seahorn.

Caine rode through the farrago of poor huts that

surrounded Serveto, drawing stares from hollow-eyed women and children in the dirt yards and unpaved streets. He wondered who these people were and how they managed to eke out a living in this destitute place.

He stopped at a water trough to let his horse refresh itself. An old woman was cranking a windlass at a nearby well. He asked her for a drink, and she handed him the bucket.

The water was cool. He let the water run across his beard and down his neck, soaking his shirt.

He handed the bucket back to the woman, then pointed at the mission. "Seahorn?" he asked.

The woman's eyes grew wide, and she quickly turned away. It was as good as an answer—better, for it told Caine something about Seahorn beyond confirming where he could be found. It told him that the people outside the walls were afraid of the man.

Caine mounted and rode toward the front gate of the mission. Atop the wall, a sentry wearing a sombrero and bandolier watched him intently. The brim of the man's sombrero moved in the hot breeze as he paced.

The front gate was closed and barred, so Caine rode to a spot nearby, dismounted, and sat down in the shade of a tree. A boy selling melons passed; Caine bought a slice and ate it. Tilting his hat down over his forehead, he dozed.

"*Señor*"

He lifted his hat. A tall Mexican stood above him. Dressed finely, the man was lean and well-groomed. His mustache was trimmed to a thin line above his straight lips. His skin was very brown, his hair curly and closely cropped.

"Señor Caine, I am Ramon Fernandez. I saw you from the east wall. We have been expecting you."

"You're with Seahorn?"

"*Sí.* You will accompany me inside?"

The massive gate opened to them, and they passed

through, Caine leading his Appaloosa. He wrinkled his nose at the crazy mix of stenches that struck him inside the enclosure: horse and chicken dung, molds, dust, hay, meat, and cookstove smoke heavy with the smell of hot Mexican spices.

Within the enclosure stood dirty adobe buildings with *vigas* jutting in a row above low doorways, *ristras* of chili peppers hanging from them in scarlet strings. Here and there, around the walls, stood pens filled with livestock or chickens that pecked the dusty ground. Lazy dogs roamed about.

The men of Serveto, though, were what drew Caine's attention most. They were a mix of Anglos, Mexicans, Indians, and half-breeds, and all looked seedy and dangerous. They were armed to a man.

"What kind of place is this?" Caine asked as they meandered through the bustle.

"Once a place of religion. Now a place of something very different," Ramon said. "For more than a hundred years, these walls have stood here. It is a good place for Neal Seahorn's purpose."

"Which is?"

Ramon smiled. His teeth were white and straight. "I speak too much. You will know soon enough."

"Where does Seahorn live?"

Ramon pointed toward a building in the center of the plaza. It probably had been the quarters of priests at some time past, Caine guessed. Two wide double doors stood open at the building's base. Two levels of balconies stretched across its front, with full-length, arch-topped windows leading out to them through the stone wall.

"Behind the center window is Seahorn's quarters. I suspect he watches us from there even now."

"Why doesn't he come down to meet me?"

"Seahorn seldom leaves his chambers now. He has

reasons, I suppose. You will meet him later in those chambers."

"Who are all the folk here?"

"These within the walls are the followers of Neal Seahorn and their families, if they have them. Many of those outside the walls fear those of us in here, but they come to us for the protection we offer."

"Protection from what? The law?"

"You are perceptive, Señor Caine. Come now. It is not yet time for you to go to Seahorn. He wishes to meet you under his own circumstances. So we will go now and enjoy a drink, eh?"

They went to a cantina in a back corner of the enclosure. Caine tethered his horse in the shade of a heat-stunted tree, and he and Ramon walked inside. Cool and rather dark, the cantina was clean and pleasant. They found a corner table.

"How long have you worked for Seahorn, Ramon?" Caine asked when they had tequila in hand.

Ramon shook his head. "I do not work for any man but myself," he said. "I merely sell my services to whoever pays me the price I demand. At the moment, that is Neal Seahorn."

"Your services?"

Ramon nodded and tapped the butt of his pistol with a long forefinger. Caine had figured as much.

"So when will Seahorn be ready to see me?" Caine asked.

"Tonight, *amigo*. For now, let us drink."

———

His hair was gray as gun steel, his eyes sparkling blue. Neal Seahorn still had the muscled build of a much younger man, but his shoulders were beginning to stoop, and in his blue eyes was a hint of deep weariness.

He stood in the arch-topped window of his quarters,

looking out over the balcony to the enclosed plaza. A crescent rim of the declining sun shone over the wall, casting an orange glow and long shadows across the plaza. A sentry paced below, and a man with a bottle weaved and staggered across the plaza, singing loudly in Spanish.

Seahorn turned away from the window and swept his eyes across his lamplit room.

Quite a contrast it was to the squalor outside. There were paintings on the wall, a fine oak sideboard, two overstuffed chairs, a long table spread with food—roast duck, boiled potatoes, rice, fresh bread—American dishes, not the over-spiced Mexican swill Seahorn had reluctantly become accustomed to since coming to Serveto more than a year ago. This was a special meal for a special guest.

Seahorn rubbed his hands together, then smiled self consciously. He was surprisingly tense. It had been many years since he had seen Simon Caine, and the prospect of meeting him made him nervous.

To relax himself, he poured a glass of wine and sat down. A tall clock in the corner ticked off two more minutes. There was a knock on the door. Seahorn quickly drained off his glass.

"Enter," he called.

The door swung open. Ramon stood in the center of the doorway, his ready smile flashing. Caine was behind him, indistinct in the shadows. Seahorn waved them inside.

"Simon," Seahorn said. "Too many years since I've seen you, my friend."

Caine nodded. His unreadable eyes evaluated Seahorn head to toe. "You haven't changed much," Caine said succinctly.

Seahorn smiled. "You flatter me. The years leave tracks on us all. But you look well; you always were a handsome man, whether you realized it or not."

"Never gave it any thought."

Seahorn waved his hand toward the table. "In your honor, Simon. A meal I think you will appreciate. We have important things to discuss, and discussion is better when the belly is full." He turned to Ramon. "Thank you, my friend."

Ramon departed. Caine took off his hat. His eye fell on Seahorn's empty wineglass.

"A drink for you, Simon? Some wine? Tequila?"

"Got whiskey?"

"I should have remembered—Simon Caine relishes good whiskey." Seahorn took a bottle from a cabinet and poured Caine an amber-colored shot. He took more wine for himself, then he and Caine talked quietly and drank. Seahorn was as tense as Caine was calm. After a few minutes and another drink, they sat down to eat.

The meal was as good as it looked. Caine was ravenous and ate heartily. Seahorn ate with tense dignity, often dabbing his napkin on his lips. A Mexican girl came in and out several times, carrying in full bowls, carrying out empty ones.

"I heard you were shot down by *federates* in Chihuahua, Neal," Caine said.

"It was a widespread story and as useful as it was false. I went away for many years. Just vanished. I fell in with a wise old Mexican man I met in a cantina near El Paso, Old Pablo, he called himself—and for years we rode together. He virtually became my father. Then other things just drew me away."

"Old Pablo lives alone now down near the bend of the Rio Bravo. Someday I'll go back and get him, take him somewhere far from this country, and give him the kind of last days every man ought to have."

The conversation drifted to the war. Seahorn spoke of it like a man talking of a lost-but-fondly-remembered lover. At last, Caine, tired of it all, sat back in his chair and looked Seahorn squarely in the eye.

"What do you want with me, Neal?"

Seahorn dabbed his lips again and poured himself another glass of wine. He stood and walked to the window with his back to Caine.

"Do you often think of the war, Simon?"

It seemed a foolish question, and Caine did not answer foolish questions.

"I know you do," Seahorn went on. "You and I will never forget those days. Neither will many others. But there are those of us who remember more and more deeply, eh? Who never forget and never turn away."

"What's your point?"

Seahorn turned. His expression was more intense than before as if a mask had been removed. He suddenly was more like the Neal Seahorn Caine had known during the old bush-whacking days. It was a funny thing: Caine recalled only now how obsessive Seahorn had been at times, how reckless.

"Have you ever heard of the Alianza, Simon?"

"A whisper or two."

Seahorn sat down at the table again and leaned forward. "The war is over, Simon. I know that. But it is a fire that still smolders. And even a smoldering fire can cast off a few sparks, eh? Maybe even enough to burn those who wander too close. That's what the Alianza is all about."

"I don't know what you're talking about."

"Then hear me out for a moment. Let me describe the Alianza. It... we... are a secret group. We talk little of ourselves, and there are many who disbelieve in us. And that is fine, for it makes what we do all the easier."

"And what is that?"

"The bluebelly government would call it crime. The Alianza calls it the due of those who lost a war they should have won. The Alianza believes that even a snake that is trodden upon can at least bite the heel of the treader. That is what we're doing: biting the heel of the Yankee government. In the process, we are taking all we can from its corrupt system—its banks, its trains, its freight lines. We of the Alianza are from the bluebelly viewpoint organized criminals — thieves, counterfeiters, extortionists, kidnappers. From our own viewpoint, we are merely taking, in whatever way we can, the good life that was wrongly denied us at Appomattox."

"This whole fortress, all these men—they are part of the Alianza?"

"A small part of it. A few ants in a hill bigger than you might imagine. I work for the Alianza, generate money for it, hire men like those around me—and it, in turn, supports me. Quite well."

"Was it the Alianza who found me for you?"

"Yes. At my request."

"So here I am. What do you want of me?"

"To join me. Become my right hand. It will be lucrative — that I promise. A way I can repay you—"

"Repay?"

Seahorn's eyes flickered down, then back up. "Yes. For what happened in Murfreesboro."

Caine understood. "So it's true—you really did let those bluebellies through?"

"Yes. But I wasn't paid off, no matter what you may have been told. It was fear, Simon. I admit that freely. For fear of my own life, I hid when they passed. I couldn't have stopped them. They would have killed me."

"They almost did kill me. And Jake Armitage and Drew Strahan, too."

"Don't you think I know that? The guilt of it will always haunt me."

"Maybe so, but I can't believe that after all this time, the only reason you've called me is to even up an old debt. What else do you want from me?"

Seahorn licked lips that had suddenly gone dry. "I want your gun. Your reputation. Your name linked with mine."

"Why?"

Seahorn glanced at the door through which Ramon had departed. "Because I can't trust them anymore. They're turning against me."

"Who?"

"My men. All of them. I'm the captain of a ship of mutineers." Caine noted that Seahorn was actually trembling.

Seahorn went on. "It's not just the men I'm concerned about. It's the Alianza itself. It's turning on me, too."

"Why?"

"I think they're beginning to believe I'm stealing from them. They think I'm skimming off more than my percentage."

"Are you?"

Seahorn forced a chuckle. "What does that matter? The point is they believe I am. I feel them turning against me on one side while my own men whisper about the wealth I'm supposedly hiding. It's becoming a nightmare, and I admit I'm scared."

"And you want me to join your nightmare?"

"You don't understand. With you with me, it would be different. People stand in awe of you, Simon. The men here see you as invulnerable, and they respect you. The Alianza would respect you, too. With you beside me, they would leave me—us—alone. You would be a cork in the bottleneck, keeping things peaceful for a bit longer. And then, very soon, we will simply disappear—as very wealthy men. All I need is your presence for a few days until a very large ransom arrives. Part is to go to me, part to the Alianza. But..."

Caine finished for him. "But you really plan to keep it all for yourself."

"And for you if you'll join me. And half of what I've already saved."

"Saved or stolen?" Caine laughed. "A thief stealing from other thieves."

Seahorn's lip twitched, and his brows lowered over his eyes. "Don't call me a thief, Simon. I don't like that."

Caine stood. "And I don't like what you're offering me. Sounds like death on a platter. I don't want any part of it."

Seahorn looked incredulous. "You're turning me down?"

"That's right."

Seahorn stood, turning over his glass. "You've leaving me to be killed!" He stopped. "Wait—is this revenge for Murfreesboro? You're betraying me now because I let those Yanks through?"

"This isn't betrayal, and Murfreesboro has nothing to do with it. I just don't want to do it." Caine turned and walked toward the door. "Thanks for the food, Neal. It was prime."

Seahorn went to him, grasped his shoulder. "You can't just walk out on me."

"Let me go."

"They'll kill me."

"Then leave. Get away before they get to you."

Caine jerked loose and turned. He put his hand on the door latch. He sensed a quick motion behind him. Instinctively he ducked and turned slightly, but something heavy came down hard on the back of his head. The room spun, and he collapsed senseless to the floor.

CHAPTER 5

Brice found the isolated residence of Drew Strahan only after great difficulty and loss of time. When he was near losing all hope of finding it, an inquiry of a hunter coming up from the Big Bend country, at last, put him right. But when he reached Strahan's, he received a hostile gunpoint reception.

Brice identified himself as Simon Caine's brother from Kensington. Strahan put his broad face close to Brice's and looked him over with squinted eyes, then nodded slowly.

"I see a lot of Simon in your face," he said. He lowered the pistol. "All right. I believe you. He said he had a brother from Kensington, and you got to be him."

"I'm looking for Simon," Brice said.

"Too late. He's gone."

Brice felt like sinking into the ground. "Where did he go?" he asked.

Strahan looked skeptically at him. "Simon told me you weren't too receptive when he came to see you. Why are you looking for him now?"

Brice told Strahan about the kidnapping and his hope that Simon could somehow help him recover Keelan. He spared no detail, even telling of Garth Kensington's inability to pay the ransom. "I don't know what to do. I've got only a few days before they'll be looking for me to bring the ransom into Serveto," Brice said.

Strahan's eyes narrowed. "Serveto, you say?"

Brice nodded.

"Well, that's exactly where Simon was headed."

"What?"

Strahan told Brice of the Alianza, Neal Seahorn, and his call to Caine to come to Serveto to meet him. Strahan told of his suspicion that Caine was to be invited to join the criminal organization. "But Simon knew nothing about your boy being kidnapped," Strahan said. "If he had, he would never have come here. He would have gone straight to Serveto to take off Neal Seahorn's head."

"So you're saying this Alianza is responsible for the kidnapping?"

"Looks that way to me. It's a crazy twist—Seahorn searching out Simon on the one hand and snatching his nephew on the other."

"What could it mean?"

"I don't know."

"There's no chance Simon will join the Alianza, is there?"

Strahan frowned. "You, his brother or not? What do you think?"

Brice said, "I don't think he'd ever join. But that doesn't help me. I got no ransom, and now I don't even have Simon to help me."

Strahan looked sincerely sympathetic. "I'd like to help you myself, son, but this is one old pistol fighter who's too old and eat up with gout to be anything but a hindrance. But what I can offer you right now is a meal and a place to sleep tonight."

"I'm obliged," Brice said. He looked out the door and across the horizon.

"What are you looking at?"

"Nothing. I just thought I saw—" He stopped.

"What?"

What Brice could have said was, I thought I saw a horseman on the horizon. But Brice looked again and saw nothing, and he thought maybe it had been an illusion brought on by fatigue.

"I didn't see anything," Brice said. "Thank you for your help, Mr. Strahan."

———

Caine awakened in darkness. He was lying on some soft but lumpy surface, surrounded by looming shapes and black shadows. Pain radiated through his skull, and at the back of his head was a tender place that made him wince when his groping hand touched it.

He lay there a few minutes, trying to make sense of where he was, but he could not. He pushed up on his elbows, then climbed to his knees and finally his feet. He moved slowly, making sure he had no injuries beyond a sore skull.

He almost tripped on his first step. He knelt and felt about him. The soft, lumpy surface on which he had been lying was a heap of old rags and sacks. He investigated the room further. The big shapes around him were crates and casks. Apparently, this was some sort of storage chamber.

He found a window and opened its shutters. Moonlight streamed in. The window was crossed with iron bars; no opportunity for escape there.

Caine sat down on a crate and massaged the back of his neck until his head hurt less. His gun belt was gone. Nothing in his pockets at all—not even matches to light one of the lamps hanging along the wall. All he had was what he had on and his hat that lay on the floor beside the pile of rags.

He muttered a curse at Neal Seahorn, then another at himself for not having listened to Drew Strahan and stayed away from Serveto.

Caine explored the room. It was about fifty feet square and had a stone-tile floor and a tall ceiling. All three of the room's windows were barred. A wide double door was the only apparent entrance and exit. On the far side of the room, a platform had been built for extra storage space, with a ramp leading up to it. There, more casks hung in parbuckles, and ropes and pulleys dangled.

Caine went to the double door. He didn't attempt to open it, for he knew it would be barred from the outside. Probably Seahorn had posted a guard out there anyway. Caine listened—a boot scuffed the floor in the hallway; a whiff of tobacco smoke filtered in through the crack between the doors.

Quietly Caine crept to the center of the room, vanishing into the shadows there. He appraised his circumstances.

He couldn't figure what Seahorn had in mind for him. Caine wondered if Seahorn was insane. Much of his talk had sounded obsessive and excessively fearful. Whatever Seahorn's state, it seemed probable that the Alianza was no madman's illusion. Only a big and wealthy entity could support Seahorn and his gunmen in a place and manner such as this.

Caine wished he could smoke but knew he couldn't. He didn't want the guard outside to come in—at least not until he had developed some plan of escape.

Returning to the window, he tried to determine his location. This building appeared to be somewhere toward the center of the enclosure. It was not, as far as he could tell, near the wall on any side. A bad situation. Once out of here, he would have to make it across open space, then find some way to mount and cross the wall without being seen.

The immediate problem, though, was simply getting out of this room. Caine looked around, but no likely options presented themselves.

He slowly walked around the room, trying to plan. He could call in the guard and then try to overcome him, but that was risky. There might be more than one guard, and a scuffle might draw attention from elsewhere in the compound.

Caine explored the main floor again but developed no new ideas.

He heard a noise at the doorway. An Anglo voice said, "Seahorn wants to know if he's stirred yet."

"I've heard nothing," said someone with a Mexican voice. "I'm tired of sitting here. Why can't we just lock him up in the carcel?"

"Seahorn said he wants him treated special. Those two rode together once, you know. Come on. Let's check him out."

After the rattle of a key in a lock, one of the big doors swung open, and the two men entered. One carried a lamp. They walked to the pile of rags and sacks in the midst of the jumble of crates and barrels. Caine lay as before, eyes loosely shut, mouth slightly open.

The Anglo man said, "Must have took quite a lick. I would have figured he'd be stirring by now."

"Perhaps he will die," said the Mexican.

The Anglo laughed. "It'd take more than a knock on the head to kill Simon Caine. All I can say is when he does wake up, Seahorn better keep out of his reach. Caine's twice the man Seahorn is."

"Such talk can get you killed here," the Mexican said.

"I ain't afraid of Seahorn. One of these days, I'll swing his scalp from my belt and jingle his money in my pocket."

The men walked away; Caine heard the door shut and the key turn.

He sat up, breathing deeply. He remained seated in the heap of rags, beginning to believe he would have no choice but to try to fight his way out.

He stood and decided to explore one more time before taking that desperate option. He quietly climbed up the ramp to the second level. He noticed a crack in the top of the wall directly across from him. He followed it down with his eyes; it disappeared behind a crate stacked against the wall.

He moved the crate aside inch by inch so as to make no noise. The crack widened here into a hole about the size of a man's head, and at its base, it was even wider. Caine lay down on his side and looked out the opening.

Beyond it, he saw the dark expanse of a flat tiled roof. The room he was in was two stories high, but apparently, the rest of the building was only one story, butting up against the taller portion.

Caine scouted about until he found a scrap of metal. As quietly as he could, he chipped away the crumbling stone around the hole, making the opening bigger. Sweat soaked his shirt, and his head throbbed.

When the hole was big enough, he pushed himself through. It was a tight squeeze, and it took several minutes for him to make it. When he was out, he crouched on the roof and looked across the plaza below.

Light poured out of numerous windows here and there around the compound. Caine heard scraps of conversation, muffled laughter in the wind. These were the sounds of people talking and smoking over tables of food and cards and liquor.

He dropped lightly to the ground, thinking of weapons. He wanted his own back again but had no way to know where Seahorn would have put them, nor if he could reach them.

The sound of footfalls nearby made him slip back against the wall. Still feeling exposed, he dropped to his belly and snaked under a boardwalk just as two men came around the corner. One was an American, a stranger to Caine. The other was Ramon Fernandez.

"No problems then?" Ramon asked.

"None except losing Juan Contero. We rode in, snatched the boy, rode out. Shot up a darky that was with the boy. I figure he's 'gwine cross de ribber' by now." The man laughed.

"Do you foresee problems getting the ransom?"

"None. That old man could pay whatever you ask without a flinch. Sit tight, and they'll deliver that ransom right to our door. You just wait."

The men went on, leaving Caine unseen below the boardwalk, evaluating what he had heard. A kidnapping, apparently—undoubtedly the same one from which Seahorn was expecting ransom, as he had mentioned. Part of the Alianza's design that Seahorn found so grand. And the victim was apparently just a boy.

It made Caine think about his own long-lost son, and he hated Neal Seahorn.

CHAPTER 6

Keeping in shadows and doorways, Caine traveled through the enclosure, searching for a way out. He heard someone whistling nearby and sank back into a dark doorway.

A Mexican with a Colt Dragoon hanging butt-forward on a cord against his thigh passed, whistling a tune. He held a jangling key ring in one hand and a stack of rifles and carbines beneath his arm. He went by Caine without seeing him.

Caine fell in behind the man's path, his eye on the weapons. The man walked to a stone building about two hundred feet away and thrust a key into the lock.

Caine stealthily approached. When the Mexican swung out the door, Caine was right behind him. The Mexican stepped inside, and in a perfectly coordinated move, Caine slammed the heavy door against him. Its timbers pounded the man's head against the doorframe and dropped him cold.

Caine dragged the bulky form into the building and pulled the door nearly shut behind him. He found matches in one of the man's pockets and lit one.

He smiled. This obviously was Seahorn's armory. Rifles

and shotguns, ranging from ancient percussion-cap weapons to Winchesters still thick with packing grease, stood racked around the wall. Flat crates held other rifles, most apparently new. Beneath tarpaulins in the corner, there were two Gatling guns, and against the wall stood casks of powder, countless packages of bullets, gun-repair equipment, ammunition-manufacturing equipment, and other such goods. There was enough weaponry here to outfit a small army—which, Caine realized, Seahorn's band really was.

Lighting match after match to see by Caine gathered arms. He took a brand-new Colt six-shooter and all the bullets his pockets would hold, then began looking for a good rifle. He selected a familiar-looking Winchester and suddenly realized that it was his own weapon, the very one he had bought in Missouri to replace the aging weapons he had carried while in the Bitterroots. His old Navy Colt he had never parted with, though, and he began digging about, hoping it had also been stored here. Quickly he was rewarded. The pistol, still loaded, hung in Caine's own gun belt from a peg on the wall, ammunition pouch intact. Gratefully Caine strapped the belt on. He loaded his new weapons and put fresh loads in the Navy Colt.

Rearmed, Caine cautiously left the hut and darted across the clearing to a double row of flat-topped adobe houses, or casas, near the west wall. There he mulled what to do next.

Suddenly, as if, at some silent signal, the compound exploded in a burst of activity, and Caine knew his escape had finally been detected.

Someone on the other side of the enclosure shouted something indiscernible in Spanish. Caine dropped to his belly. He heard his own name amid the flurry of words.

Lights flickered on here and there, and men emerged from doorways. Dogs barked. Caine began snaking off toward the compound wall, his rifle in front of him. Someone ran by not twenty feet from him but did not see him. Caine reached the corner of the row of adobes and stood in a crouch.

A grove of trees around a well at the corner of the compound appeared to be the most promising hiding place within view. Caine darted toward it. But he saw a man with a rifle slightly to the right of it, and he had to fall back again into the alley between the rows of adobe dwellings.

The man appeared to be searching. Caine impatiently waited until he had meandered off. More shouts erupted in the center of the compound as Caine stepped out again, heading toward the well and the dark trees.

"*Señor!*"

It was a lady's voice, spoken from no more than six feet away. He wheeled and instinctively raised his rifle.

A dark-haired figure, unmistakably feminine, stood in the open window just to his right.

"They will find you if you do not hide," the lady said. "Come in. Quickly!"

Footfalls, shouts—men approaching.

Caine hesitated only a moment. Then he climbed into the Mexican woman's dark house through the window, and she drew the shutters closed behind him.

She took Caine to a back room full of crockery jars, churns, water bottles, and bundles of kindling tied with twine. He hid among the latter, pulling bundles atop himself. He lay as still as possible, trying not to breathe too loudly.

He fully realized that he might have thrown his life away by trusting this dark-eyed stranger. He had entered her house because his instincts told him to and because he had no better alternative.

"They will come here, Señor Caine, and ask for you," she said in a low voice. *She knows my name,* Caine noted. "I will lie to them and turn them away."

He heard voices and footfalls outside, then the violent

opening of the door. A thick Mexican voice fired out a string of questions and demands. The woman talked back, sounding afraid.

Men moved through the house; Caine heard doors opened, furniture moved—then someone was in the room with him.

Caine peered carefully up through the kindling. A tall Mexican with dark braids about his ears was peering about the little room, pistol drawn. Caine steeled himself, but suddenly the Mexican turned away, his braids flapping from the quick motion. He said something to the lady that Caine could not understand, then laughed roughly; Caine somehow got an impression that he had also touched her improperly. Then the front door opened and closed. He heard the men retreating, then silence. Caine pushed the kindling bundles aside and rose.

She was at the door. She was a strikingly beautiful woman, wearing black. "Why are you doing this?" Caine asked. "How do you know my name?"

"I am Rosalita Contero," she said. "I help you because I hear you have offended the swine, Seahorn. He is an evil man, so if you have angered him, you must be good. Everyone here knows who you are, *señor.* The talk of you has been everywhere."

"If you despise this place so, why do you stay?"

"My husband was Juan Contero, a *secuestrador*... how you say?— a kidnapper for Seahorn. Now it has cost him his life. Do not say you are sorry; it was the justice of God against a bad man I was fool enough to love." She crossed herself and touched a crucifix about her neck. "I will go soon and spit upon my memories of Serveto and Neal Seahorn."

Caine said, "I got to get over the wall. And I need a horse."

"Hide again for now. I will tell you when it is safe."

She buried Caine beneath the kindling again. He lay

there a long time. He heard her stirring about, poking a fire, brewing something in a kettle. Then, after what seemed more than an hour, she returned. She had a shawl over her shoulders.

"There is a small door through the west wall," she said. "It is hidden by vines and was covered over with bricks, but for now, it is exposed again. The children have done it in play only this week, and the men here have not yet seen it." She gave Caine a poncho and a sombrero. "These will help disguise you."

The compound was bathed in darkness. A thin sliver of moon sailed into and out of intermittent clouds, its sporadic light watery and pale. Caine walked beside Rosalita, keeping his weapons hidden beneath the faded poncho. The hat was too large and rode low on his forehead.

Men still moved about the compound, rifles in hand. They looked in doorways, under wagons, in the brush, but without the sense of urgency evident before. Caine and Rosalita walked with deliberate slowness toward a dark alley between two buildings ahead.

"Rosalita!"

Caine winced at the sound of the voice. "Go on," Rosalita whispered. "Do not stop for anything. The door is there, beneath the vines..."

"Rosalita!" Now Caine recognized the coarse voice. That of the big Mexican man with the braids.

Rosalita, pretending to have heard only the second call, turned. Caine continued on into the alleyway, then stopped in the shadows and watched Rosalita as the big man approached her. He was a mountain, dwarfing her. He grinned, leaning toward her; his hands groped lewdly. Rosalita slapped at him, and he laughed. But suddenly, his body spasmed as Caine's rifle stock pounded into the back of his skull. The Mexican collapsed, shuddering spasmodically into senselessness.

Rosalita upbraided Caine for returning. "You are loco! You will be seen!"

"I couldn't stand by and watch him do that."

Caine and Rosalita hurried into the alley together. They rounded the back of one of the adobe buildings. Rosalita pulled aside some vines on an old arbor and exposed a small, arch-shaped door that long ago had been bricked and mortared over. But as Rosalita had said, the mortar and bricks had pulled away; they lay heaped behind the arbor vines and before the outward-opening door.

"Once there was a mission granary here, and this door opened to it from the outside," she said. "Those of us who know it is open again say nothing. I will leave through it myself as soon as I have the last pay that was to go to my husband." She looked ashamed. "It is evil money, I know, but yet I must have it."

"I understand. I'm obliged to you, Rosalita," Caine said. "Don't know how to thank you."

"Perhaps someday you will help me, *Dios mediante,*" she said. "Now go. Across the hill to the north Seahorn keeps stables, there you can steal a horse. Ride swift and far, Simon Caine."

She closed the door. Simon loped away into the night, the wide brim of his sombrero flapping.

———

At Seahorn's stables, a campfire burned brightly in the wind, and silhouetted in it, Caine saw a seated guard holding a carbine.

Caine strode up to him. "Hello!" he called. The man leaped up, turning, lifting the carbine.

"Whoa, there!" Caine said, laughing in apparent good nature. "No need to get jumpy. Just wanted to buy a horse.

How you Mexes say it *compra Caballo*—or something like that?"

The man levered the carbine warningly. Caine put on a mask of fear. He lifted his hands. "Please, *amigo*. Don't shoot me. I am a sick and weak man. I... I..." Suddenly he clutched at his chest, groaned, and fell prone.

The man with the carbine peered cautiously at Caine, then edged forward. Caine did not move. The man rolled him over. Caine swung up his pistol and cracked the butt into the side of the man's head. The man fell atop him, and Caine pushed him off. Caine was up in half a moment. But the man was not unconscious. He raised the carbine. Caine kicked it away, then followed up with a second kick, this to the man's chin. The guard did not move.

Caine levered the shells out of the carbine, tossed it into a manure stack, and entered the corral, looking for a good mount. He thanked good fortune that nobody from the compound was yet here looking for him; perhaps they still figured him to be inside the walls, hiding.

Caine grinned when he saw his own Appaloosa. He claimed it and led it to the stable, where he furiously searched for his saddle. He found it hanging over the side of a stall. Caine quickly saddled the Appaloosa, booted his weapons, and mounted.

He heard a shout from somewhere, then a shot. A bullet passed a foot above his head. He bent low. A sentry on the compound's wall had spotted him.

Caine rode into a night-shadowed street lined by crude huts. He whipped the Appaloosa into a run when he heard noise behind him. He saw dark faces peer at him from behind doors and glassless windows, but from these silent people, he had nothing to fear.

Near the edge of the cluster of hovels, he cut right, riding into a black alley between two apparently deserted buildings.

There he dismounted and, with his weight, worked the Appaloosa to the ground. He hid behind its heaving form.

A few moments later, a band of riders flashed by the end of the alley, riding on past and out of town. Caine smiled and rose. The Appaloosa struggled to its feet.

"Señor!"

Caine spun. The big Mexican with the twin braids stood behind him, about fifteen feet away, grinning. He had followed Caine. In his hand was a Colt six-shooter. Blood was drying on his head.

Caine drew his pistol just as the Mexican's fat finger began its squeeze on the trigger. Two guns fired as one. The braided Mexican's shot winged inches past Caine and his mount. But Caine's own shot punched a hole through the Mexican's broad belly, and the man fell dead.

"That one was for you, Rosalita," Caine said.

He mounted and pushed the Appaloosa into the wilderness east of Serveto, knowing that the shots would quickly draw back the riders, and he would be pursued.

———

Seahorn's face was livid. It lent him a wild, ghastly look that Ramon Fernandez had seldom seen.

"He has made me a fool before my own men and before the Alianza itself," Seahorn said. "Go find him. Bring him back to me. Alive, if possible."

"Indeed."

Ramon left Seahorn and walked through the compound. Against the west wall stood a sort of barracks building where priests once had lived. A larger building stood across from them. Long ago, it had been a mission school, but now it was the jail, or carcel, of Neal Seahorn.

Ramon walked to its doorway. A sentinel stood to the side and let him pass.

J. W. Fadden was inside, seated on a bench beside a heavy oak door.

"The boy?" Ramon asked.

"In there."

"Let me see him."

Fadden stood and lifted the bar of the door. He swung it inward, and he and Ramon entered.

A miniature tornado broke loose inside the room. Keelan, flailing, and kicking, almost knocked Ramon to the floor, then darted past him for the doorway.

Fadden's arm swept out and caught Keelan by the neck. Fadden pulled the boy back against him.

"Ain't polite to run out on your friends," Fadden said.

Keelan gurgled and choked, struggling for his breath.

Ramon leaned over, examining Keelan as if he were a colt being considered for purchase.

"He looks ill," Ramon said. "Make sure he gets plenty to eat and drink. A corpse brings no *dinero.*"

"I'm no nursemaid," Fadden said flatly.

Ramon looked at Fadden with undisguised contempt. Fadden, who couldn't care less, picked up Keelan and roughly tossed him on his cot.

"My pa will come here, and he'll kill you," Keelan said, fighting tears. "My grandpa, too—he's old, but he's got a lot of money, and he can make you pay!"

"Wrong, boy—we're making him pay, or else he gets you back one piece at a time," Fadden said.

Ramon said, "There is no need to talk to a mere *muchacho* in such a way."

"Just being truthful."

"Neal Seahorn wants you to be useful instead. Go saddle up. I am gathering men to go after Simon Caine."

"Caine got loose?" Fadden chuckled admiringly. "That explains the ruckus."

"Yes. Now go."

Fadden slowly turned and walked out, his carelessly stooped shoulders rolling with his gait. At the door, he turned. "Mexican man, watch your mouth around me from here on out. A lot here see you as Seahorn's servant boy, and when they finally turn on him, you'll be the first to chew a bullet." He smiled coldly. "Maybe it will be mine."

Ramon smiled. "I will see any such effort as a welcome opportunity for reciprocation, *amigo.*"

Fadden looked defiant but puzzled. Ramon laughed, for he knew that Fadden had not understood the meaning of what he had just heard. Fadden stalked out.

Keelan looked up at Ramon. "Will you let me go free, mister?"

Ramon merely smiled, rubbed the boy's head. "Be patient, *muchacho,* and say your prayers. Perhaps heaven will open and take you in." He laughed and rubbed Keelan's head again. The boy pulled away.

Ramon left the room and locked the door behind him.

CHAPTER 7

Drew Strahan squeezed shut his eyes until they were mere slits in his sweating brown face. Supine, he gritted his teeth and tried not to cry out as the bearded, derby-wearing man who held the Peacemaker to his throat once again ground the heel of his riding boot into his gout-racked ankle.

"Again, Mr. Strahan," said the man, whose name was Morrison Deguere, "why did Brice James come here?"

"I'll... kill you..."

"I think not. Now talk, so I can get out of here before I lose him." Deguere almost sadly shook his head as he bore down with his heel again, for he disliked distasteful things. But he disliked uncooperative old men even more.

Strahan groaned, yelled, then relented. "Mexico! He went into Mexico."

Deguere eased up only a bit. "Exactly where?"

"Serveto. Serveto."

"Why did he come here first?"

Strahan blubbered, hating himself for talking. "He came because he thought somebody might be here."

"Who?"

Strahan clenched his teeth. Deguere bore down until his victim screamed.

"Simon Caine. He was looking for Simon Caine."

"Who I happen to know is Brice James's brother," Deguere said, nodding. "Just what I suspected. Why was he searching for Caine now?"

"Needs his help."

"Go on."

Strahan hung his head. "Brice James's boy got kidnapped. By Neal Seahorn's men, I think. Brice came hoping to find Simon and get him to help get the boy back."

Deguere looked fascinated; this interrogation was proving worth the trouble. "Does Caine know about the kidnapping?"

Strahan was hurting, and his voice sounded tight. "Didn't when he was here."

"So Caine really was here? Where did he go?"

"Serveto. He was answering a call from Neal Seahorn. That's all I know. Who are you? Why are you asking all this?"

"That doesn't matter. Do you know much about the Alianza?"

Strahan looked scared now. "I've heard the name. I don't know what it is."

"I believe you do—your eyes show it. Tell me, was Caine prepared to join the Alianza?"

Strahan bit his lip, not wanting to talk. Deguere pressed again on the ankle.

"No! No. Simon just had his mind set on hearing Seahorn out. I told him not to go, but he wouldn't listen."

"Fascinating. Absolutely fascinating." Deguere lifted his foot off the tortured ankle, which Strahan immediately seized and began rubbing. "So what is Brice James going to do about his kidnapped boy?" Deguere asked.

"He's going to try to get him out alone."

"With ransom?"

"He's got no ransom. Garth Kensington's gone broke, he says." Strahan looked at Deguere with blurry eyes. "Are you from the Alianza? How do you know who I am?"

"Just count me as one who has good reason to know all I can about Simon Caine and his old partners, yourself included. I've been on Caine's trail for a long time now. I could recite a history of his life and associations in great detail. I could even tell you much about yourself, Mr. Strahan." He shifted the derby and looked ponderingly at the other. "Now the question is what to do with you, my friend. What indeed?"

Strahan squeezed his eyes shut. He cried out when the Peacemaker blasted. Half a minute later, he opened his eyes. He was unscathed. The bearded man had fired into the floor near Strahan's head, then had left. The deliberately inaccurate shot was a final cruel jest, a mercy for himself as a traitor that somehow hurt almost as much as a bullet would have.

Strahan put his face to the floor and lay there a long time.

———

Morrison Deguere sat beneath a rock, letting his horse drink at a seep and graze at the meager grasses growing around it. Deguere was eager to go on and further close the gap between himself and Brice James, but the horse was nearly exhausted. So, pencil in hand, Deguere brushed his fingers through his beard and flipped a page in his black notebook. The book held the record of more than a year of tracking Simon Caine, starting when Deguere left Henley in the Montana Territory under the hire of Caine's old enemy, William Montrose, brother of the man who had killed Caine's family in Tennessee and then had died at Caine's hand.

Montrose had hired Deguere because of his reputation as one of the most capable detectives available west of New

York. Deguere's assignment was simple: trail Simon Caine as long as it takes to bring him down.

It was the kind of assignment Deguere relished. The federal government had never been able to bring in Caine, but that didn't worry him, for he considered himself far more effective than any government agent. Besides, this was a job Deguere could stretch over many months, with Montrose funneling him money every few weeks. Caine's reputation as a hard catch made it all that much easier to extend the job for the highest cash value.

The case was proving to be more interesting and faceted than he would ever have thought. Deguere scanned his notebook, refreshing himself again on what he had learned these several months.

Through his own work and the help of investigative associates in Chicago, New York, and Washington, Deguere had pieced together a detailed working biography of Caine and his associations. Through this process, Deguere had long known, for example, how Caine's brother had changed his name to Brice James and married the daughter of famed tycoon Garth Kensington. He had noted that since leaving Montana, Caine had migrated toward Texas. That didn't surprise Deguere, given the presence here not only of Caine's brother but also of his old wartime partner Drew Strahan.

But it was another wartime associate whom Deguere found particularly interesting. That was Neal Seahorn, believed dead by the public, but who loose-tongued government sources had said was not dead at all, and who was deeply involved in a very covert Confederate-based criminal conspiracy most commonly called the Alianza. The government sources told Deguere's investigators that Seahorn was believed to be somewhere in Mexico's border country west of the Bio Bravo, or Bio Grande, between El Paso and the Big Bend region.

At first, the mysterious Alianza seemed mostly a curiosity

to Deguere, but then something unexpected happened: Caine's trail and that of Neal Seahorn and the Alianza began to converge much more closely.

It first came clear in Wichita, Kansas, when Deguere talked to residents of a boarding house in which Caine had briefly lived under his alias of Bobert Cole. Without revealing the so-called Cole's true identity, Deguere found that Caine had left Wichita after receiving a letter. A nosy fellow house resident had seen a flash of the note, enough to detect that it was calling its recipient to Serveto, Mexico, to meet a man named Seahorn.

"Unusual name, 'Seahorn,'" the neighbor had said to Deguere. "Just like the old war renegade the *federates* killed a few years ago."

Deguere had said, yes, indeed, that is unusual, tipped his hat, and left with a smile on his face and an impression that a puzzle was coming together almost of its own accord. He had just by luck discovered that Neal Seahorn was hiding out in Serveto.

Deguere had put his horse in a boxcar and headed south from Kansas, certain that in Texas, he would easily pick up Caine's trail.

It didn't prove as easy as expected. Caine seemed to have vanished like a dust devil, and try as he would, Deguere could not fall back in his track. In near desperation, he had gone to the Kensington ranch, figuring Caine had probably gone there to meet his brother and might be there yet.

Deguere found the ranch in turmoil, its personnel walking around with fear on their faces. He asked to see Brice James but was told he was gone. No, we don't know when he will return. No, you may not see Garth Kensington because he is ill. Please leave now, sir, and come again when the situation is better, and that may take a long time.

It was obvious something was amiss at the Kensington ranch, and Deguere wondered if it had to do with Caine. He made a few subtle inquiries about what had happened at the ranch but was unable to learn anything. At last, he had mounted and headed toward Serveto, hoping to pick up Caine's path in that way.

Instead, he spotted Brice James. Deguere studied the man through his spyglass and recognized him from an old photograph he possessed of the Caine family. When Brice dismounted to adjust his saddle, Deguere saw his limp and cinched the identification. Now, this was intriguing: Why would Brice James be riding alone through this wilderness? And where was Simon Caine?

Deguere followed Brice James until he came to Drew Strahan's place. Brice stayed there only briefly, then quickly rode out toward the Mexican border. Deguere had almost followed him, then decided to turn back and interrogate Strahan. Deguere was glad he had, for otherwise, he would not have learned about the kidnapping until it was too late to benefit him.

Deguere jotted more notes into his book. An amazing twist this was: Caine went to meet Seahorn, apparently not knowing Seahorn had abducted his own nephew. Now, Brice James was himself riding toward Serveto to try to rescue the boy... and in the background, a criminal organization that smelled of big money—money Deguere wouldn't mind getting his hands into even as he continued his lucrative quest for Caine.

Deguere heard something that made him put away the notebook. Distant shots were echoing across the land...

Deguere looked across the desert. Dust was blowing in a kicking wind, and he could see nothing, no one. He heard what might have been another shot, but the wind shifted and carried the phantom sound away.

After a few more minutes of rest, Deguere resettled his derby on his head, mounted again, and began riding toward the Rio Bravo and the crossing that led to Serveto.

The first shot had spooked Brice's horse, which threw him to the dirt. The second blasted sand into his face, and the third clipped off a bit of his hair.

By the time the fourth came, Brice lay on his belly amid a pile of rocks, peering through the spears of a Spanish dagger plant, trying to pinpoint the spot from where the shots were erupting.

A fifth shot, an explosion of smoke. Brice fired a responding round from his Colt —but had no clear target.

A shadow moved across him. He rolled and saw a tall Anglo, wild-eyed and seemingly big as a grizzly, descending on him, knife drawn. Brice whipped up the pistol, firing it clumsily from stomach level, and then the Anglo was atop him, dead even as his breath hissed out. The knife stuck into the ground beside Brice's ear.

Trapped beneath the dead weight of the corpse, Brice panicked. His pistol lay across his stomach, pressing into him under the dead man's belly. Straining, Brice managed to pull it free just as another man, this one Mexican, appeared over the rim of boulders. Brice fired, and the man fell back, crying out. Brice heard him writhe unseen on the other side of the rocks, then go silent.

Brice struggled out from beneath the dead man and rose to a crouched position. Nothing moved out across the undulating desert except the hypnotic waves of heat.

Something behind, a noise—

Brice spun just as a third bandido appeared. He wrenched his bad leg beneath him and fell as he shot at him. The bandido laughed and aimed at Brice's face.

"Drop it, *compadre.*"

Helplessly, Brice let his Colt fall. Two other men appeared almost magically, rising from behind rocks and cacti.

"We want money, *señor.*"

"I have no money."

The Mexican cursed in Spanish. Brice saw he was about to shoot, and instinctively he ducked to the ground, awaiting the fatal blast.

Shots fired out as expected, but Brice was surprised to find he was not harmed. He looked up at the Mexican. The man had a strange look on his face. He softly grunted, lurched, and fell sideways. The other men shouted and scattered. Brice grabbed his pistol again.

The drylands came alive with activity.

Repeated shots, fired in a steady rhythm, boomed to Brice's left. To his right, he heard more yells and screams from his surprised ambushers.

Then, as suddenly as it all had happened, there was silence. Brice lay still for another few seconds, catching his breath.

Someone trudged up to him. Brice saw a pair of booted feet. His eyes trailed up a pair of long, sturdy legs clad in canvas pants that were tucked into the boot tops to keep scorpions out. He saw a gun belt holding an 1860 model .44-caliber Colt Army pistol, well-kept despite its age. Across the crook of the man's arm lay Tandy Jones's rare and beloved Colt revolving rifle.

"Orion, I told you not to follow me," Brice said.

The handsome young black man grinned. "Yeah. Ain't you glad I didn't listen?"

"But how did you know where I was?"

"I didn't, exactly. But you said you were heading to Serveto, so I just did the same. Didn't expect to find you like this." He gestured toward the dead men. "Were they looking for your ransom money?"

"I don't think so. They asked for money, but they didn't call it ransom. I think they jumped me just because I was alone."

"You're not as alone as you think. There's someone else trailing you, too."

"Who?"

"Don't know. I've found scraps of sign here and there—enough to make me sure."

Brice shook his head. The last thing he needed was somebody following him for nonexistent ransom.

After they had talked a bit more, Orion looked again at the bodies and asked, "Should we bury them?" The corpses lay sprawled within an area about twenty feet square.

"Nope," Brice said. "Let the buzzards have them. I wonder, is one of them, Cato Blake?"

Orion shook his head. "If it was, we'd be dead now. Besides, I've seen Blake before. None of these is him."

Orion walked to one of the dead men, who stared up at the sky with his mouth open. A scorpion skittered across the man's chest, and flies were already buzzing and lighted around the staring blank eyes. Orion's expression was a bit peculiar, Brice noticed.

"First one you kill is always the hardest," Brice said. "I remember my first, during the war. I can still see the face."

Orion looked at Brice. "This ain't my first. I kilt my first back at the ranch after you left."

Brice looked amazed.

"Hosea Scruggs," Orion said.

"Hosea? For God's sake, why?"

"He went to Felipe drunk and laughing and saying it was him what helped the kidnappers get Keelan and kill my father. Felipe told me, and I just went loco. I got out Pa's old Colt rifle here and went looking. I found him."

Brice was stunned. "Why would Hosea do such as that?"

"He was paid."

Orion scanned over the bodies of the dead ambushers again and shook his head. "But I'm nothing but a common outlaw now, Mr. Brice. I've kilt men."

"Just one traitor and one common bandit is all you've killed."

"Don't matter. I kilt them, and I'm colored, and that puts me at odds with the white law."

Brice knew Orion was right. No matter what the circumstances of his actions, many Anglos would gladly string him up without worrying over finer distinctions.

"You mind riding with a common outlaw, Mr. Brice?" Orion asked.

"You're no outlaw." Brice hesitated a moment, made a decision, then went on, "And even if you were, you wouldn't be the first I've been associated with. Close associated. Blood kin."

Orion looked confused, then his eyes widened. "You ain't kin to no Jesse James, are you?"

Brice laughed. "No. But I have a brother you've heard of. He's one I've acted ashamed of a long time—but it's him I came looking for out here. If you're going to ride with me, you may as well know all the truth."

Brice told the full story: his brotherhood to Simon, his own change of name, Simon's recent return, everything. Orion listened, looking astounded, occasionally nodding as Brice went along.

CHAPTER 8

Brice and Orion forded the Rio Bravo. The water was up, and the horses had to swim. Upon reaching the other side, they let them rest.

Brice knelt and idly scratched in the dirt with a stick. "How are we going to do this, Orion?" he asked despairingly. "We're two men against Lord only knows how many."

"That won't stop me," Orion said. "That was my Pa they kilt. What did you plan to do if you had found Simon Caine?" He chuckled. "I just can't get used to thinking of you as an outlaw's brother."

"I don't know what we would have done. I suppose I had hoped Simon would know what to do. He's good at these kinds of things." Suddenly he stopped, lifting a hand. "Did you hear that?"

"I did," Orion said. "Sounds like horses. A lot of them. Bandidos?"

"Could be. Let's find out."

They began a careful exploration, and several minutes later, they hid their horses at the base of a rock formation that lay like a gigantic flat wedge against the land. They worked quietly up the long slope of it, and at the edge, where the formation cut off sharply into a bluff about twenty feet high, they gained a view of a drama being played out below.

A dozen riders were approaching a broad, shrub-filled depression about a hundred yards straight ahead. The riders pulled to a halt and dismounted hurriedly, like cavalrymen being ambushed. But it was clear that if any ambush was taking place here, the riders were the instigators, not the victims.

"What do you make of it?" Orion whispered.

"I'm not sure. They don't look like your usual bandidos. See the Mex in the fancy clothes? Dandier than any desert robber I've seen."

The gunmen below crept through the brush toward the basin. Brice noted an Appaloosa some distance beyond the depression. It was saddled but riderless, and he knew none of the visible gunmen had been on it. It must be the mount of whoever was in the basin.

"Whoever's in that hole's not got a Chinaman's chance," Brice said.

One of the men below shouted, "Don't make us kill you, Caine! Seahorn wants you back alive!"

Brice exclaimed, "That's Simon; they got down there!" He bolted up, but Orion pulled him back down.

"No, Mr. Brice. There's too many. You get killed, and what happens to Keelan? Maybe your brother will surrender, and they won't kill him."

"He doesn't surrender easy, Orion."

Suddenly the gunmen below leaped forward and fired down into the depression. The shots made popping sounds in the hot air.

Brice bowed his head, not wanting to look. "Too late," he said.

———

Fadden sat beside the fire, taking big swallows from a brown bottle of whiskey. Finally, he rose, staggered slightly, and walked to the edge of the camp where Simon Caine was tied to a gnarled mesquite. Caine had a bandage around his calf, covering a bloody scrape wound left by a passing slug. It was the only wound he had received before being struck down in the basin by one of the gunmen who had leaped upon him from behind and struck his head with his rifle butt.

Fadden took another swallow, then squatted. He shoved the bottle forward toward Caine, who shook his head.

"Suit yourself, *compadre,*" Fadden said. He turned the bottle up again; his throat moved as he swallowed. Then he corked the bottle and belched loudly and sourly from deep in his belly. "Bad stomach and bad whiskey don't mix," he said. "Hey, Caine, I thought we were going to have to kill you to get you out of that hole. You're one hellcat, you are. You ought to work for Seahorn. He could use you."

"I got no use for Seahorn," Caine said.

"You got use for *dinero,* don't you? Seahorn's got plenty of it. Connections, you know. Big crime organization of rich and crazy old Confederates. Lots of power, lots of money." Fadden laughed. "You take the power. I'll take the money." He uncorked the bottle and took another swallow and began talking again. "Now Seahorn, well, I got no use for him neither. I work for the money he pays, not for him." Fadden smiled drunkenly, leaning forward. He said in a too-loud whisper, "Someday, I might just put a bullet through Seahorn's brainpan and see what kind of cash he has squirreled away in that room he hardly ever leaves." He winked, laughed, took another swig of whiskey, and stumbled away.

Caine closed his eyes and dozed lightly. He was exhausted from the hard run. Also angry at himself for allowing himself to be cornered. Such a thing wouldn't have happened a few years ago, he thought. Must be getting old and slow.

He opened his eyes a little later and saw Ramon Fernandez standing where Fadden had been. The handsome Mexican was smoking a thin *cigarro*. He smiled at Caine.

"Are you comfortable, Señor Caine?"

"Cut me loose, Fernandez. I'll ride out of here, and you'll never see me again."

Fernandez took a drag and shook his head. "I'm sorry, *amigo*. I would gladly free you, but Neal Seahorn wants you back at Serveto."

"What does he need with me?"

"Oh, he could turn you in for the reward, but I don't think that is his plan. You are being brought back for appearances, I think. You did what Seahorn will not allow, especially at a time his men are discontented: you defied him. He cannot afford to let his men see defiance go unanswered."

"His authority is slipping, then?"

"You are perceptive, *amigo*. Seahorn has made the mistake of surrounding himself with men who care nothing for loyalty and nothing for him. Money is their motivation, their true leader. Seahorn pays them well, but more and more, they murmur about the wealth they believe he hides from them. Alianza money. Soon Seahorn's men will rise against him, and that will be the end of him and of Serveto."

Caine nodded. "I just heard the same from Fadden. It appears Neal wants me back to prove to his men; he's still strong."

Ramon shook his head. "No, *amigo*, to prove it to himself. He is a coward in his heart and ashamed of it. It is slowly driving him loco."

"Why do you stay?"

"Because at the moment, I am content to be where I am." He smiled subtly. "And because I, too, think Seahorn has much wealth in his hands. Perhaps it is wise to play along for now, eh?"

Ramon flipped down the *cigarro*. "I will sleep now." He walked away.

———

The camp lay in a wide, flat expanse encircled by an uplifted rim of rock lined with brush. Atop that rim, unseen by Caine and all others in the camp, Brice lay with a knife in one hand, a pistol in the other. Orion was beside him.

"Wish me luck, and keep me covered," Brice whispered.

"Let me go with you," Orion said.

"No. Less dangerous with one. If they get me, Keelan's rescue is in your hands."

Brice slid through the brush and dropped lightly and silently to the edge of the basin. He crouched, put the knife in his teeth, and edged forward. He could make out the form of his brother limned against the fire.

Brice saw no movement in the camp and heard snores. He crept on, almost to Simon now...

Something moved. Brice dropped to his belly and lay still.

A Mexican walked up to Caine. "You make noise?" he asked Caine in Spanish. Caine did not respond. The Mexican drew back his foot as if to kick the prisoner, but then he looked into the brush and stopped. Brice pressed himself against the earth; he felt his heart pounding the ground.

The Mexican squinted almost directly toward Brice for a very long time. Brice became increasingly unnerved, but suddenly the Mexican shrugged, turned, and walked to the other side of the camp. Brice watched him until he was outside the sphere of light cast by the campfire.

Brice remained still a long time, then crabbed up behind Caine. He reached toward him, about to touch his shoulder...

Two things happened. Brice heard a scuffle and a thud

behind him, where Orion was. At the same time, Fadden, who had been sleeping near the fire, awakened in a burst of coughing. He sat up, the firelight making his dark skin look like badly tarnished brass. Brice had no choice but to flatten again and stay frozen. Fadden sputtered and cursed beneath his breath, slid his bedroll farther from the fire, then lay down again. A few moments later, Brice heard his grating snores resume.

Up again and forward—Brice drew near to Simon, who now had noticed the stirring behind him and was trying to determine its origin without being obvious about it.

"Simon, it's me. I..."

Big hands grasped Brice's ankles and pulled him backward. He dropped his knife. Brice fell on his face as he was dragged away and rolled over. He still grasped his pistol, but a booted foot came down hard on it, and he could not lift it.

It was the big Mexican who had peered so suspiciously into the brush before. He had apparently left the camp on the far side and quietly walked the perimeter of it until he had found Brice. Brice feared for Orion.

The Mexican had a rock in his hand. He aimed it at Brice's head and came down with it. Brice shouted and rolled; the rock pounded the dirt beside his ear. The Mexican became unbalanced and lifted his weight enough to allow Brice to scramble to his feet. Brice fired but missed. At a dead run, Brice made for the brush-lined basin rim.

The Mexican drew his pistol and fired it. Brice felt the wind of the slug as it went past him. He hurried, dived for the brush, and found Orion just now pushing upright, rubbing the back of his head.

"Somebody hit me..."

"Come on!" Brice urged, pulling Orion to his feet.

Together they ran away from the camp, toward the place their horses were hidden. Voices and shouts assailed them from behind; they heard men coming after them. They ran harder.

Back in the camp, Caine struggled futilely with his bonds. He was surprised and confused. Whoever had come up and whispered behind him had sounded just like his brother. But how could that be?

Caine pulled again at his ropes but could not get free.

————

Seahorn walked across the plaza, past the well, toward the makeshift carcel of Serveto. He was uncomfortable away from his chambers; he would not have left them at all except the men he trusted least were still out searching for Caine.

A huge bonfire cast light across the hard-pounded dirt and made jumpy shadows beneath the arches of nearby doorways and portal columns. Somewhere in the darkness, someone played a guitar and sang an old Mexican lament.

A sentinel seated by the doorway stood when Seahorn approached, but seeing who it was, he first looked surprised and then stepped aside.

Inside, the dingy building lamps dimly lit the passageway. Seahorn walked down it, pausing at Keelan's door. He looked through the little barred window. Keelan lay sleeping. He counted back the days. Anytime now, the boy's father should be here with the ransom. A quarter of a million dollars, the thought of that gave Seahorn a warm feeling beneath his skin.

He went farther down the passage. Another sentinel stood by a door there.

"The key," Seahorn said. The sentinel gave it to him.

Seahorn unlocked the door and entered.

Bosalita got up from her cot. Still wearing her dress, she was unkempt and tired-looking. She picked up her blanket and wrapped it around her shoulders.

"There are rats here," she said. "They run across me when I sleep. Let me go."

Seahorn scowled. "Why should I? You betrayed me. Caine was an important prisoner, and you helped him escape."

"I am sorry. I was a fool."

"I don't dispute that. But sorrow isn't enough to earn your freedom."

"My husband died in your service. Does that earn me no privilege?"

"Your husband, my dear Rosalita, meant nothing." Seahorn's smile became different and frightening. "I hired him for one reason. You. You do know you are a beautiful woman, do you not, Rosalita?"

He advanced. She backed away.

"I would rather die," she said.

"I can easily arrange that," Seahorn responded. "But there is no need for it. Come, Rosalita. I have been thinking of you. Be cooperative, and you will go free."

"I hate you!" she spat.

Seahorn lunged at her, grasping at her dress. Screaming, she kicked his shin, then slapped him. Her fingernails raked bloody furrows down his cheek.

Seahorn swore, backed off, and touched his hand to his face. He looked at the blood on his fingers.

"You just signed your own death warrant, sow!" he shouted at her. He spun and left the filthy chamber, slamming the door shut. He pushed past the sentinels and exited onto the plaza. When he was gone, the sentinels looked at each other and laughed, for they had heard everything, and one had watched through the window.

In his room down the passageway, Keelan wrapped his blanket into a tight roll and buried his head beneath it. He had been awakened by the turmoil, and now a woman was crying in the next room, and he did not want to hear it.

CHAPTER 9

Seahorn dined alone at his table; before him stood some of his men and Simon Caine. Caine was grimed and somewhat bloody.

"How hard did he resist?" Seahorn asked.

Fadden, slouching, as usual, his lower lip drooping beneath his cigarette, shrugged with one shoulder. "Not hard enough," he said. "But I thought we'd have to kill him, I did."

Seahorn wiped his lips, stood, and approached Caine. He looked into his face and gave him a smug, tight-lipped smile. "You should have joined me, to begin with," he said. "And you certainly shouldn't have tried to escape me."

Caine's throat felt like the floor of the Chihuahuan Desert. "You're loco," he said.

"I am a leader. A leader must be followed."

"You're not my leader."

"Then I'll be your captor."

"What do you want done with him?" Fadden asked.

"I haven't decided. Perhaps we will gather a reward for him. Perhaps we will just keep him locked up for a long, long time. I could have you killed, perhaps—but we are old friends, are we not, Simon?" Seahorn waved his hand. "Take him away. Lock him up and make sure he is well guarded."

"The storeroom again?"

"No. This time the carcel."

Bamon Fernandez had been standing to the rear, but now he stepped forward. "Neal, there's something you should know. Two men, an Anglo and a black man, tried to free Caine last night. We chased them, but they escaped us."

Seahorn's face darkened. "Did Caine know them?"

"He says he didn't. But he did not see their faces."

"Who were they, Simon?" Seahorn demanded.

"Lee and Grant."

Seahorn cursed. He drew a pistol from beneath his coat and whipped it down on Caine's head. Caine fell unconscious. "Take him away," Seahorn ordered. "Get him out of my sight."

Seahorn mulled it all as Caine was carried across the broad Serveto plaza. Who could have been trying to free Simon Caine, especially from such a large armed band?

The sun was distended and red like an overripe strawberry as it edged down toward the western mountains. The evening was cloudy and windy. Seahorn poured himself a shot of whiskey. Standing at the window, he looked across the enclosure, watching the movement of people below. He watched Fadden and two others carrying Caine into the carcel, drawing much attention from others. Ramon, however, was walking across the other side of the plaza toward the cantina, having taken his leave from Fadden as quickly as possible. Seahorn could not blame him; Fadden was a repulsive man and not inspiring of trust. Trust was becoming a rare commodity to Seahorn as well; he knew even Ramon was not as loyal as he acted.

Cattle lowed somewhere to the east, and in some alleyway, two tomcats squared off in a loud and violent battle. Probably for the affections of some female—and with that,

Seahorn was reminded of Rosalita Contero's spurning. The thought was welcome as a swallow of gall.

Seahorn drained off his glass and forced his thoughts onto another track. He looked over the old mission wall toward the notch of Puerta de Serveto. Soon, if all went well, the ransom for the Kensington boy should arrive through that rock gateway.

Seahorn thought about that quarter of a million dollars and again about leaving the Alianza. He was tired of its control, but mostly he was scared. He could feel the Alianza breathing upon him, bearing down, knowing of his embezzlements, and preparing some retribution.

Maybe he should leave tonight. But if he did, he would have none of that quarter-million dollars in ransom.

Unless — the thought burst upon him — he simply took the boy with him. Kidnapped him anew, in effect, and snatched him right out from beneath the nose of the Alianza. He could take the boy deep into Mexico, find some place where the Alianza couldn't reach them, and when the time was right, demand a new and bigger ransom from Kensington. This ransom he would share with no one except Old Pablo. He would find his old mentor and take him somewhere deep into South America, and there they could live the rest of their days splendidly.

He was becoming excited now. He put down his glass and turned to a heavy door leading into a small hall just off his chamber. Dark and dusty, this passage was used by no one but himself. He lit a match and walked by its light to the end, where he fitted a key into a heavy lock and opened another door, this one reinforced with iron bands.

A squat, fat safe stood before him. He lit a candle in a wall holder and knelt, turning the combination dial. He opened the safe with a creak.

The candlelight revealed stacks of money, wages to be paid by him for the Alianza, and that he had embezzled. He picked up some of the bills and moved them between his fingers.

The light around him changed. He turned, standing, quickly putting the bills back into the safe. He closed the safe door with his foot, touched his hand to his pistol butt.

"*Saluda,* Neal."

"Ramon, I might have killed you."

Ramon's eyes flickered around the little room. This was the first time he had been here. "You spend much time here, eh, Neal?"

"It's no concern of yours."

"Of course not. Forgive me. But come out, then. I have something to say to you."

They left the chamber, and Seahorn closed the door. n Ramon's eyes was a look of concern, maybe anger, though hidden beneath his eternally calm veneer.

"What is wrong?" Seahorn asked.

"I was told you locked up Rosalita Contero."

"I had no choice. She helped Simon Caine escape."

"I want her."

A long silence followed. Peculiar emotions raged through Seahorn. He forced a smile. "I believe you care for her, Ramon."

"Call it what you want. I want her freed."

Seahorn paced in silence for a few moments, looking at the tiled floor. Though he hid it well, jealousy burned inside him. Ramon's handsome face, his calm, dignified manner—, these things would probably win the affections Rosalita had denied Seahorn, and Seahorn knew it. But he merely nodded to Brice.

"Very well. She is your care. But remember, Ramon: She betrayed me. She may betray you as well."

Seahorn went to a desk, pushed back the roll top, and wrote a directive on a piece of paper. He signed it with his unmistakable flourished signature and handed it to Ramon, who took the paper wordlessly and turned away.

"How long have you had your eye on her, Ramon?"

"Had Juan Contero not been killed in the kidnapping, I would have killed him upon his return. Quietly, secretly. Perhaps an accident."

"I will tell you something before she does," Seahorn said. "I went to her last night. She is a beautiful woman. I could not resist."

Ramon glared threateningly. "Did you..."

"No."

Ramon exhaled. "That is good because if you had, I would have killed you, *amigo.*"

Seahorn looked coldly at him. He pulled a cigarette from a wooden case and lit it as Ramon walked out, paper in hand.

Seahorn smoked and thought. This was a night for decisions, and he made one.

He went to the window and called to a man passing below: "Bring me, Fadden, at once."

He finished his cigarette and waited.

Fifteen minutes later, J. W. Fadden sat slouched in one of Seahorn's overstuffed chairs, picking at a thumbnail and looking, as always, devoid of concern about anything at all. But that was a contrived appearance; he was very interested in what Seahorn had just ordered him to do.

"When?" he asked.

"As quickly as is feasible. Do not fail. I can no longer trust him, and she has betrayed me... betrayed the Alianza already. There will, of course, be much good money in it for you."

"Mighty fine." Fadden stood, stretching like a rumpled old tomcat. "I won't let you down," he said. He walked to the door and left.

———

For seemingly endless hours, Brice and Orion had been picking their way along through rocky hills that wind and desert rains had carved into a series of piled terraces that were difficult to maneuver about. The horses had a hard time of it here, and they frequently stopped to let them rest. Orion used his hat to water them out of a water bag carried on one of the packhorses. The red sun declined, and night spread across the dry barrens.

"Can't go much farther tonight, Mr. Brice," Orion said.

But Brice was eager. "Moonlight's bright, and it's cool. Let's go as far as we can."

He was thinking much of Keelan tonight but also of Simon. He wondered what had become of his brother. Probably he was dead now. Brice regretted the years of estrangement from his brother. The old arguments and divisions seemed unimportant now.

At least, he thought, Simon died on the right side. He had apparently not cooperated with Seahorn. Based on what he had been told by Strahan and what he had seen and heard on his own, it was easy for Brice to piece together what must have happened. Simon had gone to Serveto, somehow angered Seahorn, and then escaped. Seahorn had sent the riders after him, and Simon had been recaptured and taken back. Probably he had been executed.

But maybe not. *If you're alive, Simon, and if I can, I'll try to get you out, too,* Brice inwardly vowed.

"Listen!" Orion whispered. "Somebody following us."

They quickly cut right into a small canyon, and there they waited. No sound stirred except that of the wind through the rock maze.

"I swear I heard something back there," Orion said.

"Let's make camp here," Brice suggested. "We'll post watch for a time and see what turns up."

Orion nodded. Somewhere out there, a coyote howled.

Hours passed, and Orion and Brice heard and saw nothing to indicate there was anyone on their trail. Eventually, both exhausted men nodded and fell asleep.

Morning light and the smell of coffee awakened Brice. He rolled over, groaning, and rubbed his head as he yawned himself back to consciousness. The coffee scent was enticing, but he was surprised Orion had risked building a fire to brew it.

He opened his eyes. Orion was only now stirring awake. After a few groggy moments of realization, Brice leaped up.

A stranger with a tin coffee cup in his hand sat on a rock a few yards away from a small mesquite fire. He lifted the cup as if in a toast to Brice.

"Good morning," the stranger said. He was a small-framed but solid man in fancy riding clothes, and he had a fine auburn beard parted at the chin. His derby sat on his knee.

"Who are you?" Brice demanded, looking around for his pistol.

Morrison Deguere smiled and said, "My name is Hugh Talbot." From his manner, one would surmise there was nothing unusual about his sudden appearance and his building of the fire.

"What are you doing in our camp?" queried Orion, who now had come around and ascertained the circumstances. Orion had done better than Brice; the young black man already had his revolving Colt rifle up and trained on Deguere.

"I'm here to help you, gentlemen," he said. "Let me congratulate you on leaving a rather difficult trail. For a time, I thought I would not find you."

"You know us?" Brice asked.

"You are Brice James, and prior to that, you were James Brice Caine. You are the son-in-law of Garth Kensington, the brother of Simon Caine, and you are on your way to Serveto to attempt to reclaim your kidnapped son. As for you, young man," he said to Orion, "you are a surprise. I confess I don't know you, nor did I expect to find any but Mr. James here in this camp. Nevertheless, accept my hellos."

"You'll be saying hello to Jesus if you twitch," Orion said.

"Believe me, I will remain still. I will do you no harm. In fact, I feel sure I can do you some good."

"Who are you—besides your name?" Brice asked.

"I am an agent of the United States Department of the Treasury's Secret Service."

"Secret Service?" Brice developed a sudden suspicion. "You're after my brother."

"Simon Caine? Heavens, no." Deguere laughed. "I'm seeking a much bigger game than he. I'm after the Alianza. Do you know what that is?"

"I know Neal Seahorn's in it and that he's got my boy."

"Precisely. The Alianza is also a growing source of counterfeit currency and of threats against the safety of certain federal officials and American citizens. The Treasury Department is quite concerned."

"So they send out one man? You're a liar."

"They sent out five of us as an investigative team. Two were killed, two were wooed into the Alianza. But I have no plan to attempt a single-handed overthrow of such a massive crime system. I am a fact-gatherer, that is all. However, I admit the kidnapping of your son has persuaded me to expand my role somewhat. I want to help you get him out— and in the process, get inside the walls of Serveto. There is where I can really learn what the Alianza is about and what Seahorn's role in it is.

"Seahorn is wanted very badly by the federal government at the moment, as you might imagine. We believe he might be persuaded, by threat or leniency, to provide important evidence against the Alianza."

Brice shook his head. "Why should we trust you? Show some proof of your identity."

Deguere chuckled. "A man does not enter the territory of Mexican Bandidos and antigovernment criminal conspirators and carry such identification. Such a man would find himself quickly dead."

"So all we have is your word as to who you are?"

"Precisely."

"How did you know me? And how did you know about Simon—and the kidnapping?"

"It shouldn't surprise you that a Secret Service agent would know about Simon Caine and his kin, should it? You have hidden your kinship to him well, Mr. James, but the federal government knows of it. It is our job to know such things. Consider the Alianza, for instance. What the Alianza does I find out about one way or another, sooner or later. But in your case, my knowledge isn't as mysterious as it sounds. Unfortunately, word of the kidnapping of your son has spread. You need all the assistance you can get, Mr. James."

Orion still held the Colt rifle aloft. "He's lying, Mr.

Brice. I guarantee you nobody at the ranch has breathed a word about the kidnapping. Want me to kill him?"

"No. Put the rifle down, Orion."

"But he—"

"Put it down."

Reluctantly, Orion obeyed.

"We've already been attacked by one small group," Brice said. "Orion is an old friend who came along at the right time to keep me from being murdered. The Alianza killed Orion's father; he has reason to hate it just like I do. Now, how do you propose to help me?"

"If nothing else, I will strengthen your number by one. Against bandidos and mercenaries, that counts for little, I know, but little is better than nothing. Besides, as I said, I need to get inside Serveto. Working together, perhaps we can achieve that. I don't know how I could do it alone."

"Let me shoot him, Mr. Brice," Orion urged again.

Brice shook his head. "No. Mr. Talbot, I may be a fool, but I'll trust you, partly because I can at least keep my eye on you if you're close by. And you're right: I need what help I can get. I came looking for Simon's, but that didn't work out."

Deguere said, "It's my belief that Simon Caine was headed for Serveto. Is he there?"

Brice was impressed that the false Talbot knew as much as he did. He instinctively began to trust him just a bit more, telling him briefly about Simon's apparent escape and recapture.

Deguere sipped his coffee. "Seahorn may indeed kill him," he said. "If so, he will have achieved something scores of others have failed to do. But if I were a betting man, I'd put my money on Caine. He's a hard man to kill."

He tossed the coffee on the little fire, extinguishing it. "Have some coffee while it's still hot, gentlemen," he said. "It's growing too light to keep a fire burning. Then let us move on. In following you yesterday, I found evidence of horsemen about. Bandidos, probably. By the way, do you actually have the ransom with you?"

"No," Brice said. "If I'm going to trust you, I may as well tell you. The Kensington empire is bankrupt."

Deguere clicked his tongue. "A shame. You can count on my silence. We certainly wouldn't want Neal Seahorn to hear that the well from which he expects to draw his latest fortune has run dry."

"No, we wouldn't." Brice turned to Orion. "Let's move on."

"I still think you ought to let me shoot him," Orion said.

———

The sentinel who brought food to Caine's cell looked inside, smirked, and said, "Smell the sweet perfume of this cell, Caine? It was home to a beautiful woman. Believe me; you are a far uglier sight than the widow Rosalita Contero, *amigo.*"

Caine started. "Rosalita Contero was a prisoner?"

"Do not ask about her, *amigo.* Ramon Fernandez, he may become jealous and..." The Mexican put his finger across his neck in the universal throat-cutting gesture.

Caine was dismayed. If Rosalita was a prisoner, it could only mean her help to him had been detected, and she had been punished for it.

"Where is she now?" he asked.

"Probably in Ramon's bed," the man said. "He came and took her away with him. He had a paper from Seahorn that said he could do so. You were unconscious when he came to take her."

The sentinel left, and Caine sat down on the chain-hung bunk. He wondered if Rosalita was all right and regretted that he had been the cause of her trouble. Perhaps Ramon would take care of her, protect her—but Caine didn't really trust Ramon any more than he did Seahorn.

Caine believed that unless he came up with some plan of escape, Seahorn would eventually have him killed for lack of any other good options. Caine was a threat to both Seahorn and the Alianza now, so even if Seahorn didn't really want him dead, in the end, it would probably come to that anyway. Unless...

What? Caine searched his options and found only two. The first: He could tell Seahorn he had changed his mind and was ready to join with him—but Seahorn would be unlikely to believe that. Which left only the second option—escape once more.

But this time, it would be much more difficult. Maybe impossible.

Caine ate and then lay down. He needed to gather his strength as he thought out a plan. But he was tired and, after a few minutes, fell asleep.

The sound of someone crying awakened him. It was a deep night. He pushed up for a moment, not remembering where he was.

"Hello?" he said lowly.

The crying continued. It sounded like a child, probably a boy. He remembered then what he had overheard before his escape, a boy kidnapped.

Caine rose. He cupped his hands on the wall and spoke into them, concentrating his voice so it would pass through the stone.

"Son—you all right?"

The crying stopped. He heard sniffles. "I'm all right," a youngster's voice returned. "I'm just scared."

Caine could barely hear the boy and told him so.

"There's a hole through the wall down at the floor," the boy said. "The rats go in and out through it. If we get down there, we can talk through it."

Caine did that. As he did, he had the mental experience that talking to children usually brought him: a flash of a perfectly clear memory of his own son, Marcus—-his face, his voice, his eyes. All now forever gone.

The hole was small but sufficient to allow Caine to see a little into the next room. He had to force himself to ignore the vermin droppings in which he had to lay in order to peer through the opening. Suddenly he saw the boy's eye looking back at him, no more than a foot away. Caine could see only that eye, yet he could tell when the boy smiled. He smiled back.

"Be brave, young fellow," Caine said. "I'm planning to get us out of here." And so he was; the moment he had heard the boy cry, he had, without conscious thought, expanded his hope of escape to include escape for the boy, too. If Caine thought about it, which he did not, he would have realized that the escape of the boy was now, in fact, becoming more important to him than his own.

"I am brave," the boy said. "My pa taught me to be. But in here, it's hard sometimes."

"I know," Caine said. "It looks to me like we're two jackrabbits caught in the same snare."

"Are you kidnapped, too?" the boy asked.

"No. I just happened to get on the wrong side of somebody important here."

"What's your name?"

"Simon."

"Simon, who?"

"Simon's good enough." Caine was getting an almost eerie feeling: something about the boy was uncannily familiar. Caine searched his mind to determine where he might have seen him.

"My name is Keelan. I'm kidnapped. But my pa and grandpa will pay to get me out. Then they'll have the bad men arrested, and the Texas Rangers will hang them all." "So they might, Keelan. Who's your folks?" "My grandpa is Garth Kensington. My pa is Brice James." There was no sound from the other side for a long time.

The boy looked through the hole again; no one was looking back.

"Mister? Are you there? Mister?"

The eye returned, looking back into Keelan's.

"Mister? You all right?"

"I'm all right, son. And you're going to be all right, too. I promise."

CHAPTER 11

Ramon Fernandez strode back toward his quarters with two long loaves beneath his arm. It was not yet dawn, but he was hungry and stirred the baker early from his own bed and bought the loaves for his breakfast and Rosalita's.

Ramon lived in an upper-level room in the building that once housed the Serveto Mission nuns' quarters. He had never particularly liked the drab place, but now that Rosalita was with him, it seemed much brighter and inviting—even if so far Rosalita had spurned his affection, treating him with an uncomfortable combination of gratitude for his rescuing her from the carcel and seeming disgusted at his touch. Ramon didn't really mind—so far. She was an interesting challenge. He had cast his eye on Rosalita a long time ago, well before the death of her husband.

Ramon climbed the stairs and mounted the balcony, but at the full-length window, he paused, some instinct warning him. He touched the latch and cautiously pushed the window open.

"Rosalita?"

He dropped the loaves and drew his pistol. "Rosalita?"

She was not inside the main room. He slipped to the bedroom and saw her there, her face twisted in fear. J. W. Fadden held her from behind. His pistol was jammed against her temple.

Fadden's drooping lip curled into his typical sneer of a smile. "Hello, Ramon."

"Let her go."

"No can do. Got me a job, you see. Got to take care of a big Mex rat that's been nosing around Seahorn's grain pile too long. He wants rid of it."

Ramon took a long breath. He seemed to grow taller. "Seahorn sent you?"

"Surely did. But don't worry—I ain't inclined to do what he said to do."

"What?"

"I aim to let you do it yourself."

"No!" Rosalita cried. "Run, Ramon!" *Ironic,* Ramon thought; *at a time like this, she seems to care something about me.*

Fadden laughed. He squeezed Rosalita and cut off her breath. "Ramon won't run, pretty lady. He don't run from nothing," he said. "He's a brave man, you see. Brave enough to plug his own brain rather than see you lose yours all over these walls."

Ramon's finger moved microscopically on the trigger of his long pistol.

"Put that pistol to your noggin, Ramon."

Slowly Ramon's pistol went up. Rosalita began to cry.

"That's good, Ramon. That's right. Put it to your head... no—even better, in your mouth. That way, you can't miss."

Ramon, his eyes boring into Fadden's, obeyed. Rosalita was near collapse; she hung in Fadden's grip.

"Adios, Ramon," Fadden said. "Do it."

"No!" Rosalita cried. *"Madre de Dios!"*

The sound of the shot echoed across the plaza of Serveto,

awakening sleepers. Neal Seahorn was among them. He leaped from his bed, raced to the window, and flung it open. Below, people emerged into the plaza. Seahorn heard a woman scream, then another shot.

"Where?" Seahorn shouted at a man below.

"In Ramon's rooms," he said.

Seahorn looked across to the old nun's quarters. He smiled to himself as he turned.

But motion at Ramon's window suddenly caught the corner of his eye. The window swung open, and someone emerged. Seaborn quailed. It was Ramon, and he was carrying the body of J. W. Fadden. Blood dripped from a hole in the forehead of the corpse.

The people in the plaza sent up sounds of surprise. Several laughed. Ramon walked down the stairs, carrying the body as if it weighed nothing, and strode across the plaza with it. Ramon looked up at Seahorn as he approached. He went out of sight, then Seahorn heard him coming up the stairway. With dread, Seahorn went to his door and opened it.

Ramon came down the hall. Fadden's draining body was gruesome and pale.

Ramon dumped the corpse at Seahorn's feet. "Yours, *compadre?*" He wheeled and walked away.

It took Ramon a long time to comfort Rosalita. The bullet he had fired into the head of Fadden had passed within two inches of her own. Fadden's blood had splattered her, and even though Ramon had scrubbed it from her until her skin was coppery red, she still talked of it and wiped at her face.

At last, she calmed as he held her.

"I want to leave this place," she said, her voice quaking.

"We will leave, soon, very soon. I will take you away."

"No. I want to go alone."

Ramon put his hands on her shoulders and pushed her back to look into her eyes. "Even now, you will not have me?" he said. "Do you not realize he would have killed you had I not shot him?"

"I realize. But if I stay here, and if I stay with you, there will always be more of such things. I want only to live a quiet and peaceful life."

"Then live it with me. We will go away. I will learn to live differently."

"As what? A farmer? A merchant? You would have no patience with such things. Men such as you cannot change, Ramon. I lived too many years with one to believe differently."

"So you are rejecting me?"

"I am asking you to let me go. And another thing—to help me free Simon Caine again. I saw them bring him back to the carcel before you came for me. He looked almost dead."

Ramon's expression slowly hardened. Anger welled up. "So it is Caine who interests you," he said. He shoved her to the floor. He drew his pistol and thumbed back the hammer. "I ought to..."

Rosalita closed her eyes, fully expecting to die. But Ramon restrained himself. He lowered the hammer and holstered the pistol, then reached down and roughly pulled her up.

"Come, Rosalita. If it is Caine you want, you can have him. And the rats of the carcel."

"Let me go!" she shouted, trying to tug away.

Ramon smiled. "No. No. I was loco to free you. Let Seahorn and Caine have you. I don't want you."

He dragged her out and down the stairs. She screamed and fought, drawing stares and laughter from those in the plaza. Ramon ignored them all as he carried the writhing woman across the courtyard toward the makeshift carcel.

Neal Seahorn heard the commotion and walked out onto his balcony. He watched Ramon disappear around the carcel toward the door on the far side. Surmising that Rosalita was being reincarcerated, Seahorn smiled. She must have rejected Ramon, too. But his smile quickly faded, for he was worried.

Fadden had failed to kill Ramon, and Ramon obviously knew that Seahorn had been the one who was behind the attempt. Ramon would not let that pass.

Seahorn made up his mind: It was time to go.

———

The first slug came from above and almost took off Deguere's head. He dropped from his horse and scrambled to the rocks beside the narrow trail. He drew his pistol but wished he had been able to unboot his saddle carbine.

The packhorse spooked and tugged at its ties, broke free, and ran back down the trail. Orion Jones dropped out of his saddle, managing to take the burnished revolving Colt rifle with him. Brice reacted more slowly. A second shot winged down from the high rocks and almost struck his mount before he threw himself out of the saddle and landed roughly on the rocky trail. He popped up, drew out his own long arm, and ran for the trailside boulders.

"Where?" Brice shouted across to Deguere and Orion.

Orion answered by lifting the revolving Colt and firing upward above Brice's head. Someone above cursed in Spanish and scrambled back.

More bandidos.

Now Brice saw movement above the other side of the narrow pass. "Look out!" he yelled. A huge boulder, dislodged by someone above, rolled down toward Orion and

Deguere. They threw themselves to either side just in time to avoid being crushed, but the tail of Orion's duster was caught beneath the stone.

A bandido whooped like an Indian and appeared briefly where the boulder had been. He fired down, slugs spanging around Orion, who could not twist around sufficiently to retaliate. But Brice and Deguere fired simultaneously. Neither hit the bandido, but their shots forced the man to draw back behind the rocks above.

Orion was tugging at his duster tail, then he gave it up and began slipping out of the long trail coat. The move left him momentarily but helplessly bound up—and precisely then, two horsemen pounded up the trail from behind, riding straight toward him.

Deguere stood, leveled his pistol, and fired. One of the riders pitched out of the saddle, then rose and ran for cover, gripping a bleeding arm. His riderless horse sped on by, kicking up dust and gravel. The second rider cursed and levered a carbine. Brice fired at him, missed, and Deguere lifted his pistol a second time. But a second boulder, much smaller, came tumbling from above and struck his shoulder, felling him roughly. He dropped his pistol as a miniature follow-up avalanche of gravel and fist-sized stones descended upon him, virtually burying him. Above, a jubilant bandido cheered at his success.

The bandido on the horse fired at Orion but missed. Brice was about to shoot at the man again when something struck the chamber of his rifle just above the trigger. A slug, fired from above and intended for his head, had missed and destroyed his gun instead. Brice tossed down the weapon and drew his pistol. But now, two more riders came up the trail to join the one already there, and another horseman appeared from behind Brice. This one was a tall Anglo with deeply tanned skin and hair the color of the dust that now swirled through the little rocky pass.

The Anglo leveled a Smith & Wesson on Brice. "Drop it, friend. Now."

Brice obeyed. "You too, dark!" the man shouted at Orion. Orion's face twisted in a snarl of frustration as he complied.

Deguere dug himself out from under the pile of dirt and rock. He spat out dirt, glared angrily at the Anglo bandido leader, and began picking grit from his beard.

"Money," the Anglo said.

"We got no money," Brice returned. "That's the God's truth."

The Anglo fired a shot that almost pierced the toe of Brice's boot.

"Kill me, and it won't help you," Brice said. "We don't have any money."

The bandidos were gathering around their leader, leaving their various ambush perches and mounts. The wounded one who had run away came back, right hand around the left arm, blood running through fingers. In Spanish, he urged the Anglo to kill them all.

"Shut up," the Anglo said. "I kill them after I find where the money is."

"You seem to have a problem with either your hearing or your comprehension, my friend," Deguere said.

"The Apaches have been known to pluck out white men's beards a hair at a time," the Anglo responded. "It's a skill I've learned from the best of them."

Deguere arrogantly lifted his brows. Even in the midst of this crisis, Brice almost laughed; this man had looked uppity even while sprawled on his rump.

"I know you," Orion said to the Anglo. "You're Cato Blake."

"Ah!" Deguere said. "Comanchero turned Mexican highwayman. A fitting step up for such an infamous gentleman."

The Anglo started to say something to Orion, but he got

no further than opening his mouth. In silence, he regarded the young black man, looking at him as if he recognized him. Suddenly he wheeled and looked at Brice just as closely. He tucked his Smith & Wesson back into the cross draw rig he wore.

"*Amigos,* you got my apology," he said. "I didn't recognize you. You'll suffer no harm from Cato Blake."

CHAPTER 12

The pronouncement left Brice and Deguere confused and casting glances at each other.

"You're married to Garth Kensington's daughter if I ain't mistaken," Cato Blake said to Brice. "I see you one time — though you didn't see me."

"I don't understand," Brice admitted.

"Old man Kensington was good to me once when I was down and out," the outlaw said. "It was maybe six years ago, and I was on the run from some rangers. I'd stole a few sheep from an old Irishman about Presidio. Your pappy-in-law hid me out, gave me some food, steered them rangers the wrong way. Said he liked the look of my face. I never forgot that. No, sir."

"But Garth always said..." Brice trailed off. He had started to comment on his father-in-law's apparent hatred of the infamous desert bandit Cato Blake, but he realized such might be dangerously imprudent at the moment. Thinking about it, though, it made more sense. Six years ago, Blake was not the widely known criminal he was today, and it was just like Garth Kensington to take pity on some dusty loser on the run.

Deguere stood, dusting himself off. "Well, it's good it was sheep you stole. Had it been cattle, Kensington would have strung you up."

Cato looked at Deguere with a threatening expression. Brice stepped up quickly and thrust out his hand, hoping to avert trouble. Cato looked like the kind of man who might shoot an irritating stranger the way a man swats a bothersome fly.

"My name's Brice James. I'm not happy to have been shot at, but I appreciate you not killing me."

"Wouldn't have jumped you if I'd known you. The fact is, we were waiting for a group what's supposed to be hauling guns, dynamite, and whiskey into Serveto when you come along. One of the men got trigger-happy."

"Dynamite, you said?" Deguere's face had lost its smug expression. He now looked keenly interested.

"Yep. I don't exactly know what's going on in Serveto, but for the last month, they've hauled in guns, freight, liquor. Even one kidnapped boy, so I hear."

"The boy—is he all right?" Brice asked eagerly.

Cato looked like a slow-thinking fellow, but the appearance was deceptive. He cocked his head and looked piercingly at Brice. "He wouldn't be your boy, would he?"

Brice nodded.

"Don't know whether he's all right or not. I didn't see him myself. Rico did, though." He waved toward the bandido with the bleeding arm, who glared back with his teeth gritted.

"These dynamite couriers, when will they be through?" Deguere asked.

Cato asked Brice, "Who is this jackass?"

Brice said, "A friend. He's going to help me get my boy back."

"Out of Serveto? You know what you're getting into?"

Deguere said, "When a small force takes on a large fortified one, a little equalization helps. That's why I asked about the dynamite."

Cato frowned. "I figure to keep that for myself. I don't recall making you any offers."

"It's your chance to repay your debt to Garth Kensington," Deguere urged. "You take the whiskey, the guns—just let us have some of the dynamite."

Cato said, "My debt to Garth Kensington was repaid the moment I let you boys keep breathing."

Orion, who up until now had been standing to the rear in silence, stepped up and joined Brice. He looked at Cato. "I remember you, mister," he said. "You hid out behind the grain bin for a day or so. I brung you your food."

"I remember, boy. I'm obliged to you."

"What about the dynamite?" Deguere said.

"Shut up," Brice cut in. He could tell the bandit disliked Deguere, whose pushiness might make his mercy wear thin. Brice turned to Cato. "Mr. Blake, as far as I'm concerned, you owe none of us a thing. But I do ask you this: For the sake of my boy, we could use at least a few sticks of that dynamite. I don't know how we'll use it or whether it will help, but it just might."

Rico of the bleeding arm began chattering angrily in a mixture of Spanish and English, protesting Brice's request. Cato listened to him until he was finished.

The outlaw sat down on a rock and put his elbow to his knee. Fingering his chin, he thought. The others silently watched as the wind whistled through the rock pass, and the strayed horses began meandering back into their owners.

Finally, Cato stood. "All right," he said. "There'll be some dynamite for you. But you got to help me get it. After all, I didn't kill you, and you did wing Rico in his gun arm."

The way he said it made it sound as if not having murdered them before was an act of great magnanimity.

Brice felt a burst of the first authentic hope he had known since starting on this impossible venture.

With dynamite, they might just be able to fight their way out of Serveto if it came to that. They just might be able to rescue Keelan after all. Maybe even Simon if he was still alive.

"You got a deal," Brice said. He extended his hand, and Cato shook it. The bandit's palm felt like the underside of an old boot worn out by sharp gravel.

"I'm just glad I was able to arrange this," Deguere said.

———

Caine sadly watched Rosalita Contero crying in the corner. The guards had brought her in shortly before and cast her roughly to the floor. They had lingered long enough to jest lewdly about the carnal opportunity they had just provided Caine; then, they slammed the door shut. Rosalita had crawled to the corner and cried, and there she remained.

"I won't hurt you, Rosalita. You know that" Caine said.

He had said it to her several times before, but she had not responded.

But now, she turned her reddened eyes on Caine. "I know," she said. "But Seahorn will. He has already tried to kill Ramon, I think because of me."

"What happened?"

She told him about the attack and resultant death of J. W. Fadden.

"Interesting," Caine said. "The powers that be in Serveto fighting among themselves. What will Ramon do now that he knows Seahorn wants him dead?"

"I think he will kill him. But first, he wants to steal his money."

Caine said, "Listen to me. There's a boy in the next room, and I aim to get him out of here. You, too. You helped me out once; I'll help you out now."

Rosalita wiped her face. "How?"

"I haven't fully figured that yet," Caine said. "Seems to me there's only a couple of things that would persuade our guards to let us slip: the threat of death or the promise of reward."

"But we have no weapons and no money," Rosalita said.

"No money, you're right. But there's always a weapon."

Rosalita smiled and nodded. "Sometimes a woman can be the best weapon, no?"

Caine smiled, too. "That's a fact."

———

Despite the pact between Brice and himself, Cato insisted on thoroughly searching his new partners. He found a hip flask of good whiskey on Deguere and immediately claimed it as his own. He began drinking it as the band hid among the boulders above the rocky pass, and his tongue loosened and gave forth his personal history.

"I was borned in Arkansas, but my ma, she died a few days after, and I don't remember her. Pa wasn't no good, and I wasn't either. We come across Texas, mostly running from the law, and crossed the Pecos. Apache trouble, Comanches, other outlaws, nothing stopped us. Pa up and died on me one night. Got drunk and choked to death on a piece of melon rind. I come across the Bravo into Mexico and started waylaying folks here and there, stealing what I needed, just trying to make a dollar or two…"

Brice rose, not interested in hearing more. He picked up the Winchester carbine Cato had given him to replace his own damaged weapon and wandered away some distance. Keeping his head low so as not to be potentially visible from below, Brice settled back against a rock that had been shaded through most of the day and thus felt deliciously cool through his sweat-soaked shirt. He looked over his grimy self, considering that he hadn't been this filthy and reeking since the war years. His bad leg ached, and he rubbed it.

"Mr. Brice?"

Orion had crept up on him unseen. It made him start — and also realize the natural stealth of the young man. Orion had the stance and grace of a natural outdoorsman; he seemed comfortable in these rugged barrens.

"Sit down, Orion. Keep your head down, or Cato might shoot it off for fun."

"Yeah. He's a strange one. I still can't figure out why he didn't kill us."

"He might yet, or at least get us killed. I wonder how many will be in this cargo team we'll be jumping?"

"Hadn't thought about that."

Orion settled himself down with the effortlessness of a young cat. "Mr. Brice, is it stealing to take something a man has dropped?"

"I don't know. What are you talking about?"

"This." Orion reached into a pocket and pulled out Deguere's notebook. "Old Redbeard, he dropped this out of his riding jacket after the rocks and scrap fell on him down there. I kind of picked it up. I ain't the best for reading, but it looks to me like he's been lying to us. The name on it sure ain't Hugh Talbot."

Brice looked over the notebook. "Deguere. M. Deguere. Where have I heard that name?"

Brice read further. "Look at this, Orion. Records about my brother. The old wolf is after Simon. And here, look— 'Payment received. W Montrose, six hundred dollars.'" Brice slapped dust from his knee. "He's played me for a fool. Using you and me and what's happened to Keelan to get at Simon."

He flipped pages. "Look at this: 'June second, Detouring away from Wichita, hear from Washington office that bank robbery in St. Louis is thought to be Alianza crime. Murder of county judge in southern Illinois in newspapers. Also Alianza, government believes.'"

Brice skipped farther down.

"August fifth—Little doubt now that Caine is going to visit brother. Also may visit old companion Strahan. Suspect Caine also to see Seahorn.

"Seahorn working for Alianza, involved in several robberies. Bank robbery in Dallas possibly led by Seahorn underlings."

Brice stopped and closed the notebook. "I'm a fool, Orion. To think I accepted him as a government agent just because he said he was. What are we going to do about him?"

"Do? Go face-to-face with him, that's what!" Orion said. "Shoot him if you need to. I'll do it! I'm already in trouble with the law as it is."

Brice firmly shook his head. "I won't murder a man nor see you do it. But once we get the dynamite, we break him off clean."

"I still say kill him."

At that moment, one of Cato's gunmen gave a low whistle. Cato, who had seemed totally drunk before, now appeared to be stone sober. Deguere lifted his derby from his brow and slid over to the natural breastworks overlooking the enclosed pass. The atmosphere became tense.

"Look yonder," Orion whispered.

Coming in from the east was a line of packhorses, led by a line of riders. Eight men, it appeared.

They checked their rifles and waited. Suddenly the air seemed very still and hot.

CHAPTER 13

Ramon Fernandez wiped his mouth on his cuff and stood. He staggered, for he was drunk. Plunking money onto the table, he weaved out of the cantina.

Drunkenness was not characteristic of him, especially this early in the day. He mostly drank when having trouble with women, and at the moment, the face of Rosalita Contero was all he could think about.

He hadn't really wanted to return her to the carcel, particularly to the same cell as Simon Caine. It had been rage that made him do it. Rage was the one force in his life that Ramon could not keep in check—it had been like that since the time when as a young man, he had assaulted a village priest who criticized him for his habits. From that time on, it had been evident to Ramon that he was destined for something other than a life of following somebody else's rules.

He kept to the shade of the buildings as he walked. Some of the people who passed him spoke or nodded, but he ignored them. He fought the urge to free Rosalita once again from Seahorn's carcel. No. He wouldn't do it. She had scorned him, so let Seahorn have her. If he wanted, he could toss her to his two-legged animals for whatever fate they could dream up for her. Ramon didn't care. Wouldn't care.

He turned into an alley and sat down. He lit a small *cigarro* and let the smoke sooth him. He thought again of Neal Seahorn's safe full of money. When he had finished the *cigarro,* he stood, feeling a little more stable. Looking around the plaza, he realized how sick he was of this place. The sun-blasted compound with its crumbling, century-old buildings and human-maggot inhabitants offended Ramon, who had always thought himself more refined than the average man. He decided on the spot that it was time to complete his work and go.

Ramon thought it over. He had heard that soon, maybe tonight, a shipment of weapons and whiskey was expected at Serveto. Then there was the ransom for the kidnapped boy—that should also be here soon. Ramon suspected that when the ransom did arrive, Serveto would see the last of Neal Seahorn and the contents of his safe. Unless, of course, somebody else moved more quickly.

"Tonight," Ramon whispered up at Seahorn's window. "Tonight, we settle our debts."

He waved off across the compound toward his own quarters, ready to sleep.

———

For a small group, the Alianza weapons couriers put up a valiant battle. But their efforts were futile against Cato's brutal attack. Brice fired off three ineffective shots, then stopped, feeling that somehow this ambush was wrong, even if its victims were nothing but gunrunners and whiskey traders in commerce with scum like Neal Seahorn. Orion seemingly had no similar qualms, for Brice saw his tense enthusiasm as he fought with the revolving Colt rifle—though his shots seemed uncharacteristically inaccurate.

Deguere also joined Cato's attack eagerly, blasting at anything that moved below him, and it was clear he was trying to connect.

As the battle progressed—much longer than Brice expected—the narrow pass filled again with orange dust mingled with gunsmoke; Several packhorses and burros, laden with boxes and bundles covered with waterproof canvas, thrashed about and bucked in the confusion. They sent up a ruckus of brays and trumpeting. The men who had driven them sent up their own horrible wails, one by one, as Cato's men picked them off.

We shouldn't have agreed to this, Brice thought. *That's a massacre happening down there.*

Cato was perched about fifteen feet from Orion and Brice on the rim of the pass wall. He stood now, carefully took aim, and fired a shot that brought a short, final-sounding shriek from below. Cato whooped like an Indian, enjoying his work.

Brice took a quick look below. Two men remained alive out of the original eight. One threw down his rifle and raised his hands. His companion shouted at him and kept on firing. Cato's band released another volley, arid both of the men below fell. One lay still immediately; the other writhed for a moment until Cato pumped one more slug into him.

The pass suddenly grew quiet. Luminescent smoke and dust rose and dispersed. The burros, packhorses, and rider-less mounts milled about, bumping each other, some of them escaping the pass, and then they, too, grew still.

Cato stood and let out another whoop. He raised his rifle above his head and shook it. At that moment, he was the most clear image of pure savagery Brice had ever seen.

Already Cato's men were descending into the pass as quickly as they could. One leaped right over the drop and landed squarely in an empty saddle. The startled gelding beneath it trumpeted and bucked, throwing him off and drawing much laughter from his companions. The man rose, laughing, too, then did something that chilled Brice: He shot the gelding dead.

Lord above, get us out of here alive, Brice prayed. These are men who would help you one moment then blast out your brains the next.

Deguere was standing, smiling at Brice and Orion. "Quite a battle, eh?" he exulted.

"More like murder," Brice returned.

"Come now, my friend! Exterminating desert vermin is a high calling. This is war! Aren't we fighting to get back your son?"

"I am. You're not," Brice said.

Deguere looked puzzled, maybe even a little concerned by that remark, but he had no time to inquire. Cato shouted at them from below, waving whiskey bottles in each hand.

"Good whiskey, amigos! Join the celebration!"

"I don't want whiskey," Brice said. "Just dynamite."

He, Orion, and Deguere descended a southward slope that led them gradually back into the pass. The bloody bodies, lying with eyes and mouths open, were terrible to see. A scorpion skittered across the shattered forehead of one of the dead men. Already turkey vultures circled above.

Cato was still trying to push whiskey on his new friends, and Brice finally accepted a bottle to humor him. He took one small swallow, but he was in no mood to drink.

"Where's the dynamite?" Deguere asked Cato.

One of Cato's Mexicans ran up to him, dangerous-looking blasting sticks in hand. He dropped one; Brice thought he would not get his breath back again for at least ten seconds.

"*Dinamita!*" shouted the exuberant Mexican. "Blow Serveto into hell!"

"Not to mention us, unless you exercise a bit more care,

my friend," Deguere said as he gingerly took the dynamite. "Much more?"

"*Muy dinamita.* Three men make an army with *dinamita.*"

"Indeed."

"Come aside. I want to talk to you," Brice said to Deguere.

"Certainly." Deguere was carefully placing the blasting sticks into his pockets and spoke inattentively.

"I think maybe you lost this—Mr. Deguere." Brice held up the notebook.

Deguere's expression became stern. "Where did you—"

"I ought to kill you, Mr. Deguere. Kill you and leave you for the buzzards. I've heard your name before. Just who are you?"

Deguere looked sincerely stunned. He seemed to be faltering about for a lie, then he stopped. His words came with the flat sound of truth.

"So you've caught me. I'm a detective, and I work for William Montrose."

"You're after Simon."

"I'm after money. Whether it comes from Montrose in reward for your brother's death or if it comes from elsewhere makes no difference to me."

"Elsewhere?"

"Serveto. There must be great wealth there. I figured that by accompanying you, I could possibly get my hands on it. If not, at least I might complete my job for Montrose. It was worth a try."

Brice drew back his fist and pounded it into Deguere's mouth. The lip split, and blood poured into Deguere's auburn beard. Deguere shook his head as if to clear it, touched his lip, but otherwise seemed unaffected, even unangered.

"I suppose I deserve that, from your viewpoint."

"You deserve castration," Brice said. "What would you have done once we got into Serveto? Turned us over to Neal Seahorn to get his favor and maybe his money?"

Deguere lifted a finger. "Now, that's an idea I hadn't thought of. You've a devious brain, my friend. Actually, I was really ready to help you if I could, as long as I could pursue my own quest in Serveto as well. I'm not heartless, you know— the idea of a kidnapped boy is most unpleasant."

Brice was so angry speaking was difficult. "You're a lucky man, Deguere. If I were my brother, I'd be taking your scalp right here. But I'm more merciful— I'll let you ride out, and as long as I never see you again, you'll be safe from me. If I do see you, you die. Whenever, wherever."

Deguere had produced a handkerchief and was using it to staunch the blood flow from his lip. It slightly muffled his voice. "Come now don't you see I can still be of use to you? I'm still as capable as I ever was. And what do you care what happens to Simon Caine?"

"Keep talking, and I'll gut you."

"All right. I'll give you my word: I'll not harm Simon Caine —if he's alive, which I doubt—and I'll do all I can to help you free your son. All I want is a fair crack at Seahorn's money. It's a long shot, certainly, but worth the trying. You've got my word."

"Your word is so much spit. Get out of my sight. And leave that dynamite here. We need it all."

Deguere shook his head. "Well, it was a good effort." He straightened his derby. "Gentlemen, it's been too brief a pleasure, and I'm sorry it has come to this. You need not worry about seeing me again, Mr. James. You will not survive your mission, I fully believe. With my help, perhaps you could have." He smiled coldly. "Perhaps I can go to work for Seahorn later. I think he might need a good gravedigger. One who can dig holes sufficient for grown fools—and perhaps one just the size for the corpse of a boy."

Brice was on Deguere then, his fury coursing into his arms like blood through his veins. He hit Deguere again, again, but the bearded man expertly swept him off. He deftly kicked two times, knocking Brice to the dirt. Orion lifted his rifle, but before it was leveled, Deguere was pointing a derringer into the handsome black face.

"Don't be just another dead nigger," he said. He laughed in contempt, lowered the derringer, and walked away, and Orion, somehow, could not summon the nerve to shoot him.

CHAPTER 14

Under cover of falling darkness, Brice and Orion slipped unseen through the rocky notch of Puerta de Serveto. Above them, the western sky clung to the last fading traces of a rich crimson sunset as if reluctant to give in to the darkness. And the darkness would be deep tonight, for the clouds were pouring over the horizon and piling themselves thick against the sky. Thunder sounded, the wind kicked up, and the two travelers knew they were about to be struck by the fury of a rare desert storm.

As they led their mounts through the pass on hooves muffled with cloth wrappings, Brice felt his heart pound in his chest and his blood surge in his temples. Serveto lay just ahead, and in there, somewhere, was Keelan.

Being this close to his son did strange things to his emotions. He experienced both an intense longing for his son and a deep grief for him. He also missed Agatha terribly and wished he could touch her for a moment to gather strength for the coming ordeal.

They had abandoned the packhorses a mile back, but on Brice's horse was strapped a box with several sticks of dynamite. More than enough, Brice figured, to blow much of

Serveto off its century-old foundations. And God help him, he would love to do just that, if he could —after, Keelan was safe.

"Mr. Brice?"

"What?"

"You got any idea how to get into that place?"

"Cato said there is some sort of stream running through a grate at the northern wall, up against the hills. Maybe we can get through there some way."

Lightning arched across the sky, followed by a jolting round of thunder. Brice's horse whinnied and almost spooked.

"Whoa, boy. Calm down." Brice stopped. A deep sadness came over him. He turned to Orion.

"I can't have you go through with this," he said. "I have no real plan, no good chance of succeeding. I'm doing this because it's my boy in there, and I've got to. You should turn back while you can."

"Like I told you before, Mr. Brice. That was my pa they kilt."

Brice nodded. "All right. But you know that—"

"That we probably won't come back? Yeah, I know it. What does it matter for me? I've kilt now, and there's nothing but a rockpile or a noose for me—or just the trail and looking over my shoulder the rest of my days."

Brice said, "You're a friend, Orion. Best kind a man could have."

Orion seemed uncomfortable with the praise. "We'd best keep going," he said.

They went on farther, winding along the trail. The wind rose and fell. They topped a rise just as a big flash of lightning cracked the sky from end to end. By its light, they saw it: the town of Serveto, the big walled former mission, and presidio looming in its center. To Brice, it looked like a vast prison, gray and oppressive.

"God help us," he said, for the sight made him and Orion and their few handfuls of dynamite seem insignificant and helpless, like ants assaulting a bank safe.

Orion seemed to be having similar thoughts. He stood quietly, staring across at the seeming fortress.

"We're never even going to get in, Mr. Brice," he said hopelessly.

"I'll get in," Brice said. "I'll get in even if I have to scratch down the wall with my fingernails."

Lightning flashed again, and it started to rain.

———

Neal Seahorn watched the rising storm from his window and tossed down another glass of tequila. *Edgy tonight. Nervous about something—don't know what...*

Yet he did know. And he heartily wished that he had fled earlier in the day, simply run out rather than sit here and wait for the inevitable coming of Ramon.

He looked at his empty glass. His hand shook, blast it, shook like that of a doting old man! He slammed down the glass, angry at himself.

Why was he so afraid of Ramon? Was Neal Seahorn not the equal of any man in a fight?

At one time, maybe. Now, maybe not. He was growing older, though he disliked admitting it. How long had it been since he squarely faced a man in a gunfight? Or even in a fist-and-knuckle brawl? What Neal Seahorn was afraid of tonight was the unknown, and in this case, the unknown was himself.

The rain began, a sweeping storm that would pound the plaza into mud and wash red silt from the hills down through the gullies and gulches. A storm to drive everyone in Serveto inside their quarters...

Suddenly he realized it: he hadn't missed his best opportunity to leave Serveto after all. Nature was giving it to him right now. But he must move quickly. He went to a wardrobe and brought out saddlebags, which he stuffed with clothing, what food he had about, ammunition, and other goods. Then he opened the door into the hallway that led to the room where his safe stood.

When he knelt and began working the lock, he had a moment of doubt. If he double-crossed the Alianza, he would not be forgiven nor forgotten. They would look for him, they would find him, and he would die. The Alianza was a rattler with no rattles, and it could strike him when he was not expecting it.

He refused to think about it. Since when did Neal Seahorn run from any man or organization? And who could find Seahorn when he did not wish to be found?

But they found Simon Caine, he remembered. Found him when the federal government could not.

The heavy safe door creaked open, and Seahorn saw the stacks of bills in the safe. He forgot his fears then and knew he was doing the right thing. Outside, the storm grew louder; he could hear the rain driving against the thick-tiled roof. That was good—he would leave no tracks in such a storm.

A shadow, a subtle sound. Seahorn felt something like ice against his spine. Slowly he turned.

Ramon was very drunk. That Seahorn could see at once. The handsome Mexican stood, drenched from the storm, and toyed with his pistol, repeatedly turning the cylinder.

"*Saluda,* Neal. I have come to kill you."

Seahorn stood. He gulped, and it was like swallowing sand. "You're drunk, Ramon. You don't want to do this. Go home."

"No. No."

"Where is Rosalita?"

"Don't speak of her. You have made a blunder, Neal. You

sent a fool like Fadden to do a job too big for him—and that is too bad for you, for now, it is you who must die."

Ramon's bloodshot eyes drifted for a second to the open safe. "You were leaving, maybe? Taking the money with you?"

Seahorn's mind desperately searched for some scheme. "You always did see right through me, Ramon. Perhaps I was wrong about you. I'm glad Fadden didn't succeed. Listen— we can be partners, closer than ever before. You take half the money, I take half—"

"No! First, you die, then I take it all."

Seahorn stared coldly at him. "You want the money, then take it. Here—I'll even get it out for you."

He knelt at the safe, turning his back on Ramon. He was risking a backshot, but he had a good reason: a loaded Remington pistol he had hidden beneath the stack of cash as a precaution.

"There is enough here for both of us, Ramon," Seahorn said. "I hope you'll reconsider—"

Still crouched, he spun. The Remington blasted, deafeningly loud. Ramon pitched back against the wall, stood there for a moment, and then his pistol dropped to the floor, and he slowly slid down, leaving a red trail all the way down. The bullet had passed completely through him.

———

The wall at which Brice and Orion stood was thick and tall, impossible to scale, but near one corner, there was a narrow channel through which a small wet-weather stream ran. The builders of the Serveto presidio had not diverted it because it provided easy water for livestock, and so it remained. The channel was, in effect, a tunnel through the wall, but in its midst was a barrier of crossed iron bars.

Despite the rain, the water in the stream was no more

than ten inches deep at the moment, a muddy swirl that drenched Orion as he knelt in the passage and sought to work loose enough of the rusty bars to let himself through.

Brice hugged the wall outside, looking about for sentries. Every flash of lightning made him feel exposed. But he was grateful for the storm, too; it had apparently driven the guards from the walls and now covered the noise Orion made at his work.

Brice noticed the stream beginning to rise. He knelt and, in a whisper, called into his partner, "Any luck yet?"

As if in answer, Orion heaved back. A metallic wrenching noise heralded the removal of the first iron bar. The young man turned, grinning, and showed it to Brice.

"Good," Brice said. "How much more?"

"Couple more bars, and we can squeeze under the bottom."

He went back to his task, tugging at the ancient metal. The second bar came off easier than the first. He started pulling on a third.

"Water's rising," Brice whispered in.

Orion had been too busy to notice, but now he saw Brice was right. The water reached almost to his waist as he knelt.

He worked with greater vigor. At last, the iron bar gave a moaning creak of surrender and pulled away in his hand. One end, though, remained attached. No time to break it loose; Orion put his weight against it and bent it back as far as possible.

He looked over his shoulder to where Brice peered at him at the end of the channel.

"I'm going under—you shift in the dynamite," he said. He took a lungful of air and disappeared under the water.

In a moment, he appeared on the other side, soaked but smiling. Brice smiled, too. Success so far, they had found a workable entrance into Serveto.

Brice picked up the box of dynamite, covered in canvas,

and waded in a stoop back into the tunnel. At the grate barrier, he said, "Pull it up as fast as you can and try to get the water out. This may ruin some of it."

He submerged the box and pushed it through the opening Orion had made. It was a tight fit but sufficient. Orion brought up the box on the other side, quickly removed it from the protective canvas cover, and drained the little bit of water that had leaked in.

"Appears to be all right," he said.

Brice went back out and picked up their rifles and sidearms. These he passed to Orion through the grate.

Brice said, "Slip on out into the compound, find a place to hide. I'm coming through."

Balancing the box of dynamite and the weapons with difficulty, Orion crouch-walked to the inside mouth of the water channel. Brice saw him outlined there against the backdrop of the rain-battered grounds of Serveto, then he moved out and to the right.

Brice was on his knees in the stream, and the water was up past his waist. He filled his lungs with air and descended. Beneath the dark, swirling water, he could see nothing. He groped for the grate, found it, and began pulling himself through.

The storm seemed to give a massive shudder and cast off sweeping sheets of water. The hills outside Serveto belched out gushes of brown liquid. The passageway all but filled even as Brice struggled through the opening.

He was broader in the chest and stomach than Orion, and he barely fit the hole. Holding his breath, he fought to pull through, but it took a long time. His brain began to spin, stars to burst beneath his eyelids. *No, not like this. Don't let me drown this close to finding Keelan. Don't end it like this—*

Orion was becoming concerned. He had emerged into what appeared to be a large, empty livestock pen. He was hiding behind a small stable about five yards from the mouth of the water passage. The stream ran through the pen, filled nearly to the top.

And Brice still had not emerged.

He heard a shot—muffled and coming from the other side of the compound. He heard a voice calling, then another. The shot had apparently drawn attention. It might generate investigation, men in the compound, sentries back on the walls.

Still no Brice. Orion swore and put down his weapons. He ran back to the channel mouth and looked in.

He saw nothing but blackness vomiting out water. He could not see Brice at all.

"Mr. Brice?"

Suddenly there was movement nearby. He spun. A man was moving across the compound on the other side of the stone wall that formed one portion of this stock enclosure. Orion saw the up-and-down movement of his hat above the edge of that wall.

Though frustrated and fearful for Brice's life, he had no choice but to scurry back behind the stable. Voices. Two men there now and coming this way.

Orion picked up the weapons and the dynamite and moved along the back of the stable to its far side. There the pen wall was broken and low. He crossed it, entering a little grove of trees. He vanished into the shadows.

CHAPTER 15

Caine held up the sharpened piece of metal and examined it critically. Then he nodded in satisfaction. He had found the scrap beneath the straw on the floor, and he had patiently worked it to a point against the stone. Rosalita had altered between watching him work and watching the storm outside the barred window.

"You will kill the guard with that?" she asked.

"Nope," Caine said. "I doubt I'd get close enough to him. The point is for you to kill yourself."

"What?" Her expression almost made Caine laugh.

"Look, if we're to share the same cell, you might as well call me Simon—not that I intend either of us to be in this cell much longer. Don't worry; you won't really kill yourself. You'll just threaten to, very loud and very sincere."

Rosalita tried to surmise his plan. "But why would the guards try to stop me? Why would they care?"

"They may not. But I'm going to try to make them."

"And then?"

"Let's skin this bear before we tackle the next one. You get back into that corner, where they'll have to come all the way in to get you. Put the sharp part to your neck... wait a minute." Caine probed his arm with the point and drew blood. He let a little of it pool on his arm.

"Smear some of that on your neck and touch the point there," he said. "Makes it more convincing. And you've got to sound completely plumb stark loco; else, they won't buy it. Understand?"

She nodded as she dabbed some of Caine's blood at her throat. She crossed herself, took the sharp bar, and went to the corner. There she looked back at Caine.

"Go to it," he said.

Her first scream was enough to convince even Caine she was in utter despair. She gave another and another and began babbling Spanish words Caine could not understand.

The guards appeared at the door, looking through the little window. One of them shouted at Rosalita, but she continued crying out, probing the sharp point into her throat.

Caine waved at her. "Aren't you going to stop her? She's ready to carve out her own throat!"

The guards looked disturbed and uncertain. One ordered Rosalita to stop, but Caine laughed.

"She's given up, figures she's going to die a worse death if she doesn't do it herself."

One of the guards said, "Well, what does it matter? No one will care if she lives."

Caine laughed. "You're a fool, then. Neal Seahorn and Ramon Fernandez both love that woman—the only reason she's in here now is that they're too busy fighting over her to know what to do with her. She dies; you'll die."

Rosalita gave a particularly startling scream. Caine was amazed to see her actually cut the skin of her throat a little. Fresh blood flowed down her neck.

The guards mumbled between themselves, then opened the door. One of them went to Rosalita; the other lifted his rifle and covered Caine.

Rosalita then did something Caine had not anticipated — she jabbed the blade deep into the arm of the guard closest to her. He screeched and leaped back. He examined the bleeding wound, cursed Rosalita, and raised his rifle.

The stabbing had distracted the guard covering Caine just enough to allow Caine to reach him a second before he would have shot Rosalita. Caine pulled the rifle away. The other guard saw it and spun away from Rosalita toward Caine. Rosalita lunged forward again, this time driving the sharp metal bit deep into the guard's side. He collapsed, then a moment later died.

The other guard, now weaponless, fell on his knees and begged Caine for mercy. Caine pounded the butt of the rifle into the man's forehead, and he fell unconscious. Caine stripped the shirts from the guards and, with them, tied up the survivor.

"Come on!" Caine urged.

He gave Rosalita the first guard's rifle. He dug in their pockets for spare ammunition and found only a little, but he also discovered a loaded double-barreled derringer, which he gave to Rosalita. She dropped it into the pocket of her dress.

Caine and Rosalita entered the hallway of the makeshift carcel. A ring of keys hung at the far end, and Caine got it. He went to Keelan's cell, fumbled the lock open, pushed the door open.

"Come on, son, it's time—"

He stared in surprise into an empty cell. Keelan was gone.

Caine spun on his heel and went back to the tied-up guard. He picked him up by the collar and slapped at his face until he came to.

"Where is the boy?" he demanded.

The Mexican talked as if his tongue were too thick for his mouth. "Seahorn... came... took him."

Caine let go of the man's collar, and the back of his head

thumped against the stone floor, knocking him unconscious once more.

"But why would Seahorn take him?" Rosalita asked.

"I should have known he would do something like that. He'll probably try to ransom the boy off himself and take the money for his own."

"So he betrays the Alianza?"

"Betrayal," Caine said, "is in Neal Seahorn's blood."

———

There were two of them, and they found Brice floating face down in the muddy, foaming water that gushed in through the wall channel. One of them, a tall Anglo, pulled him out and rolled him over. He leaned his ear to his chest.

"Alive," he told the bandoliered Mexican with him.

"Seahorn will want to know of this."

"Yep." The Anglo disarmed Brice, stood, and hefted him onto his shoulder like a sack of oats. The pair, like several others, had come out into the rain to investigate what had sounded like a muffled gunshot somewhere in the enclosure. They had not found its origin, but what they had found here was much more interesting. And perhaps a source of reward from Seahorn.

The Anglo and the Mexican reached Seahorn's quarters and climbed the stairs; the Mexican reached the door first and knocked on it.

No one answered, so he knocked again. A moment later, the door creaked slowly open, and both the Anglo and the Mexican stepped back in surprise.

Ramon Fernandez stood before them, his usually swarthy face almost drained of color. Blood, a lot of it, soaked his clothing. He wobbled on his feet, clinging to the door.

"Seahorn has killed me," he said, just before he collapsed.

The Mexican knelt beside him, felt him. He looked up at his partner, his brown eyes wide. "He is dead," he said.

The Anglo looked wildly around. Suddenly he dumped Brice's unconscious form on the floor beside Ramon's corpse. "Let's get out of here," he said.

Brice lay still for several more minutes. Water slowly drained from his lungs and spilled out of his mouth, and his shuddering, weak breathing steadily became stronger. Color began returning, and at last, he opened his eyes.

Slowly he pushed himself up until he saw the dead man beside him. He looked around, utterly confused. How had he come here, wherever here was? The last thing he could recall was struggling beneath the water, trying to squeeze through the opening at the bottom of the iron grate.

He stood, holding the wall until his strength returned. He assessed his situation. He guessed he was somewhere inside Serveto. Had he wandered here in a daze? Or had he been carried here, by whom? And where was Orion?

He examined the body on the floor. A finely dressed Mexican shot through the chest. Apparently, the man had bled to death.

Brice looked around the hallway, dimly lit by a lamp on the wall. A door stood open behind the dead Mexican. Brice carefully peered inside. A living quarters, it appeared. Nicely furnished, too, with overstuffed chairs, a big table, a large sideboard, paintings on the wall. He listened and heard no movement inside. He stepped across the Mexican's body and entered.

A trail of blood showed where the bleeding man had moved across the room to the door. He followed the trail back to another doorway leading into another hallway. Brice walked into it, wondering if maybe Keelan was somewhere in this building. His foot struck something on the floor. A pistol. He picked it up. The grip was slick with blood. The

Mexican must have dropped the pistol from his weakening fingers as he came down this hallway.

Brice passed down the hall and entered the room at its end. A safe stood there, open and empty.

There was nothing else in the room, so Brice turned and went back into the main chamber. There were two more doors. One led into another long passage; the smell of food drifted up it to him. A kitchen beyond, probably. The other door, though, led into a bedroom.

This, too, was empty. The bed was rumpled and unmade. Clothing hung in an open wardrobe against the far wall. Brice went to it, examining what it held. He noticed a gun belt hanging from a peg inside. No pistol, just an empty holster. But then he saw the name neatly etched into the leather: N. Seahorn.

This was Seahorn's room. The room of the very man who held Keelan captive.

Brice took one of Seahorn's shirts and wiped the blood from the pistol and his hands. He spat contemptuously into the wardrobe, then at the bed where Seahorn had slept.

Tucking the pistol under his own belt, he went back into the main room. There he blew out the lamps that burned here and there, and in the darkness, he went to the tall window that opened onto a balcony.

He was in Serveto, all right. Below him spread the plaza, still being pounded with rain. Lightning showed him various buildings here and there, their shapes rectangular and stark, as they were limned for a second against the backlighting sky.

He studied each building, hoping for some clue to indicate where his son might be held. But he found no sign. He saw two men move across the plaza and ducked farther inside Seahorn's room.

It struck him that he should quickly get out of here. Seahorn might return at any moment.

Brice headed back to the hall, but he heard voices. After

looking frantically about, he darted into Seahorn's room again and slipped into the big wardrobe. Pulling the clothing around him, he eased the door almost shut. Through the open space, he could see just a bit into the main room.

"He's dead, all right," a man said. "You didn't see who did it?"

"No. But Seahorn is gone. He was seen running across the plaza toward the carcel, and since then, he has vanished. I have heard that somewhere here, he has a safe full of money. I'll bet it's empty now."

"But why would Seahorn shoot Ramon?"

"Haven't you heard what's gone on?" a voice with a Mexican accent said. "They say Ramon and Seahorn fought over Rosalita Contero, and then Seahorn sent J. W. Fadden to kill Ramon. Ramon killed Fadden instead—and now it seems Seahorn has done the same to Ramon."

A pause, then one said, "If Seahorn has run off, he's probably taken everything for himself. Our wages, too, I'll bet."

"Well, then there is nothing holding us anymore—and no reason for us not to take what we can find."

Brice watched through the opening; he saw forms moving about as the men talked.

"And what of the kidnapped boy? Who will collect his ransom?"

Brice closed his eyes and breathed a prayer of gratitude for the indication Keelan was still alive.

"Maybe we will," one of the men said. "The ransom is due at any time."

"Well, I don't plan to hang around waiting for no ransom or anything else. Think about it—maybe Seahorn took off because he knew something bad was about to happen. There may be a passel of rangers crossing the border. Or the whole damn Mex army."

"That's right," one of the others said. "Let's take what

we can find and leave. Let's look for that safe of Seahorn's. Might be something left in it."

Brice tried not to breathe as the men began searching the rooms. One of the men did come into the bedroom and begin looking about, moving pictures, shoving aside the bed. Then he walked toward the wardrobe. Brice saw his face clearly through the opening and his hand extending

"We found it!" one of the others called.

The man turned and quickly left the bedroom. Brice exhaled a long, relieved sigh.

CHAPTER 16

Caine could almost smell a difference in the atmosphere of Serveto. The place simply felt different. Neal Seahorn's absence was as tangible here as the moisture that hung in the air as the storm finally gave out.

Caine and Rosalita moved along the base of the wall, hugging it close, letting the shadows swallow them. From the carcel, they ran toward a row of empty adobe houses around the back of the old mission chapel. From there, they cut toward Rosalita's adobe house, dangerously exposed to view.

Someone shouted nearby, and a shot was fired. Caine at first thought they had been seen, but an exultant whoop followed, then three more shots in succession. He saw the gunman—someone firing at the sky.

"What is happening?" Rosalita asked.

"Word is probably, spreading that Seahorn has gone," Caine said. "Serveto is about to come apart. If we're found here, they might buy us a drink, or they might kill us. I'd bet on the latter: a lot of men would like to say they brought me down. Then there's the price tag on my head."

They reached Rosalita's house. Rosalita went to the door and started to open it, but Caine motioned for her to stop.

Then she heard it, too: someone inside. Moving, knocking things about.

"Looting," Caine whispered. "The door through the outside wall—is it still open?"

"I don't know." Come on. We'll try it.

They ran across the plaza. While they were in the open, men emerged from various buildings. Caine heard angry shouts; someone cursed Seahorn's name.

If Caine and Rosalita were seen, they were not noticed, for no one reacted to them. They darted into the tree-shaded alley and through to the little door through the wall and found it sealed shut.

"I figured they would have done that," Caine said. "Any way out besides the front gate?"

"Nothing but over the wall."

Caine looked up. The wall was twelve feet high, and its smooth stone surface offered no handholds.

"I'll find something to climb on," he said.

An empty barrel stood against the wall farther down, and Caine went to it. As he touched it, a shot blasted somewhere nearby, and a slug knocked chips out of the wall inches from him.

Caine wheeled, pumped two shots from his rifle in the general direction from which the slug had come, then shouted for Rosalita to run. She did.

"It's Caine!" someone yelled. "He's loose!"

More shots, more slugs were chipping the wall, digging the dirt at Caine's heels. He ran to his right, then cut between the rows of adobes again. A shading overhang, or *portal*, was built onto one of the adobes, and beneath it was a plank porch built about eighteen inches above the ground. Caine dropped to his belly and slid under the porch. Moments later, he watched three pairs of boots stomp by as his pursuers went after him.

Something touched his hand, and he started. It was Rosalita. He exhaled in relief.

"Lucky I didn't put my fist through your face," he said. "I didn't know you were under here."

"There was nowhere else."

"I got to get you out of here."

"How?"

"Hush!"

Some had stepped onto the porch. The clunk of the boots was loud. Caine and Rosalita hardly breathed. Two men above.

"Got away," one said. "But he couldn't have got over the wall."

"Then let's keep looking."

"Forget Caine," the first responded. "Go after Seahorn. Get back the money he took, and the boy, Garth Kensington, would pay a lot to get the boy back. That's why Seahorn took him. I figure the kid to be worth more than Caine."

"Maybe so. But the storm will have washed over Seahorn's trail," the other said. "By morning, he'll have such a jump we'd have a hard time catching up to him. But Caine's inside these walls, and we ought to be able to spook him out. Let's give it a try."

The other grunted apparent assent, and the men moved away. Caine shook his head. Always it was the same—having either to hide for his own protection and, if not hide, to kill.

"There's got to be some other way out of here," he said to Rosalita. "Think hard."

Rosalita concentrated. "There is a passage for the stream. It is dry except when it rains—I think it is blocked."

"It's worth trying," Caine said.

Carefully they crawled out from under the porch. Men still moved about the plaza, and it was impossible for the pair to remain fully hidden. Fortunately, Caine realized, either not everyone here was aware of who he was, or if they were, did not care, so he and Rosalita moved along without being molested.

Near the stone armory, Caine saw two men moving together, and something about them made him suspect they were the two who had been on the porch moments before. Though they apparently did not see him now, Caine and Rosalita were dangerously in the open.

On impulse, Caine tried the armory door. He was surprised to find it unlocked. He went inside and pulled Rosalita after him, then closed the door almost completely.

The two men walked nearby; one looked directly at the armory. But they did not stop.

When they were gone, Caine turned. He was going to tell Rosalita they could go on now, but he found himself staring into the black muzzle of a long revolving Colt rifle held by a very intense-eyed young black man.

"You twitch, and you die," the man said.

"I won't twitch," Caine said.

The man lowered the Colt rifle a bit. "You look like somebody I know," he said. "Who are you?"

"What does that matter?"

The rifle came up again.

"My name is Robert Cole."

"Why you come in here?"

"To save my hide. There's some men after me."

The black man suddenly looked at Caine very intently, cocking his head slightly to the side. "You're Simon Caine," he said. "I know because you look like Mr. Brice."

Caine couldn't mask his surprise. "You know my brother?"

"Yeah. I come here with him to get his boy. My name's Orion Jones."

"Where is he?"

Worry skirted across Orion's face. "I think he's dead."

Caine felt as if he were sinking into deep water. "How?"

"We come in the place where the water flows in through the wall. There's metal bars there—I think he got hung up under the water. Men come along run me off before I could help him loose."

Through Caine's mind flashed memories of his brother as a child, as a young man, and as he had seen him last, atop the stone tower near the Kensington ranch. Emotion threatened to overcome him, but he dammed it up and swallowed it down. "Who are you, Orion?"

"Me and my pa worked for Mr. Kensington and Mr. Brice. My pa, he got shot dead by them what kidnapped Mr. Brice's boy."

"Orion, this is Rosalita Contero. She and I were locked up by Neal Seahorn Keelan was in the same place."

"Where is Keelan now?"

"Seahorn took him and left Serveto. That's why there's all the stir outside. Seahorn robbed the place blind, and hell's busted loose."

"I want to get Keelan back— for Mr. Brice," Orion said.

"We'll do it together."

Orion nodded.

"What do we do now, Simon?" Rosalita asked.

"Well, we at least got plenty of weaponry," he said, looking around.

"I got dynamite," Orion said.

"How'd you get—"

"It's a long story."

"Tell me later, then. Just bring the stuff out."

———

Brice watched the growing commotion in Serveto and didn't know what to make of it. Men moving about, doors and windows being smashed, goods being strewn across the plaza, looting going on everywhere. At first, it dismayed him

—how could he find Keelan in this turmoil? But then he realized the hubbub might be an advantage, for, in it, he could probably move unnoticed.

But he wished he had some weapon besides the blood-stained pistol he had found on the dead Mexican. And he still wondered what had happened to Orion.

Brice stepped out into the plaza. He felt dangerously exposed, but the men who passed him, carrying items taken from one of the adobes, did not even glance at him. Nor did the horsemen a dozen yards away who were chasing down a hefty, screaming woman they had apparently driven from her home. Their intent Brice could guess.

He crossed the plaza, holding his pistol, not knowing where to go. It was almost funny, he thought. All his worry about entering Serveto, about remaining hidden and safe once here—and now he was walking openly through the heart of it.

A man stumbled by several bottles of liquor under his arm. He apparently had already partaken of much of it, for he smiled cordially at Brice and extended a bottle. Brice ignored the offer but asked, "The prisoners... where does Seahorn keep the prisoners?"

The drunk slurred out, "Yonder. But they're all gone. Empty."

Brice felt an inward lurch of dismay. "The boy?"

"The kidnapped one? Everybody says Seahorn took him for hisself and run off."

"Run off..."

"Yep." The drunk turned and weaved away, turning up his bottle as he went. Brice stood there, hands hanging at his side, and felt as if he could not move. Suddenly he turned and trotted after the drunk. He grabbed the man's shoulder. One of the bottles beneath his arm fell and broke.

"Hey! What are you—"

"Simon Caine—is he alive?"

"Live as you or me. I ought to kill you—you broke my bottle." The man weaved off.

Suddenly the door of a nearby stone building swung open, pushed from inside. Brice spun, instinctively raising his rifle.

It was equally instinctive when Simon Caine fired at the figure before him. Through the blast of his rifle's fire and smoke, he saw the man jerk and fall. An unexplainable feeling of sickness suddenly swept over Caine.

Orion cried out, "It's Mr. Brice! You shot him!" He ran to the still form on the ground and knelt by him.

Caine leaned against the door, his legs suddenly weak beneath him. After a moment, he went to his brother.

"Brice? I didn't know it was you..."

Brice opened his eyes. "Keelan," he said. "Where is..." He fell unconscious.

Caine stood and breathed deeply. A man with a gun darted around a nearby corner; Caine caught a glint of gunmetal. Caine spun, lifted his rifle, and shot the man through the heart. He walked to the body and picked up a lighted cigar that had fallen from the man's lips. Caine dusted it off and put it in his own mouth.

"The dynamite, Orion," he said.

———

Orion knew as he watched the destruction of Serveto that never again would he see a fury like this. They had moved Brice to the relative safety of an alleyway, and then Caine had walked into the plaza, sticks of dynamite stuffed into each pocket and beneath his belt.

The first stick he cast into Seahorn's quarters, and it blasted out the full-length window and the wall around it. In the night, the explosion was strangely beautiful, an eerie blossom of sparks bursting out in magnificent destruction.

Two men rose from behind a wagon, leveling rifles on Caine. Orion was about to shout a warning when Caine lit another fuse with his cigar, turned, and threw the stick directly under the wagon. Orion averted his eyes as the blast splintered the wagon and killed the men behind it.

On Caine continued, seemingly untouchable there in the plaza, throwing dynamite wherever he went, downing buildings, destroying stables and barns and walls. The few who dared try to stop him failed, fatally, and finally, Serveto seemed to empty so that Caine was left unchallenged. Orion and Rosalita watched him silently, a lone figure in the broad plaza that now was lighted with leaping flames.

"He is an amazing man, no?" Rosalita said.

"He is, ma'am. The most amazing I've ever seen."

And then it was done. Caine strode back to them, knelt again beside Brice. Brice's eyes moved, lids lifting for a moment, then falling again.

"I'll get the boy back for you, brother," Caine said. "Don't you die! I'll get him back."

An hour later, they rode out of Serveto, Brice lying on a horse-drawn litter. Caine rode slightly ahead of Orion, who noted two remaining sticks of dynamite sticking out of Caine's pocket.

"What's those for?" he asked.

"Seahorn."

"How will we find him?"

"We?"

"Yeah. I'm going with you."

"We'll find him."

"But we don't know where he's heading."

Caine said, "I know. He's heading for the Big Bend country to find a Mexican called Old Pablo."

CHAPTER 17

D ays and miles away from Serveto, Rosalita Contero stood in the doorway of a bedroom and watched Brice as he lay slightly propped up in bed, staring out the window; before him lay a plate of food, barely touched.

"Do you need anything else?" Rosalita asked. Without looking at her, Brice shook his head.

Rosalita took the plate. She scraped the scraps out the door, where three scrawny dogs immediately devoured them. A plump Mexican woman, Rosalita's sister, and the owner of this *casa* stood at an oven outside, poking the fire as she prepared to bake bread. Rosalita took the plate back into the house and immersed it in a big crockery basin filled with water. She then went back out to her sister.

Rosalita and Brice had been here almost two weeks now. Her sister, the widowed, impoverished, and very plump Ria de Velasco had freely opened her home to Rosalita and Brice despite having not seen her roving younger sister for the past seven years.

Ria had asked Rosalita what had become of her husband, Juan, of whom she had not approved, and when Rosalita told her simply that he had been killed, Ria nodded as if she had expected that answer. She had pointed a stubby finger at Brice and said in a too-loud whisper that this one, Rosalita, looks much better for you. We will take good care of him, no?

Yes, we will, Rosalita had said, and she had realized the idea was appealing. Brice was a fine-looking man, like his brother, and seemingly a good one. Ready to die in the effort to retrieve his son—that impressed Rosalita, for she had seen too little of love and loyalty in the circles in which she had run these past years.

Rosalita approached her sister, wiping her arm across her forehead as she bent over the round-topped oven. The house was surrounded by a handful of outbuildings, including one small building that Ria called her *granero,* or barn, though it hardly was big enough to merit the designation. Around the little enclave rose rocky Texas hills. Miles northward stretched the Sierra Diablo, and to the northeast, the Delaware Mountains.

"So again, he did not eat?" Ria asked.

"No."

"Ah, that's bad. Bad. Why does he waste himself away so?"

"Because his son is still captive, and he can only lie in bed while others go after him," Rosalita said. "It is hard for him to do that and hard for him to be unable to walk."

"It will go bad for the boy," Ria said, shaking her head. "They say Neal Seahorn is a man without mercy. If the boy angers him—"

"Don't talk so, Ria. I don't want to hear it."

Ria smiled in a self-deprecating way. "Talk, talk, that is all I do. Pay no attention to me, *Hermana.*"

Rosalita walked away, glum and a little angry. Angry not at Ria's words but at the fact she probably was right.

She had not, in the beginning, understood why Seahorn had taken Brice's son with him when he fled Serveto, but

Simon Caine had surmised it was because the boy might be a useful hostage if Seahorn were cornered by the law. Furthermore, he said, Seahorn could now hold Keelan James as his own prisoner, demanding a new ransom.

Caine and Orion had ridden off in search of Seahorn and Keelan just as quickly as Brice and Rosalita were settled in at the widowed Ria's home. Rosalita tallied the days: two weeks now. They had no trail to follow, but Caine was confident he could find a lead somewhere. Ask a few questions, keep your ears open, and you'll pick up word of a man traveling with a boy, he assured them. He and Orion had ridden out of sight across the hills, generally following the southward course of the Rio Bravo. Seahorn will go south, Caine had said, down into the hilly, empty Big Bend country where a man can hide and where he can find his friend Old Pablo, whoever that might be.

Brice had wept in frustration when they left, but he tried to hide it, so Rosalita pretended not to notice, even though she would have liked to comfort him. Now he did not weep. He merely stared out the window, said almost nothing, ate almost nothing.

The worst part was that now he could barely move his legs. Whether it was a delayed effect of the bullet he had taken in Serveto or some blunder of the amateurish medical man Ria had brought in to dig out the slug, they did not know. All they knew was that after the slug came out, Brice had lost most of the movement and feeling from the waist down. The so-called doctor muttered apologies, waived his fee, and rode away. He took for a souvenir the bullet he had not too gently dug out.

Rosalita went back to Brice's door. He still sat as before, just staring.

"You want coffee?"

Nothing.

"Water, then? Or I will go to town and bring you beer if you wish."

"Just leave me alone," he said, and the way he said it hurt. She withdrew, closing the door after her.

Brice tried again to move his feet, but he could not.

———

Though he had spent all his life in Texas, Keelan had never before seen a dust storm like the one that loomed before them now. It was as if some superhuman painter had dipped a broad brush in the too-dry pigment of dirty orange and roughly slapped it across the sky. Except in this painting, the smear of color was moving, almost writhing, rolling across the desert like a hoop snake.

As he had since they had left Serveto, Neal Seahorn turned in the saddle and looked behind him. Again and again, and each time seeming concerned, maybe even scared.

He looked that way all the time now, Keelan noted. Sometimes in the night, Seahorn would start upright, breath whooshing out and eyes wide, as if he was looking back into a nightmare. "Alianza," he would say. "Alianza." And then settle back to sleep with Keelan's wrist tied to his.

Now Seahorn watched the dust storm, about a mile away from them, and smiled. "That'll hide our trail well enough," he said. "Let them find me through that!" He turned and looked behind them again.

Keelan looked, too. "There's nobody there," he said.

"Alianza is there, boy. Alianza is everywhere you look."

Seahorn pulled his bandana across his face. He reached into his vest pocket and pulled out another, which he gave to Keelan. The kerchief smelled like sweat and cigarette smoke, but Keelan tied it across his face anyway, for he knew how a dust storm could choke a person.

"They'll never find us now," Seahorn said again as they moved forward into the storm.

It seemed to roll down to meet them. Stinging pieces of sand and grit against the skin, burning the eyes, making the hair feel like a skullcap of dirt on Keelan's head. He hunched over his saddlehorn, squinting, suffering under the buffeting. Seahorn's shoulders were pulled up to hug his neck, and he rode low in the saddle, but Keelan could tell he didn't mind the storm. Maybe even was enjoying it. Keelan wondered if Seahorn was crazy.

The distance was almost impossible to calculate in this hell of wind and sand, direction even more so. Yet Seahorn seemed determined to continue. The storm did not abate.

At length, Seahorn stopped; Keelan did the same. Seahorn pointed wordlessly at a little house of adobe, alternately visible and invisible through the storm. One moment it was stark and clear, the next invisible as a ghost place when the wind kicked up more dust.

"Come on, boy."

Keelan dutifully put his heels into the flanks of his wind-tortured horse. They rode slowly toward the house. A little shed came into view through the dust storm, and Seahorn motioned for Keelan to follow him there. Once inside, Keelan pulled down the foul-smelling bandana, coughed, and spit out sand, then took a deep breath of fetid air. Sand blew in through cracks in the wall.

A nearly starved burro stood in a stall nearby. There was water in a wooden bucket for it, and Seahorn took some and gave it to the horses.

"Shouldn't we ask?" Keelan suggested, then realized how foolish that must sound to Seahorn.

"Come with me, boy," Seahorn said to him. He pushed open the door, and they went out into the storm.

It seemed to take forever to trudge to the house. Keelan

expected Seahorn to knock, but he didn't. Instead, he just pushed open the door and walked in.

An old man was inside. His eyes were strange, looking in the wrong direction. He pulled back fearfully at the sound of the door; in Spanish, he asked who was there.

"Just some dust-bit riders, old man," Seahorn said. "You speak the English, Mex?"

"*Sí*, some English, some English. Please do not shoot me. Blind. I am blind."

Seahorn was patting dust off his clothes. He stopped, leaned over, and looked into the man's face.

"Be damned, so you are," he said. "You got any food, old man?"

"Little food, *señor*. My son, he is gone for many days, working to north. He was to come back, but he has not."

"Why he might be dead, old man," Seahorn said, laughing. "You might just starve like a rat out here in the middle of these godforsaken badlands."

He began stalking about the little house, looking in boxes on the table. "Haven't you got anything but tortillas, old man?" he said. "Look at that—covered with ants—not fit to eat."

Keelan approached the old man. The blind eyes were a filmy blue, cocked at a strange angle. "I'm sorry," Keelan whispered as Seahorn continued to thrash about. "He is a bad man."

"You are only a *muchachos*," the old man whispered.

"Yes. I don't steal. He steals."

The old man's voice dropped to a whisper. "You are, you are..." He was struggling for the right word. "You are — kidnapped?"

"Yes. How did you—"

"Much talk for a long time—ones who pass talk of a boy kidnapped many days ago in Kensington—"

"Shut up in there," Seahorn barked. "Get away from him, boy."

Keelan drew away. He had a peculiar feeling, though, that the old man was looking at him with those blind eyes, trying to tell him something. The man's head was twitching in an unnatural way as if he were trying to shake a fly off his nose without using his hands. Suddenly Keelan understood: the old man was gesturing to his right. Keelan looked.

An old rifle, its stock thrusting out from under a cloth-draped table. Keelan's mouth went dry. He felt frozen in his place.

Seahorn stomped back in and went to the door. He opened it and peered out. The wind howled in, blowing in grit. Seahorn drew his pistol.

"They're out there," he said.

"Who?" Keelan asked.

"Alianza, you little jackass!" Seahorn thrust his pistol out the door and fired. The report made the old man start and moan. The blind eyes rolled in their sockets.

Seahorn fired again, then cursed as if he had missed. Keelan went to a window and peeped out through a cracked shutter.

"There's nobody there," he said, and there wasn't. Nothing but blowing dust and sand and the far-stretching barrens.

"I can see them. I can even smell them. Everywhere I go, they follow me."

He really is crazy, Keelan thought. Keelan had heard vague scraps of talk around the dinner table about the Alianza, and he had gathered that it was something most people, his grandfather included, didn't even believe existed. He had heard the word mentioned by his guards in Serveto but still had only an imprecise notion about what it might be.

Whatever it was, though, Seahorn certainly believed in it

and was scared of it. So scared he saw it where there was nothing.

I've got to get away from him, Keelan thought. *He's crazy enough that sooner or later, he'll just get tired of dragging me along and kill me.* The thought made Keelan's empty stomach knot up like a wad of wet twine. He looked once more at the old man's hidden rifle.

An old musket of some kind. Something out of Civil War times, maybe, or even before. Keelan glanced again at Seahorn, who was still peering through the storm at his imaginary enemies.

The stock of the rifle seemed to attract Keelan's eyes, magnetlike. The old man was rolling his head again, obviously trying to get Keelan to pick up the weapon.

Keelan swallowed and went half a step toward it. He watched Seahorn, edged a little closer, a little more. Seahorn did not turn.

Keelan suddenly was afraid he would cry. He bit his lip and forced back the tears that brimmed in his eyes. Could he even aim a weapon at a living man, much less squeeze the trigger?

I've got to, he thought. *Else he'll kill me, leave me dead out there for the buzzards.*

In one sweeping motion, he reached the rifle and drew it out. The old man heard the motion, smiled. The hoary old head with its unseeing eyes bobbed up and down.

Keelan was shaking as he raised the old cap-and-ball rifle. He prayed that the rifle was loaded and at the same time half-hoped it was not. It seemed to weigh a hundred pounds as he leveled it, aimed it—

For what seemed a much longer time than it really was, he stood there, holding up the heavy old rifle, trying to stop the muzzle from waving back and forth as he hoped it in on Seahorn.

Seahorn raised his pistol and fired into the storm again

just as Keelan numbly squeezed the trigger of the rifle. The hammer fell on a dead cap, the snap of it masked by Seahorn's pistol blast. Keelan felt tears erupt. He slid the useless rifle back into its place. The tears would not stop, and now he was starting to blubber. He sank to the floor, trembling and hiding his face behind his upraised knees. The old man's head was still bobbing, but now he was praying to the Virgin, a weird chanting that sounded like an Indian death song.

Seahorn suddenly laughed. Keelan choked off his tears by sheer will, wiped his eyes, and looked up. Seahorn was holstering the pistol.

"Why there wasn't anybody there, to begin with!" he said. "Imagine that! Just shapes in the dust."

I wish I could go find my father and be home again and never, never leave, Keelan thought.

CHAPTER 18

I t was a little community where trails crossed—a half-dozen adobe houses like squat boxes on the land, a round well with a block wall, a stable with a horse corral, a general store, a blacksmithy, and a cantina. The name of this smattering of buildings they did not even know. Here Simon Caine and Orion Jones rode as the sun edged down on the hills and made the sky look like a ruby.

A few miles westward, the Rio Bravo flowed slow as syrup, unhurriedly moving south toward the rugged place where it would bend east and then northeast. Before reaching there, it would run in a speeding torrent through three canyons and past some of the most rugged and inhospitable country in all of Texas. It was in that country, Caine believed, that he would find Seahorn and young Keelan. With any luck, he would learn something in this cantina that might help him toward that end.

Caine's eyes swept over Orion as he dismounted. It struck him that in the brief time he had known the young man, he had become more hardened. The gaze of his black eyes was more flinty and piercing than before. Orion could have been an offspring of the very barren landscape through which they traveled. This life was transforming him.

"You getting down?" he asked Orion.

Orion rested his right hand on the stock of the booted revolving Colt rifle and shook his head. "Don't feel very comfortable here, somehow."

"Suit yourself. I'll bring you a bottle."

"I don't drink."

"A man with no vices is hard to be nice to, Orion."

There were only three men inside the cantina. All three quit talking and openly stared at Caine when he entered. One of them rose and went to the other side of the home-made bar.

"You got beer? *Cerveza?*"

"*Sí.* Good beer, but hot."

"I'll take what I can get. And buy some for my friends here."

That brought smiles. The two other men rose and came to the bar to accept their unexpected gift. One was an Anglo, the other a Mexican who looked as if he might have some Apache or Comanche blood mixed in.

"*Gracias,*" said the half-breed. The Anglo said thanks in English with a flat Texas accent.

"Been riding far, *amigo?*" the Anglo asked.

"Far enough," Caine said. "Looking for somebody. Maybe you've seen him."

"Maybe. Who?"

"Fellow about my age, maybe a couple years older. Riding with a boy maybe ten or eleven."

Something changed in the look and stance of all three men. The barkeep turned away and busied himself, wiping out his kiln-fired beer mugs with a towel. The half-breed took a long swallow and looked at Caine out of the corner of his eye, the Anglo coughed a couple of times unconvincingly and took some gulps of beer as if to settle his throat. He backhanded foam off his mouth.

"Man and a boy... let's see. Nope. Don't recall seeing any such."

Caine smiled. "I see. When was it you didn't see him?"

For a moment, the Anglo took offense at the delicate sarcasm, but his half-breed partner laughed, and that softened him. He smiled.

"No offense, mister, but I like to know why a question is being asked before I answer it."

"Easy enough. The man stole that boy away from his kin. I want to get him back."

"You his pappy?"

"Uncle."

The Anglo took another swallow and looked as if he was thinking something over. Finally, he gave a quick, resolute nod.

"All right, I'll level with you. I did see him, maybe a day, day, and a half ago. Right here. Seemed nervous, looked behind him a lot." The man paused before he added, "And he looked a heck of a lot like Neal Seahorn to me."

"So he is."

"And you're tracking him? Seahorn's not to be fooled with, I hear tell."

"He fooled with me first."

The half-breed laughed again and spoke for the first time. "You are a confident man, *señor*."

"Just concerned about my nephew. Which way were they heading?"

"South. He didn't say, but I'd guess he's bound for the Chisos Mountains. If you're hiding, that's the place to go."

"He buy anything?"

"A couple of water bags and a canteen. A little liquor, a new bridle. Had his horses reshod! Bought some flour and such at the store."

"So he had money."

"Biggest wad I ever seen. Lord, why am I talking so free? He comes back through; he might plug me if it gets out I blabbed on him."

"He won't come back through."

The half-breed said, "Who is the buck outside with the rifle?"

Caine glanced up in the bar mirror. In its reflection of the street outside the open door, he saw Orion still tensely mounted. He had drawn the Colt rifle.

"Friend of mine," Caine said.

"What a rifle! Made like a pistol."

"Yeah. What's in the Chisos Mountains?"

"Mostly jackrabbits, turkey vultures, scorpions, and your occasional bandido. You may have trouble finding him once he gets there."

"I'll find him." Caine drained his mug. "Obliged, gentlemen."

"Not meaning to be forward, but what's your name?"

Caine smiled and touched his hat. He walked out the door without another word. The two men came after him and stood in the doorway, watching. Orion stared back at them nervously.

"You look jumpy as a hot frog," Caine said to Orion as he untethered.

"I don't like it here. Let's go."

"Hold your horses. Where we're going, we're going to need more supplies."

Orion looked displeased. He nudged heels into horse flanks and moved to the center of the dusty street. Caine led his horse to the general store that stood diagonally across from the cantina and retethered there. Orion rode farther down and then held up at the end of the street, sitting mounted with his rifle butt parked on his hip. Caine frowned. To any casual observer who did not know him,

Orion would look as if he were pondering gunning down the entire populace— something he could probably do in this tiny place with only one reload, Caine noted. Caine determined to give Orion some lessons at first opportunity in how to be inconspicuous.

Caine had little money, so he tried to spend it wisely. Brice had carried this cash hidden in his boot and had not lost it at Serveto. Caine bought jerked meat, flour, hard biscuits, coffee, some extra ammunition, and other supplies. He walked out laden with goods, trying to figure how best to divide the load between their horses. Then he stopped cold.

Two men were talking to Orion, and Orion looked none too happy about it. Caine glanced at the cantina; the half-breed Mex-Indian guiltily slipped back into the interior darkness just as Caine saw him. Caine remembered the 'breed's question about Orion and realized there might have been more behind it than idle curiosity. The half-breed might have sent out some kind of alert while Caine was occupied in the store.

Trying to look casual, Caine untied his horse and walked steadily toward Orion, leading the horse and carrying the supplies at the same time. Orion shot a disturbing glance at him that let Caine know the situation could quickly get out of control. *Take it easy, Orion. Be calm,* Caine mentally commanded.

"Howdy, gentlemen," Caine said. "Pretty day."

One said hello, and the other nodded. "I'm Dorthal Abemathy," the first said. "I'm sort of a constable here, you know. Just talking to your partner for a minute."

Caine smiled. "He's careless about flashing that rifle. You'll do better, won't you, Fred? Sure you will."

"Fred?" Dorthal Abemathy swung his skinny frame toward Orion. "You said your name was Orion."

Caine winced inwardly and added how to lie to Orion's list of overdue lessons.

Orion looked at Caine in wild-eyed helplessness. Caine shrugged.

Suddenly Abemathy had a big Dragoon pistol leveled on Orion. His partner, an equally skinny man whom Caine suddenly realized might well be Abemathy's son, had Caine staring into the black eye of a cut-down Winchester rifle with a sawed-off stock.

"There's reports of a young nigger buck with a revolving rifle killing a white man up at Kensington," Abemathy announced. To Caine, he said, "Don't know just who you are, mister, but you're both coming with us."

"Pa..."

"What, boy?"

"We ain't got no jail."

Under other circumstances, Caine would have laughed at the way Abemathy's eyes widened at that comment. Abemathy stood there with his mouth steadily drawing up like a sphincter.

Orion quietly leveled the revolving Colt and thumbed back the hammer. Abemathy swallowed. The Colt rifle shook as Orion trembled.

Caine turned to Abemathy's son. "You don't want your daddy to get hurt, do you?"

The young man shook his head.

"Put down that chopped-off rifle, then."

Abemathy, meanwhile, still had his Colt Dragoon leveled on Orion. The two men looked at each other in a hopeless standoff.

The younger Abernathy stooped and laid his unusual weapon on the street. Dorthal Abernathy harked up and spat in disgust, then lowered his Dragoon. He handed it to Caine.

"Never wanted to be constable no how," he said.

"Mister, I've seen places do a lot worse for law officers with grit," Caine said as he took the Dragoon. He also picked up the sawed-off rifle. "I'll leave these on the ground about a mile south. And if you'll excuse us now, gentlemen, we've got to go kill Neal Seahorn."

Orion had little to say for a long time after they rode out. Night spread its ink over the sky, and they made camp under a large basalt escarpment whose black upright plane surface blended up into the dark sky as if it had no end.

Orion unloaded the Colt rifle and carefully began cleaning it in the light of the small fire they allowed themselves. They built it near the escarpment base, piling stones around it some distance away to help hide its glow from any direction.

"Where did you get that revolving rifle?" Caine asked.

"My pa's. Don't rightly know where he got it." Orion lifted his eyes for a moment. "I think maybe it was stole."

"Oh."

"Pa said these rifles come out in '57. Mr. Sam Colt made them for a regiment up in Connecticut that they named after him. They busted up in '61, and all the rifles was supposed to go back to the armory."

"But not all of them did."

Orion smiled. "This one didn't, at least. But I really don't know how Pa got it. He sure wasn't in no Sam Colt regiment during the war."

"Pretty gun. Takes a.44?"

"Yeah. But I'll have to get myself something newer and better soon."

Caine understood. "You're on the run."

Orion nodded. "You heard what they said hack there. They're looking for me."

"Did you really kill somebody?"

"Sure did. Didn't really mean to. A man who worked on the ranch—he's the one who told Seahorn's kidnapper's where to get Keelan and my pa."

Caine had been making coffee, and now he took the pot off the fire. He poured a cupful for Orion, then for himself. "I know what it means to lose kin to killers," he said.

"If I can get vengeance, I'll be all right," Orion said.

Caine took a swallow of the scalding black coffee. "Don't throw away your life for the likes of Seahorn."

"How can you say that? What about all you did? Robert Montrose and all that?"

Caine had no answer.

Orion rubbed an oily cloth over his rifle's cylinder, working silently for several minutes. "How you reckon Mr. Brice is doing?" he finally said.

"Well, I hope. If he dies—"

"He won't die, Mr. Caine. And you just wait—he'll walk again. I'll bet he is already."

———

But Brice wasn't walking. In fact, it was a struggle for him even to stand. He could drag himself along with great effort, but rarely could he take a real step. Usually, it was more like heaving one rag-doll leg forward, locking the knee, vaulting over, heaving the other leg, locking the knee, doing the same. All the while clutching the bedpost or leaning against the wall.

Brice had long ago overcome the self-pity he had felt after the wartime injury that had left him with a permanent limp. A limp, after all, could be lived with. A man didn't have to walk smoothly to get around.

But this, he thought as he lay awake tonight—this was much worse. He was a cripple. Just like Garth Kensington had been just before he—

Brice realized he had just thought of Kensington as dead. And dead he probably was, judging from the shape he had been in when Brice left. Maybe that was for the best. It was likely, after all, that Keelan would never come home. Seahorn would kill him out there somewhere. Likely they would never even find the body. Keelan would be dead, Garth would be dead, and Brice himself a cripple—

Brice pushed himself up in his bed. No! He would not surrender hope for Keelan, not until he certainly knew that he was dead. Nor would he quit trying to walk.

He threw his legs over the edge of the bed. He wiggled his toes—at least he could do that. His spine was injured, not broken.

Closing his eyes, he took a deep breath, then pushed himself to his feet. He wavered, reached for the bedpost to steady himself. He wiggled his toes again—and felt it, though his legs still seemed wooden and detached.

Here goes, he thought.

In her own bed in the next room, Rosalita heard the sound of his collapse. She bolted up and, in her gown, rushed to Brice's room. He lay just inside the door, facedown.

"Brice—"

She knelt beside him as he rolled over. He took her hand and squeezed it. He was smiling broadly.

"Six steps. Six steps before I fell."

He put his arms around her neck, drew her down, and kissed her.

CHAPTER 19

"There they are, boy," Neal Seahorn said as he pointed. Keelan was already looking. Ahead, rising from the sprawling desert floor, stood a hazy line of volcanic mountains. Their contrast to the red-brown landscape was remarkable, for along the mountain crests were green forests of madrone, pine, and juniper. These were the Chisos Mountains, which seemed to grow from the parched Chihuahuan Desert like some hardy plant.

"A man can get himself swallowed up down there," Seahorn said with satisfaction. "That's just what we're going to do, boy." He gave another habitual glance over his shoulder, then spurred his tired mount forward. Keelan's own horse also lurched into step again, its head low with weariness.

Keelan rode with his wrists bound together and roped to the saddlehorn. The ropes were too tight and burned him, but he did not ask Seahorn to loosen them. The last time he had asked, Seahorn had sworn at him and pulled them tighter.

The closer they drew to the mountains, the more the desert became a place of life. Keelan saw two roadrunners dart among the scrubby desert brush. Mice scampered, hawks circled, a jackrabbit watched them from a safe distance before loping off, and scorpions vanished off rocks like bugs escaping a newly fired stove.

Vultures circling overhead lent an ominous cast to the area, but even Keelan couldn't miss the beauty into which they were riding. But he dreaded going farther into it. He had no idea what would become of him once they were hidden in the mountains. His father, whom he had never doubted was searching for him, might never find him in the Chisos. Eventually, Seahorn might tire of having a boy along, even a boy who could potentially bring him a big ransom, and what would happen then?

Keelan quietly tugged at his ropes. He had to find a way to escape.

Noon waned into afternoon, but the heat remained intense. Such was the way of the desert: reflecting back intense and unfiltered sun rays all day, making the desert floor hot as a skillet, then casting off all its accumulated heat at night until land and atmosphere were almost bitterly cold.

Ravines began marking the land, deep ruts that led to the Rio Bravo to the west. The vegetation here was almost exclusively thorny mesquite. They pushed on.

At last, the trail began to rise; they reached a high point and then descended into a gulch filled with juniper and pinon. The north slopes of the Chisos range stood uplifted before them, their sheer volcanic walls defying penetration. Into the gulch, they descended, leaving the true desert behind. They reached at length a wide depression particularly rich in vegetation, including madrone, oak, ponderosa pine, even quaking aspen. The night was nearly upon them now, and Seahorn halted. "We'll sleep here," he said. He said it reluctantly; Keelan could tell Seahorn wanted to push on into the mountains.

"Where are we going?" Keelan asked.

Seahorn smiled. "Old Pablo lives yonder. He'll put us up where even Alianza won't find us."

They ate a meager hardtack supper and lay down. The horses grazed on the wild grasses and drank at a little seep into which Seahorn had dug a water collection trench.

Keelan did not go to sleep as quickly as usual, even though he was very tired. His thoughts ran like a runaway wagon; he had a strong notion that his time with Seahorn was approaching an end—one way or another. *Well, if that is to be it, then let the end be tomorrow,* he thought. *Whatever happens, and however it happens, the end of this will be tomorrow.*

Seahorn kicked Keelan awake the next morning. "Come on," he barked. "We're going to Old Pablo's place."

"I'm hungry."

"Pablo will have grub."

Seahorn busied himself tensely. Still, he looked around and back constantly, searching for the Alianza pursuers who were, in his mind at least, always just behind. But today, he also bubbled with seeming anticipation. Keelan realized that Seahorn saw this Old Pablo's place, wherever and whatever that was, as a sanctuary where he would, at last, be safe. It gave Keelan an uneasy feeling. He remembered his mental pledge, *Today; somehow, I will be free of him.*

They mounted. Seahorn tied Keelan again. They rode through bigtooth maples and beneath red cliffs until the land finally began transforming back to something more resembling desert. They crossed a sand wash and picked their way through long stretches of creosote, ocotillo, and cacti. The day stretched itself awake after the cool night; the sun grew hotter and more intense, flaring like a blacksmith's bellow-fed fire. The night had been characterized by the buzzing singsong of insects, but that gave way to stillness. The desert became quiet except for the sound of the wind, of their horses plodding along, of Seahorn whistling a tune Keelan did not know.

They rode for a long time, occasionally stopping to water themselves and the horses and to rest in whatever shade they could find. During those times, Seahorn would first sit a few moments, then rise and scan the horizon, sit again. Over and over. Keelan had been brave throughout his whole ordeal, but now his courage began to waver. It was hard to keep back tears. He began to think that the only way he would escape today would be through death whenever they reached this Old Pablo's place that Seahorn apparently regarded as his mecca.

But Keelan did not cry. After each stop, they remounted, Seahorn tied Keelan again, and they rode on. At last, they came to a canyon about four hundred feet deep and descended into its limestone depths. The horses moved eagerly, with new energy, for they smelled water below.

The floor of the canyon featured numerous tinajas or natural water tanks. They rode to the nearest one, frightening off an array of birds, a rattlesnake, and a porcine-looking javelina. Seahorn filled their canteens and water bags as the horses drank. Here at the base of the canyon, it was much more cool than above. Also darker, the undulatory walls casting deep shade.

Seahorn slapped a mosquito on his neck and wiped it on his trouser leg. "Old Pablo's isn't far now," he said. He almost sounded friendly, even fatherly. It made Keelan despise him all the more.

The boy asked, "When will you let me go home?"

"This is no time to think of that," Seahorn returned.

After the horses were grazed and watered, they rode on. The sun dipped toward the west. Keelan realized they hadn't eaten all day, not even during their stops. Yet he wasn't hungry; the sense of dread that had ridden on his shoulders all day kept him from it.

After another hour, the noticeably excited Seahorn stopped and pointed up a ridge. "There it is, boy!" he said. "Pablo! Hey, Pablo! It's Neal!"

Keelan had to squint to make out the rough stone wall built onto a wide ledge up the ridge. The spot apparently was inaccessible but for a steep dry wash that cut into the side of the slope. A rider could pass this place and never know it was there. The dark door and two windows that seemed to peer down at them blended into the natural colors of the stone.

"Pablo!" Seahorn shouted again. No sound in response.

Their tired horses labored up the wash, their hooves kicking down avalanches of gravel. Finally, they reached the ledge and stopped. Seahorn dismounted.

"Pablo?"

He edged forward toward the door. Keelan saw now that this dwelling was merely a front stone wall built over a natural deep depression in the slope.

Seahorn's heart hammered. Something was wrong here, and he could feel it. He slipped silently to the door, then went inside. No one there.

"Pablo?"

A half-filled lamp lay on its side on a table made from a stone slab: Seahorn sat up the lamp and lit it. He lifted it and looked around the room.

"No, Pablo. No..."

The old man apparently had died months ago, for bones were all that remained of him. Most of them lay about the back of the dwelling, and others were scattered all across the room—probably by coyotes. From beneath a stool, Pablo's skull, still retaining a few tufts of hair and bits of leathery skin, peered back at Seahorn, the toothless jaw open.

Seahorn turned and sadly walked outside again.

It took him a moment to notice that Keelan was gone. The boy had slipped his ropes and run away on foot.

———

Keelan ran scared, not well. He left a clear trail, and most of the time, he stayed in the open. The farther he got from Seahorn, the more sure he felt that he had done the wrong thing. Seahorn would quickly track him down and kill him.

Keelan hadn't even thought to take one of the canteens with him, nor any food. But none of that could matter now —he must run as hard and far as he could.

By the time Keelan stopped, he had gone more than a mile. He was exhausted and collapsed in a shaded arroyo, panting.

———

Simon Caine knelt by a tinaja and studied marks in the wet sand. "They were here, all right," he said to Orion, who was still mounted. "And not only them—there's tracks of another rider."

"Another rider? Who would that be?"

"Don't know. But it appears whoever it is, he's tracking Seahorn just like we are."

Orion dismounted and studied the marks. He was not the tracker Caine was, but even he could see that Caine was right.

"You think the Alianza has somebody following Seahorn?" Orion asked.

"Don't know. Anything's possible. Whatever, we're going to have to look sharp. If we know about him, he may know about us."

"But why haven't we spotted these tracks before now?"

"I have, but never clear. I didn't want to say anything until I was sure."

Caine mounted, and he and Orion rode for another hour deeper into the rugged country. The wind rustled through the acacias; somewhere, an owl hooted. The air began to grow cool, and the light dimmer.

"Going to have to give it up for tonight," Caine said.

Orion nodded. "Too bad. I was hoping we'd—"

The bullet struck a moment before the sound reached them. Chips of blue-gray stone exploded from a boulder against which Orion had been outlined. He reacted instantly — bent low over his saddle horn, spurred his mount forward and into a cluster of brush growing around a seep.

Caine, meanwhile, cut to the right, gracefully leaped from his saddle when his horse was safely behind a wall-like limestone face and freed his rifle from the saddle boot. He scanned the upper lines of the ridges, searching for some movement against the rich, blue-black sky.

Another shot and this one almost hit Caine. He saw where it had come from—lower on the ridge, maybe from a ledge. Caine strained his eyes in the growing dark. He thought he made out the outline of the door, maybe windows, against the cambered ridge. Some kind of dwelling built up there—and occupied by somebody with an unfriendly way of welcome.

"Who are you?" The voice echoed down from above. "Why have you been following me?"

Orion whisper-shouted to Caine, "That Seahorn?"

"Yep," Caine returned.

Another blast of fire; Caine pinpointed this one even more exactly. He lined up his sites.

"Who are you? Are you Alianza?" Seahorn yelled.

Caine shouted back. "The boy, Neal. Give him to me."

A long pause. "Simon? How the devil..." Another pause, then another shot. This time Caine fired back.

"There's two of us to one of you, Neal," he shouted. "Let's talk. All I want is the boy."

"Why? What's he to you?"

"My nephew, Neal. Believe that or not. But I want him."

He heard a strange vocal sound echo down: Seahorn's laugh, distorted as it bounced down between the facing ridges. "Well, Simon, you can't have him! Couldn't give him to you if I wanted, now!"

Orion said, "That must mean he's dead, Simon."

Caine gritted his teeth; a deep rage surged inside him and geysered out. "You're a dead man, Neal!" he shouted.

Caine moved out from behind the stone face and darted along the edge of a tinaja. Two shots from above, sent bullets into the water. Caine leaped from one side of the natural water tank to another, rolled, and came up firing. He apparently got close enough to worry Seahorn; no gunfire came in response for several seconds.

"Simon! What are you doing?" Orion shouted. When Caine didn't answer, Orion came out after him.

Now Seahorn fired repeatedly again, almost hitting Orion three times. Orion slipped and fell into the tinaja; his rifle dropped from his grip and sank to the bottom of the tank.

Caine backtracked and extended his hand to Orion. Above, he heard Seahorn laugh, then Seahorn fired again, and Orion grunted and fell. The water turned pink around him.

Caine yelled and reached again for Orion. The black man struggled to his feet, gripping a bleeding shoulder.

"Give me your good hand!" Caine shouted. Orion did, reaching out with gory fingers. Hands clasped, Caine heaved back, and Orion was almost out of the tinaja when another slug tore through him and jolted him back in.

Caine dropped his rifle and went in after Orion. He dragged the limp form out, hefted him across his shoulder, and carried him to cover as Seahorn laughed and fired from above. Amazingly, Caine made it. Then he ran back to where his rifle lay, picked it up, and found meager cover behind a pile of stones.

Caine looked up, and now in the last light of the day, he saw Seahorn. The man had recklessly exposed himself at the edge of the bluff.

Caine lifted his rifle, got Seahorn in the sights.

"Where's the boy?" he shouted.

Seahorn laughed again. "He's gone, Simon. Got loose and ran away. What, you thought I'd killed him?"

Suddenly Seahorn moved back, firing carelessly down as he did so. Caine lowered his rifle.

"Keelan! If you're there, let me hear you!" Caine shouted. Nothing in response but Seahorn's laugh, more muffled than before, for Seahorn had gone back inside Old Pablo's cliffside dwelling.

"Keelan? Are you there?"

Still nothing.

Caine reached inside his jacket and drew out two sticks of dynamite wrapped in canvas. He loosened the canvas's ties, then used them to bind the sticks together. He intertwined the fuses.

Something moved above. Seahorn fired down again. He missed Caine, but not by much.

"I know Alianza sent you, Simon!" he shouted. "Don't tell me different!"

"I don't work for the Alianza; you know that," Caine shouted back as he struck a match on the rocks and lit the fuses. "This is a family matter, Neal."

The long fuses burned steadily down toward the deadly sticks in Caine's hand. "I got ransom for you, Neal!" Caine yelled. "I'm sending it up!"

He stood and threw the dynamite. It was almost dark now, and the fuses made a sparkling line as they arced up. Caine's aim was true, but he had miscalculated by a second the burn time of the fuses. The twin explosions came just before the sticks would have landed in the doorway of the house of Old Pablo.

The blast illuminated the night as it blew in the wall with incredible force, throwing stones back into the interior as if shot from cannons.

A few minutes later, when Caine had found Seahorn amid the rubble, the dying man looked at him and said, "Simon... you swear to me that Alianza didn't send you?"

"I swear it, Neal. I came on my own, for the boy. If I had wanted to work for the Alianza, I'd have taken you up on your offer in Serveto."

Seahorn smiled. "So, Alianza didn't get me after all. Looks like the joke's on them."

"Looks like it."

Seahorn closed his eyes. "Never wanted to let those blue-bellies through at Murfreesboro, Simon. I'm mighty sorry."

"We made it out all right."

"I'm tired. I want to rest."

"You do that, Neal."

Seahorn nodded. His breathing deepened and became steady, and then it stopped. Simon Caine laid the body down and crawled back out over the rubble.

CHAPTER 20

Caine gave a final check to Orion's bandages and said, "You're going to be fine, son. You were lucky you got hit no worse than you did."

"It don't feel lucky," Orion said. "It hurts."

"We need to sleep now. Come first light; I'll be leaving you here so I can look for Keelan."

The sunrise was clear the next morning; the day would be one of those searingly bright ones the desert often served up. As Caine saddled his horse, he worried over Keelan. He hardly knew the boy despite his kinship; Keelan, indeed, had no idea that Caine was his uncle. Still, Caine found his concern for Keelan was hardly less than that he would have felt for his own son in such a predicament.

"I won't be gone too long, Orion," Caine said. "Keelan probably didn't get far, and besides, I can't just run out on you with you shot up."

"I'll make it fine. You find the boy," Orion said.

Caine had no idea at what point Keelan had escaped Seahorn, nor which direction he would have taken, so he decided to trust his instinct and his own memories of how the mind of a boy works. Keelan, he figured, had probably tried to put as much distance as possible between himself and Seahorn, meaning he probably kept mostly in the clear when running away. But he might have taken to the rocks, too, to find a place to hide.

Caine followed the most obvious route through the rugged terrain, gambling on the chance Keelan in his haste, had done the same. At last, he came to a place requiring a turn either south or north, and there he stopped and dismounted. Slowly and carefully, he studied the earth all about and at last found what he thought might be a portion of a boy-sized footprint. He went in the direction it indicated, passed over an expanse of bare gray rock, then beyond that found another footprint, this one deeper and more obvious. Caine nodded— he was on the right track.

He returned to his mount and rode along the path Keelan had followed, but eventually, the route sloped up, and he had to lead his horse. Finally, even that became difficult, and he looked for a place to hobble his mount while he continued on alone.

He saw a narrow passage between two rocks, and beyond it, a little natural cove filled with grass. A good place for his horse if he could get it through the small opening. He tried and succeeded, but once inside, he stopped and stared.

Another horse already was here, grazing. It had a saddle on its back.

Something moved above. Caine turned, drawing his pistol. He saw nothing but almost mentally detected a presence behind a line of rocks above the enclave. It seemed for a moment that he also heard a muffled exclamation of some sort—the voice of a boy.

"Keelan?" Caine said. "That you?"

Movement at another place now, Caine turned again, looking up. He was facing east and had to stare almost directly into the sun to see the figure that rose above him on the rim of the rocks enclosing this place. Sun-blinded, he could make out no details, but the figure was too large to be Keelan. Then he saw a smaller form beside the larger one.

"Keelan? You all right?"

"For now," the man with the boy said. "Hello, Caine. I've been waiting a long time to meet you."

Caine still held his pistol. "Who are you?"

"My name is Morrison Deguere. Perhaps you've heard of me."

"Afraid not."

"Strange. Like you. I've got something of a reputation. I've also got your young friend."

Caine moved slightly to his left to get a better view. He could ascertain a bit about Deguere's looks now—rather long beard, derby on the head, and clothing that looked too heavy for this clime. "I want the boy safe," Caine said.

"Certainly. For a price."

"What are you talking about?"

"First, drop the pistol, then lack it away. It makes me nervous." Deguere moved a bit, and Caine saw he held a gun on Keelan's neck. "Drop it, or I will have to do something unfortunate to your nephew here."

Keelan frowned, confused by Deguere's reference to him as a nephew of the man whose voice he recognized as that of the occupant of the cell adjacent to his in Serveto. For Caine's part, he could do nothing but comply. He dropped the pistol and toed it away.

"Very good, Caine. Let me tell you something about myself. I am a detective, and I work for William Montrose. He is paying me quite well to see you dead, and though you don't know it, I've trailed you since you left the Bitterroots. More recently, I've been trailing Neal Seahorn and this young man instead, ever since they left Serveto. You see, my goal is to gain whatever money I can; however, I can get it, and I figured Seahorn to have a lot of it. I was surprised, I admit, to find the boy wandering alone out here. He tells me he evaded Seahorn."

Caine said, "If Montrose wants me, take me. Let Keelan go."

"Oh, no. He's a good source of insurance—I know you'll try nothing as long as I've got him. But tell me, Caine, where is Seahorn?"

"Looking for his lost hostage, I figure. Probably drawing a bead on you right now." Caine lied without missing a beat.

Deguere laughed. "I can see you're still a conniver, Caine. I'll get no straight talk from you. I'm coming down with the boy now. You move, and he's dead. Now I'm going to—"

Neither Deguere nor Caine anticipated Keelan's next move. With a quick, catlike twist, he pulled away from Deguere's grasp, then elbowed Deguere in the crotch. The man's eyes bulged, his breath burst out, and he doubled over. Keelan scrambled away, and Caine made a dive for his pistol.

Deguere roared and fired a shot in anger at Keelan, but the boy darted behind some rocks, and it missed. Then Deguere remembered Caine and trained his pistol down on him. Caine reached his own pistol and fired just as Deguere also did. Neither man hit his target. But Deguere knew better than to wait for Caine to have a second shot, so he backstepped away from the edge of the bluff and Caine's potential line of fire.

Caine exited the rocky enclave as fast as he could, then cut back to the left and up a wash. He searched for both Keelan and Deguere but saw neither. Suddenly something exploded behind him, and a bullet struck the earth at his feet. He overreacted and fell, rolling back several feet down the wash. He heard Deguere laugh, then another shot. At first, he was amazed that this one, too, had missed, but then he saw blood and realized he had been grazed in the calf.

He made it up the wash and came out on the same rocky area on which Deguere had stood earlier when he still had

Keelan prisoner. Caine heard motion behind him, turned, and caught a glimpse of Deguere moving from behind one boulder to another. Between the two, Deguere fired, almost hitting Caine in the face. Caine tried to fire back but found his pistol had become jammed as he scrambled up the wash.

He ran, trying to fix the weapon at the same time, but it was no use. After Seahorn had been killed, Caine had stashed his other pistol in a saddlebag, figuring he would not need it. He now wished he had it.

He ran along the rocky area, hearing Deguere follow. Caine made a zigzag pattern among the rocks to present a hard target, but he did not know what lay ahead and was afraid he was about to box himself in unwittingly.

Still, there was nothing to do but go on. The rocks became more rugged and sloped upward, and as he scrambled up, his grazed leg throbbed. He came across the crest of the rise, teetered for a moment, then fell into space.

He caught himself on jutting stones that felt like razors under his fingers. He was swinging over a rock pit about thirty feet deep. He looked down; in the cool shadows at its base, he saw slithering, writhing motion. He heard a brief rattle. His fingers slipped a little on the stones.

Deguere was above him then, laughing. "Simon, my friend, you've done it now! And I do believe I see rattlers down there. Dark, cool places attract them, you know. It's a pity because they will make it hard to get your corpse out. But I'll manage. Have to take some identifying portion to Montrose, you know.

"I almost hate to kill you, Caine. All these months of following you have made you something like an old friend to me. But all things must end, eh?"

Deguere thumbed back the hammer of his pistol and aimed. Caine fought the reflexive tendency to close his eyes; he would die looking Deguere in the face, unflinching.

From nowhere, Keelan appeared directly behind

Deguere. With a shout, the boy pushed with his arms, shoving Deguere out. The detective screamed, sent winging into space the bullet intended for Caine, then fell writhing inches past Caine. He dropped into the pit. Caine and Keelan both heard the horrible crunch when he hit the rocks below and then the rattling and movement of the rattlers that sank fangs into the fleshy form that had disturbed them.

Keelan, crying, reached down for Caine.

"It's no use, boy. I'd just pull you in," Caine said. "It's going to be up to me to get out."

Caine closed his eyes now, summoning his strength. Muscles contracting, he pulled up, inch by inch, then groped out with his right hand to find a better handhold. He did find one, then his left foot located a toehold on the rock. On it, he pushed up, which enabled him to find a hold for his left hand. From there on, he climbed carefully and slowly, sweat pouring off him in the sun and blood running down his hands from torn fingertips.

"You can do it, Mr. Simon," Keelan urged through his tears. "Just an inch or two more."

One final heave and Caine was up. He rolled onto the rocks beside Keelan and caught his breath. Keelan knelt and touched Caine's shoulder, patting and stroking it almost as if he were giving affection to a pup or a kitten.

"Are you really my uncle?" he asked.

"I sure am," Caine said, still panting for air.

———

Ria de Velasco was the first to see them returning. She was out emptying a washpot about sunset and looked up when she heard a whinny. Orion was well-bandaged and rode gingerly, hanging back somewhat behind Caine and Keelan. Ria lifted her hands toward the sky and let out a yelp of delight, then ran back into the house shouting for Rosalita and Brice.

Caine watched the doorway in nervous anticipation, hoping against hope that Brice would walk out on his own legs. The guilt of leaving his own brother crippled was a torment to Caine.

"Where's my pa, Uncle Simon?" Keelan asked.

"Probably inside, Keelan." He swallowed, dreading to tell the boy that his father might be unable to walk out to meet him. "Keelan, when I left, he was—"

Brice came to the doorway. On foot. His limp seemed worse, but he was walking. Caine's face brightened with a big grin.

"Pa!" Keelan yelled, dismounting and running toward him. "Pa!"

Brice walked clumsily out, knelt, and spread his arms. Keelan ran into them and wrapped his own arms around his father's neck. With smiles, kisses, and tears, father and son were reunited.

Caine dismounted and helped Orion off his horse. They had waited two days after Keelan's rescue to begin the trip home, allowing Orion some time to start healing, though not nearly as much as he had really needed. Caine was grateful the bullets had passed cleanly through—otherwise, they would have faced a much rougher prospect.

Rosalita came to Caine and Orion. Caine greeted her and realized just how much he had been thinking about the beautiful Mexican lady while he was away. She went to Orion's other side and slipped her arm around his back; in so doing, she touched Caine, and to him, her touch seemed electric.

"You are badly hurt, Orion?" she asked.

"I'll make it. Just let me lie down."

They got him inside and into bed, then Caine and Rosalita went back outside. Caine paused at the door, where

Ria already stood beaming, and Rosalita went to Brice and Keelan. She knelt and hugged the boy.

"They make a good family, no?" Ria said.

"Family?"

"*Sí*, Señor Caine. In the time you have been gone, many things have happened. Brice and Rosalita are to be married."

Caine looked the other way for a few moments. "I'm happy for them," he said at last.

———

That night, Orion told Caine that when he was healed up, he would become his partner. Ride with him from there on out.

No, Caine responded. Everywhere I go, men try to kill me. I've got a name and a reputation, and I'd just be a danger to you.

Orion said, that doesn't matter, I'm already wanted for killing, and it'll be just the same for me. Besides, I'd be proud to ride with you.

So Caine smiled. I'd be proud, too, he said.

Brice and Rosalita talked about the wedding, about the family they would become, and about how they would start with little but somehow build a happy home. Brice told Keelan that he had heard only two days ago that his grandfather was gone, and now they would be on their own. The Kensington empire was no more, and there was no inheritance but debt and trouble. Keelan was saddened by the news about Garth, but a glow of happiness so permeated Ria de Velasco's *casa* that bad feelings just couldn't last here tonight. Soon he was smiling again.

Caine sat in the corner and watched it all. Brice came to him late in the evening.

"Simon, things aren't like they were before. From now on, we'll be together, brothers again. I don't know just what I'll be doing, but I'll have a good wife in Rosalita, and Keelan will have a good mother again. I'll make a place for Orion. And I want you to be with us, too."

"Thank you, Brice. I'm obliged for that."

"Good. We'll talk more about it in the morning, then."

"So we will."

It was hours later before they settled for sleep. In the darkness, Caine rose and gathered his things. Keelan heard him and got up.

"Uncle Simon? What are you doing?"

"Hush, Keelan. I got to go."

"But Pa said?"

"I know. But it can never be that way. Do me a favor and don't wake them up, all right?"

"All right." Keelan watched Caine a while longer. "Will you come back?"

"Maybe. If I can."

Caine put on his hat and went to the door. He stopped and looked around the *casa*, remembering again his own home and family, long gone from him.

"So long, Keelan. You take care of your pa and your mother. Be the man I know you are."

"I will."

Caine opened the door and stepped into the darkness.

"I love you, Uncle Simon," Keelan said as Caine walked away.

Caine did not turn. "I love you, too," he said. He kept walking until he reached the barn. He saddled his mount and rode away, and when he looked back, Keelan had closed the door.

A Look at: The Complete Dave Hunter and Ash Mawson Series

By Gordon D. Shirreffs

Take a journey with Dave Hunter and Ash Mawson in this four-book western collection by Gordon D. Shirreffs. If the terrain doesn't kill them, the bullets certainly would...

In *Hell's Forty Acres*, Bounty Hunter Dave "Treasure" Hunter enters the Colorado River area searching for a lost silver mine, but finds a woman with a mysterious past, hostile Paiutes, and betrayal. It was rich with the promise of silver—and sudden death. In *Maximilian's Gold*, Hunter teams up with his buddy Ash Mawson to find the Mexican Emperor Maximilian's gold, stashed somewhere on the treacherous Chihuahua Trail. Gold can make a man as rich as a king. If it doesn't kill him first.

In *The Walking Sands*, South of the Arizona border is the Gran Desierto, a vast area of shifting sand hills. It is there that a church was buried beneath the sands, never to be found again. Hunter believes the Jesuits' treasure is there for the taking—but so do some other very dangerous people. And in *The Devil's Dance Floor*, Hunter returns, this time doing fancy footwork for a religious figurine. His search for the Virgin Mary figurine means crossing the Sonora Desert—the Devil's Dance.

The Complete Dave Hunter/Ash Mawson Series includes: *Hell's Forty Acres, Maximilian's Gold, The Walking Sands,* and *The Devil's Dance Floor.*

AVAILABLE NOW

About the Author

Cameron Judd is the author of more than fifty published novels of the American frontier, two of his works having been national finalists in the Spur Awards competition of the Western Writers of America. He has written under his own names and pen names including Judson Grey, Tobias Cole and Will Cade. A native and lifelong Tennessean, he has three adult children. He and his wife, Rhonda, share their Northeast Tennessee home with a cornbread-loving dog named Lola. He is a former award-winning newspaper journalist and editor.

ABOUT THE AUTHOR